Halfhyde
to the Narrows

Historical Fiction Published by McBooks Press

BY ALEXANDER KENT
Midshipman Bolitho
Stand Into Danger
In Gallant Company
Sloop of War
To Glory We Steer
Command a King's Ship
Passage to Mutiny
With All Despatch
Form Line of Battle!
Enemy in Sight!
The Flag Captain
Signal–Close Action!
The Inshore Squadron
A Tradition of Victory
Success to the Brave
Colours Aloft!
Honour This Day
The Only Victor
Beyond the Reef
The Darkening Sea
For My Country's Freedom
Cross of St George
Sword of Honour
Second to None
Relentless Pursuit
Man of War

BY DOUGLAS REEMAN
Badge of Glory
First to Land
The Horizon
Dust on the Sea

Twelve Seconds to Live
Battlecruiser
The White Guns

BY DAVID DONACHIE
The Devil's Own Luck
The Dying Trade
A Hanging Matter
An Element of Chance
The Scent of Betrayal
A Game of Bones

On a Making Tide
Tested by Fate
Breaking the Line

BY DUDLEY POPE
Ramage
Ramage & The Drumbeat
Ramage & The Freebooters
Governor Ramage R.N.
Ramage's Prize
Ramage & The Guillotine
Ramage's Diamond
Ramage's Mutiny
Ramage & The Rebels
The Ramage Touch
Ramage's Signal
Ramage & The Renegades
Ramage's Devil
Ramage's Trial
Ramage's Challenge
Ramage at Trafalgar
Ramage & The Saracens
Ramage & The Dido

BY ALEXANDER FULLERTON
Storm Force to Narvik

BY PHILIP MCCUTCHAN
Halfhyde at the Bight
    of Benin
Halfhyde's Island
Halfhyde and the
    Guns of Arrest
Halfhyde to the Narrows

BY JAMES L. NELSON
The Only Life That
    Mattered

BY V.A. STUART
Victors and Lords
The Sepoy Mutiny
Massacre at Cawnpore
The Cannons of Lucknow
The Heroic Garrison

The Valiant Sailors
The Brave Captains
Hazard's Command
Hazard of Huntress
Hazard in Circassia
Victory at Sebastopol

BY R.F. DELDERFIELD
Too Few for Drums
Seven Men of Gascony

BY DEWEY LAMBDIN
The French Admiral
Jester's Fortune

BY C.N. PARKINSON
The Guernseyman
Devil to Pay
The Fireship
Touch and Go
So Near So Far
Dead Reckoning

BY JAN NEEDLE
A Fine Boy for Killing
The Wicked Trade
The Spithead Nymph

BY IRV C. ROGERS
Motoo Eetee

BY NICHOLAS NICASTRO
The Eighteenth Captain
Between Two Fires

BY FREDERICK MARRYAT
Frank Mildmay OR
    The Naval Officer
The King's Own
Mr Midshipman Easy
Newton Forster OR
    The Merchant Service
Snarleyyow OR
    The Dog Fiend
The Privateersman
The Phantom Ship

BY W. CLARK RUSSELL
Wreck of the Grosvenor
Yarn of Old
    Harbour Town

BY RAFAEL SABATINI
Captain Blood

BY MICHAEL SCOTT
Tom Cringle's Log

BY A.D. HOWDEN SMITH
Porto Bello Gold

The Halfhyde Adventures, No. 4

Halfhyde
to the Narrows

Philip McCutchan

MCBOOKS PRESS, INC.
ITHACA, NEW YORK

Published by McBooks Press, Inc. 2004
Copyright © 1977 by Philip McCutchan
First published in Great Britain by George Weidenfeld & Nicolson Limited
First published in the United States by St. Martin's Press, Inc.

Cover painting: *Coaling a Warship* by Norman Wilkinson in *The Royal Navy,*
1907. Courtesy of Mary Evans Picture Library.

Library of Congress Cataloging-in-Publication Data

McCutchan, Philip, 1920-
Halfhyde to the narrows / By Philip McCutchan.
p. cm. — (The Halfhyde adventures ; no. 4)
ISBN 1-59013-068-5 (trade pbk. : alk. paper)
1. Halfhyde, St. Vincent (Fictitious character)—Fiction. 2. Great Britain—
History, Naval—Fiction. 3. Dardanelles Strait (Turkey)—Fiction. 4.
Russians—Turkey—Fiction. 5. British—Turkey—Fiction. 6. Torpedo-boats—
Fiction. 7. Ship captains—Fiction. I. Title.
PR6063.A167H37 2004
823'.914—dc22

2004007948

Distributed to the trade by National Book Network, Inc.,
15200 NBN Way, Blue Ridge Summit, PA 17214
800-462-6420

Additional copies of this book may be ordered from any bookstore
or directly from McBooks Press, Inc., ID Booth Building,
520 North Meadow St., Ithaca, NY 14850. Please include $4.00 postage
and handling with mail orders. New York State residents must add
sales tax to total remittance (books & shipping). All McBooks Press
publications can also be ordered by calling toll-free
1-888-BOOKS11 (1-888-266-5711).
Please call to request a free catalog.

Visit the McBooks Press website at www.mcbooks.com.

Printed in the United States of America

9 8 7 6 5 4 3 2 1

Chapter 1

TALL AND LEAN, his skin burned brown by sun and wind, Lieutenant St Vincent Halfhyde stood in the "at ease" position in front of the fo'c'sle division. The men were fallen in for entering harbour, wearing sennit hats and anticipatory grins as they considered the forthcoming delights of a run ashore to Strada Stretta, known in Her Majesty's Navy as The Gut. After an uneventful voyage from Portsmouth dockyard to join the Mediterranean Fleet at Malta, the ship's company of the *Lord Cochrane* were ready enough for wine, women, and song, and Halfhyde knew that tomorrow would bring a muster of men pale from a night's vomiting, and that succeeding days would bring a long line of sufferers from worse ailments to attend the doctor's surgery.

Halfhyde glanced upward and a little astern, his eye caught by sudden movement and colour: as the ship turned slowly and ponderously towards the Grand Harbour, her numeral pennants began climbing on their halliards to the starboard fore upper yard-arm, so as to identify her to the signal station at Lascaris, the eyes and ears of the admiral superintendent of the dockyard and of the commander-in-chief, Mediterranean Fleet, under whose orders the bombardment monitor would now come. The bright colours of the pennants, the polished brass of bollards and stanchions and picket-boat's funnels, and the paintwork of buff, white, and black stood out sharply beneath a strong sun, the heat of which made men glad enough of their white foreign-service uniforms; white and blue and gold, traditional colours of the sea . . . Halfhyde felt at peace with himself and with the world at large. He was pleased to be sailing in to Malta, to be joining a great Fleet and to be becoming once again, after some years of half-pay followed by a variety of special missions on detached service, a part of the mainstream of naval life: as an ambitious officer he knew well that some degree of mainstream service was essential to promotion, and Malta in the 1890s was as pleasant a station as any in which to qualify.

From the monitor's flag deck more signals were made: the captain was now asking permission to enter, his engines stopped until the answer came. From Lascaris, within minutes, the Queen's harbourmaster signalled permission; blue water boiled up beneath the monitor's counter and, with the white-helmeted band of the Royal Marine Artillery playing on the quarterdeck beneath the snow-white, scrubbed canvas awnings, Her Majesty's Ship *Lord Cochrane* headed inwards to join the proud assembly of the warships anchored in the Grand Harbour. As the music of the band blared towards the rock and the clusters of yellow-white buildings that closed in the Grand Harbour, the monitor moved slowly past Fort St Angelo to the anchorage allotted her by the Queen's harbourmaster. Halfhyde's division was now fallen out, the hands standing by to let go the starboard bower anchor on receiving the signal from the bridge. As Captain Bassinghorn lowered his green flag, Halfhyde passed the order to the blacksmith to knock away the slips; in a shower of red rust the great links of the cable flew out around the out-of-gear centre-line capstan, rattling across the deck and down the cavernous mouth of the hawse-pipe to take the harbour bottom and hold the ship steady in her position. With the fourth shackle on deck, Halfhyde ordered the brake on the capstan, and as soon as the ship had "got her cable" the slips were re-secured. The hands were fallen out to go below, to await the piping away of the first of the liberty-boats.

In the wardroom St Vincent Halfhyde dropped into a worn leather armchair, thrust out long legs, and called for whisky: gin was the usual drink in Her Majesty's Navy—it was said that the aroma of gin was less obtrusive to senior officers' noses than that of whisky—but Halfhyde preferred whisky and refused to make concessions to other people's customs. His whisky, a double tot, would cost him twopence on his wine bill, and was more extravagant a drink than gin; but Halfhyde, as yet a single man, could afford the indulgence. He had by now made up the leeway of his impoverished years of half-pay on the Admiralty's unemployed list, to which he had been consigned as a result of his predeliction towards argument with his seniors when he considered himself in the right: for in naval eyes, perhaps the most heinous sin was to be right when a captain or an admiral was wrong. Prudent men were content to acknowledge this fact of service life and to mutter only into their beards or their gin . . . Halfhyde grinned as he sipped the whisky brought by the wardroom servant: he was not a prudent man, except in one respect—he would not, whilst in Malta, be sampling the pleasures offered by the ladies of easy virtue who traded in The Gut. Unpleasant diseases were strictly for the lower deck, and officers had to stiffen their upper lips and wait either for the end of the commission or for the advent of young ladies of cleaner bodies, such as those upon whom Halfhyde had on occasions waited outside the doors of theatres and music halls in London, Portsmouth, and Devonport. These young ladies of the stage stood halfway between harlotry and the virtuous respectability of officers' wives and daughters, and as such were worth a risk when a single man felt the urge of desire. In between, it was a matter of whisky and the wardroom piano, or of very long walks and games of hockey . . .

Halfhyde yawned, got to his feet and wandered over to a large square port to look out at the Grand Harbour, at the great battleships and cruisers of the Mediterranean Fleet lying at anchor in orderly lines, attended by busy picket-boats or by native *dghaisas,* curious craft with high-pointed bows and sterns, propelled by a single oar, that had often enough proved salvation for officers and men who had missed the last liberty-boat off shore—to the delight of the *dghaisamen,* whose instincts told them unmistakably of their passengers' misfortune and who doubled the fares accordingly . . . Malta, island of the Knights Hospitallers, lived by and for the British Mediterranean Fleet, without which it would surely sink into the sea.

Hearing a knock at the open wardroom door, Halfhyde swung round. A seaman messenger stood waiting, his cap beneath his left arm.

"Yes?"

"Mr Halfhyde, sir. Captain's compliments, sir, and he'd like to see you in his cabin, sir."

"Right, thank you."

The messenger turned about smartly, putting his cap on. Halfhyde finished his whisky, staring moodily into the glass when it was empty. He and Captain Henry Bassinghorn were old shipmates who had been through many difficulties together in the China seas and off the West African coast; but a captain's summons inevitably held overtones of some criticism, of something either left undone or done improperly. As he went aft to the cuddy Halfhyde's mind flickered over the recent past: had there been inefficiency in anchoring, had one of his division been slack, or slow to obey an order, such as would reflect upon his divisional lieutenant? Halfhyde believed his own eye to be as true as Bassinghorn's, as sharp to spot improprieties, but it had to be acknowledged that the navigating bridge gave a superior view . . . as he passed the rifle racks Halfhyde absent-mindedly returned the butt-salute of the armed Royal Marine Light Infantryman on sentry duty outside the cuddy, then tapped once on the captain's door.

"Come in," came Bassinghorn's deep voice.

Halfhyde tucked his cap beneath his arm and went in, standing at attention. "You sent for me, sir?"

"I did, Mr Halfhyde, but at the behest of someone else who has also sent for you."

Halfhyde raised an eyebrow. "Sir?"

"The vice-admiral commanding the Inshore Squadron, Mr Halfhyde." There was a gleam in Bassinghorn's eye, a suspicion of humour. "Do you know who the vice-admiral is, Mr Halfhyde?"

"I do not, sir."

Bassinghorn moved his heavy body slightly in the chair, looking at Halfhyde from under massive brows, grey turning to white. "When last you and he met, he was a commodore. Commodore Sir John Willard—at Hong Kong. He wishes you to dine with him tonight—seven-thirty for eight—I also was bidden, but pleaded a signal to dine with the commander-in-chief aboard the flagship, so you'll go alone."

"A sorry fate, sir," Halfhyde said involuntarily, thinking his own thoughts. "Not that I intend disrespect, but—"

"Miss Mildred?"

"Precisely, sir."

"My presence would scarcely have helped. I'm a confirmed bachelor—you are not. I wish you very good luck, my dear Halfhyde—and remember that admirals' daughters can be double edged swords to an officer's career!"

True words indeed, Halfhyde reflected as he left the cuddy; and especially in the case of Miss Mildred Willard. An admiral set upon marrying off an unattractive daughter would need tactful handling. Halfhyde pulled out his timepiece: six-thirty— one bell in the last dog watch. He went to his cabin, washed, shaved for the second time that day, and put on the starched shirt and white bum-freezer laid ready by his servant, the gold stripes and curl of his rank as an executive lieutenant gleaming from his shoulder-straps. Dressed, Halfhyde took up his white covered cap, strode along the steel-lined alleyway of the officers' cabin flat and climbed the ladder to the quarterdeck. He had a word with the officer of the watch, a lieutenant wearing an empty sword-belt to indicate his duty status and carrying a telescope beneath his left arm. The next officer's boat for the shore would leave at three bells, too late for Halfhyde's purpose; but the duty steam picket-boat could be called away.

"I'll take a *dghaisa*," Halfhyde said, unwilling to have men disturbed for himself alone. "If you'll be so good?"

The officer of the watch passed the order to his midshipman, who stepped to the starboard guard-rail and hailed a passing craft: this immediately altered course for the foot of the monitor's accommodation-ladder. Halfhyde descended, returning the salutes of the gangway staff, stepped into the *dghaisa* and sat upon a thwart while the brown-skinned, bare-foot Maltese pulled him towards the quay opposite Fort St Angelo's frowning battlements, ancient stone that in its long history had looked down upon Lord Nelson's wooden Fleet and upon the valiant old ships of Collingwood and Cochrane, Troubridge and Codrington, Hood and St Vincent. But as he was pulled for the shore and what he felt in his bones would prove an awkward and constrained evening, Halfhyde's thoughts were centred, not upon the famous names of England's history, but upon the basically pointless words of a naval ditty that seemed currently apposite to marriage-broking admirals: *"You may pass, kiss my arse, make fast the* dghaisa . . .*"*

At the vice-admiral's residence, Halfhyde stepped down from the carriage that had awaited him at the landing-stage. As he approached the magnificent front door it was opened by the admiral's chief steward in person, a portly chief petty officer with a lock of grey hair greased down with brilliantine over his left eye like a misplaced Nelson's patch, and a curious habit of lifting one corner of his mouth in a series of jerks as though it were some kind of Morse transmitter. Memory stirred in Halfhyde.

"I'll be damned!" he said. "It's Barty!"

"Chief Petty Officer Steward Bartholomew if it's all the same to you, Mr Halfhyde, sir—"

"Well, it isn't. Barty you were aboard the old *Britannia*, Barty you are still. How are you?" Halfhyde extended a hand, and shook the steward's warmly.

"None the better for seeing you, young sir," Barty grumbled, but the light in his eye was friendly enough. "Last time I see you, you'd cut me 'ammick netting through far enough for me to fall on me arse the moment I climbed in. I'll say one thing: you owned up like a man, and then apologized 'andsome." His mouth jerked. "Ruddy cadets. Enough to make a man shit a brick if you'll pardon the expression."

Chief Petty Officer Steward Bartholomew turned away across the admiral's hall, leading Halfhyde to the drawing-room, where he announced the visitor in loud tones and then closed the door behind him. To Halfhyde, the group by the fireless chimney-piece seemed frozen into attitudes struck long ago, in Hong Kong. Now as then, though adorned with more brass, Sir John Willard, with a face like a rock and a distant, haughty expression on it, stood flanked by wife and daughter. Lady Willard was as nervous as ever in her husband's presence and had lost none of her bulk—if anything, the years had increased it. Miss Mildred seemed poised on the brink of her dreadful horsey laugh; and her resemblance to her father was even more marked now. At about twenty-eight by Halfhyde's calculations, she had grown decidedly spinsterish, with no breasts and a broad behind. Halfhyde felt positively carried back in time, as though once again he and Bassinghorn were about to take the old *Viceroy* out across the China seas to plant the flag of Empire on what had since gone down in the Admiralty charts as Halfhyde's Island. Even the portrait over the fireplace was the same: Her Majesty Queen Victoria, garter ribbon, cap and bun, had made the journey from far Hong Kong to Malta and still stood looking out upon her beloved Scotland from behind the drawn-back tartan curtains of Balmoral Castle . . .

"Good evening, Halfhyde. Glad you could come."

Halfhyde bowed his head politely to each in turn, then said, "My captain, sir, sends his apologies—"

"He's already sent 'em by signal." Sir John turned, and tugged at a bell-pull; Chief Petty Officer Steward Bartholomew silently appeared and the admiral snapped his fingers at him. "Sherry." Bartholomew vanished again and the admiral addressed Halfhyde once more. "You've met Bartholomew? He remembered you."

"Yes, sir. Dear old Barty." The admiral stared from under raised eyebrows. Halfhyde cleared his throat. "In Hong Kong, sir, he wasn't—"

"With me. No. Man I had there died. Drink—*my* drink! Damn thief." There was a long pause, during which Bartholomew came back and poured sherry. Halfhyde, no sherry drinker, found it thin and tasteless, much too dry. It was quickly gone and no more was offered. Into another pause came the chief steward's voice announcing dinner, and the admiral immediately shepherded family and guest towards the dining-room. They sat at a long table with Sir John at one end and, distantly, Lady Willard at the other. Rather closer together amidships, Halfhyde and Miss Mildred faced each other. The meal was frugal and fast: soup, fish, meat, pudding, and coffee flashed by as speedily as in Hong Kong. The admiral was no gourmet. The conversation was sparse also: the admiral was preoccupied, silent, frowning, continually tapping a hand upon the table; Lady Willard clearly had nothing to say, and the moment she ventured to say it she was snapped into silence by the admiral. Thus the conversation was left to Halfhyde and Miss Mildred, and to Halfhyde dinner was torture. Miss Mildred spoke of Ascot, Lincoln, Newmarket, the Row in Hyde Park, and of little else; and Halfhyde, in spite of his farming background in the Yorkshire Dales, had no interest in horses. His relief was great when the ladies withdrew, and Sir John Willard—precisely as in Hong Kong—poured the port and gruffly said, "Now then."

Now then was, for the second time in Halfhyde's experience, the admiral's personal signal for getting down to the real business, the business for which dinner was in a sense mere cover. The fact was that the lieutenant in command of a torpedo-boat destroyer of the Inshore Squadron, a ship outside the strict command of the Mediterranean Fleet itself, had died of Malta fever.

"Otherwise known as undulant fever," the admiral said. "Nasty. Enlarged spleen, profuse sweating, constipation, rheumatic pains, and swelling of the joints. Get it from the damn goats. Steer clear of goats, Halfhyde."

"Yes, sir."

"This TBD, now. Her Majesty's Ship *Vendetta*. Fast and well-armed, and of shallow draft. Interesting to handle." Sir John Willard stared hard at Halfhyde, eyes boring into his guest from a face of granite. "Does it interest *you*, Halfhyde?"

"In what capacity, sir, if I may ask?"

"Command."

Halfhyde gaped. "*Command,* sir?"

"Kindly don't repeat my words back at me. I said command, yes. A temporary and local appointment, such as lies within my jurisdiction to make, with the necessity simply to inform the Board of Admiralty after I've made it."

"So that the Board of Admiralty will find it too late to object?"

The rock of the admiral's face showed the small fissure of a smile, briefly. "You have your past record in mind, no doubt?

Rude, insubordinate, disrespectful towards your seniors and betters?"

"I dispute—"

Sir John raised a hand, peremptorily. "You shall not answer me back, or you will regret it most mightily. Remember that your record stands as a monument to your capacity for annoying your superiors and to your tactlessness and forthcoming manner towards authority."

"Then why choose me for command, sir?"

"Do you doubt your ability to command, Mr Halfhyde?"

"By no means, sir."

"Then do not look a gift horse in the mouth." The admiral refilled the port glasses, held his up against the table-lamp's shaded chimney and looked thoughtfully at the ruby glow. "I am well disposed towards you, Halfhyde, as it happens. In the North Pacific you performed your duties admirably and with dash, and the Navy is sadly short of dash today. To a large extent it disappeared with sail." There was another pause, and then the admiral said, not looking now at Halfhyde, "I can be of much assistance to your career . . . given certain conditions."

"And the conditions, sir?"

Sir John Willard got to his feet abruptly without answering: the evening was at an end. "I shall be in communication with your captain tomorrow, and after that I shall pass your orders. For now I can tell you this: you'll be sailing under conditions of secrecy with the Fourth TBD Flotilla under Captain Watkiss in the leader—and you'll be sailing for the Dardanelles."

"I see, sir. May I ask—"

"No questions for the present, Mr Halfhyde. You'll not sail

before next week. In the meantime, my daughter has expressed a wish to be taken round the island, and I'm unable to spare my flag lieutenant . . ."

The possible computations were many, and Halfhyde, making his way back to the *Lord Cochrane*, reflected much upon them, and with cynicism. Miss Mildred Willard loomed in those reflections: Sir John Willard had indicated that in fact he had only recently been appointed to his position as flag officer commanding the Inshore Squadron. It was certainly possible, if unlikely, that Miss Mildred had not yet found time and opportunity to look round . . . it was possible, and equally unlikely, that the flag lieutenant and other younger officers had managed to find excuses that could be tactfully put to the combination of Admiral and Father . . . but Halfhyde had a strong feeling that Miss Mildred was being as it were held free and ready against his own arrival on the Mediterranean station. And another strong feeling was this: the length of his so-far local and temporary command might very well lie in the horsey hands of Miss Mildred Willard . . . Halfhyde, waving from the landing-stage for a *dghaisa* to take him off, forced unwelcome thoughts from his mind. The Dardanelles, that narrow passage from the Aegean into the Sea of Marmara, beckoned him intriguingly. What was the secrecy about, what were Their Lordships of the Admiralty up to this time? Beyond the Sea of Marmara lay another narrow passage—the Bosporus, gateway to the Black Sea and the naval might of the Russian Empire, a part of the world that had not been unknown to St Vincent Halfhyde in the past.

Chapter 2

"BLOODSTOCK—"

"St Paul's Grotto," Halfhyde said firmly, "is most interesting, Miss Willard." He glared out over the side of the horse-drawn carriage that had been provided by the admiral: the yellow sandstone and dust of Malta was a better prospect than Miss Mildred and her chaperoning mother. The day was hot and Halfhyde, in civilian dress, found gritty dust between neck and high, starched collar, though the ladies appeared remarkably fresh beneath fashionable parasols, despite the weight of their immense hats. Gloved hands reposed in laps, and skirts descended to the floor of the carriage; the only visible flesh was between hat and neck-choker of lace and whalebone. Halfhyde reflected sourly that the *Lord Cochrane*'s lower deck ratings would be having a much better time of it in The Gut, not that he had any designs at all upon Willard flesh. He was aware that his manner was chilling; that it had even, at least temporarily, chilled Miss Mildred into silence; and in a sense he was sorry, for the poor girl was obviously finding life difficult in Malta. Socially, apart from a certain attentiveness demanded from young officers by her father's position, she was a wallflower; and her consuming interest in horseflesh was likely to find scant response in a small, dusty island dominated by seamen and the sea. To the majority of seamen, as to Halfhyde himself, a horse was an unknown quantity best avoided: one end bit, and the other kicked. Certainly there was the occasional officer, usually a senior one, who fancied himself upon a horse: the result was invariably a pathetic sight. In the early hours of the morning Halfhyde, in order to circumvent prospective horse-talk, had taken pains to study an encyclopaedia provided by the captain's clerk whom Halfhyde had woken from sleep on his return aboard. From this he had stored knowledge and had compiled an itinerary. St Paul's Grotto, where St Paul had lived after his shipwreck on the island in 62 AD, was of obvious interest; so were the underground catacombs that extended for many miles in three tiers, largely below Valletta, the capital. The catacomb alleys were narrow enough to necessitate a single-file progress, thus lending themselves less to conversation than did the open air on the surface. Halfhyde launched himself into an exposition.

"A labyrinth of galleries and chambers cut out of the sandstone, ma'am," he said to Lady Willard. "I understand the third tier reaches a depth of some eighty feet. The walls to either side of the passages have been cut away into recesses to take the dead . . . the effect is said to be rather like a passenger liner's cabin alleyways, except that each berth is occupied by bones alone."

"How very extraordinary, Mr Halfhyde."

"Merely an ancient burial custom, ma'am."

"I think I prefer the sunlight," Miss Mildred said.

"Indeed, Miss Willard, but the mind should not be neglected for the body. I beg your pardon," he added as he saw the slight shock in Miss Mildred's face: he wondered, wickedly, if she knew how horses came to be born.

"I understand," Lady Willard said, "that it is easy to become lost in the catacombs?"

"There's a guide, ma'am, with a candle."

"But are there not draughts?"

"Indeed there are, but there is also the forethought of Her Majesty's Service. I have not come unprepared—but you shall see." Shortly after this the carriage drew up at one of the entrances to the catacombs, an unprepossessing-looking hole in a sandstone surface, from which came a barefoot Maltese to act as guide. Halfhyde beckoned to the rating who was sitting beside the coachman on the box of the carriage. "The kitbag, Turner."

"Aye, aye, sir." Able Seaman Turner scrambled down and walked to the rear of the carriage. Opening the boot, he brought out a regulation-pattern naval kitbag of stout canvas, nipped at the throat by a length of codline rove through brass-eyed holes. The kitbag seemed heavy; Turner dragged it towards the catacomb entry and opened its top. He handed the end of a length of spunyarn to Halfhyde.

"Thank you," Halfhyde said. He placed his back smartly against the wall, where, just inside the entrance, a vulgar hand, belonging, no doubt, to a seaman or a soldier from the Malta garrison, had drawn that portion of the female anatomy dearest to the heart of men on foreign service and much missed in the farthest-flung corners of Her Majesty's Empire. So hirsute an artist's impression thus concealed from matronly and maidenly gaze, the ladies entered behind the candle-holding Maltese with Halfhyde bringing up the rear, still clutching the spunyarn.

A terrible day, with Miss Mildred breathing hotly down his neck and Lady Willard complaining of faintness and of the hard ground underfoot in the catacombs: it was with much relief that

Halfhyde returned the ladies to the vice-admiral and found himself bidden to the study for sherry and to render his report of the outing.

"Spunyarn, hey? Spunyarn! I'll be damned!" Sir John Willard's eyebrows rose high above the facial rock. "Could show two things, Halfhyde, diametrically opposed one to the other!"

"Sir?"

"Initiative and enterprise—or too much damn caution."

Halfhyde shrugged. "For myself alone, sir, I'd not have bothered, of course. But with the ladies whom you had placed in my care, sir—"

"Nothing left to chance?"

"Quite, sir. It was a high responsibility."

The admiral frowned, glared, and Halfhyde felt that possibly his tone had been not quite right, or his choice of words too fulsome. He said, "As events proved, the spunyarn was not needed. The guide's candle held its flame."

"And the man had lucifers, no doubt."

"Yes, sir."

"Well, *some* caution's not necessarily a bad thing in an officer," the admiral conceded. "It's going to be useful when you reach the Dardanelles. I'm inclined to be impressed with you, Halfhyde."

"Thank you, sir." Halfhyde waited for the admiral to elaborate. Sir John approached the point: Halfhyde was informed that Captain Bassinghorn's objections to losing his services had been overruled and that the commander-in-chief was prepared to place him at the disposal of the Inshore Squadron for temporary reappointment.

The admiral glanced at a clock above his fireplace, checked

it with a timepiece of gold and blue enamel which he pulled from a waistcoat pocket, then said, "Captain Watkiss is due to report shortly with his Commanding Officers—of whom you are now one."

"I see, sir. And then the orders will be passed?"

"Just so, Halfhyde, just so."

The wait was tedious; the admiral seemed slightly on edge, frowning over his thoughts and saying nothing further. After some fifteen interminable minutes, Bartholomew announced Captain Watkiss and his flotilla captains, three lieutenants, one of them wearing the half stripe between the two full ones to indicate that after more than eight years in his rank he was now a senior lieutenant. Sir John Willard made the introductions briefly.

"Captain Watkiss, commanding the flotilla in *Venomous*. Mr Soper, Mr Cholmondeley-Ross, Mr Lavington. Mr Halfhyde, reappointed from the *Lord Cochrane*."

Captain Watkiss, a short stout man, with a very red face and protuberant eyes and the tail of a tattooed snake protruding below the cuff of his white uniform, pressed a monocle to his left eye and stared Halfhyde up and down. "Bombardment monitor, all spit and polish and never goes to sea."

"I beg your pardon, sir?" Halfhyde coloured angrily. "With respect, I must insist—"

"That'll do, Mr Halfhyde." There was a snap in the admiral's voice, a clear indication that Halfhyde's past record of insubordination had again flashed before his inner eye. Halfhyde gave Captain Watkiss a frosty look, but said no more. A better time would come to show the senior officer of the flotilla that he had his full sea-time in and that he was no barrack stanchion.

The officers were sat in a half-circle before the admiral's desk; the admiral himself remained standing and began with an adjuration to strict secrecy. What he was about to say was not to be discussed with anyone else at all, not at any rate until the torpedo-boat destroyers had left Malta on their easterly course, when the various first lieutenants could be confided in. It would be up to Captain Watkiss to decide how much to reveal to the ships' companies thereafter.

"As little as possible, sir," Watkiss announced at this point.

"Consistent with efficiency, Captain," Sir John said mildly.

"Consistent with the mentality of the lower deck, sir. Efficiency is best maintained by maintaining discipline. Discipline is not served—"

"Captain—"

"—by treating the lower deck as though they had intelligence, which they have not. That is fact—I said it. They shall be told nothing whatever, sir." Captain Watkiss sat back with his tattooed arms folded across his broad chest and bulging stomach, his single eyeglass daring anyone present to contradict him. Halfhyde now understood the admiral's earlier edginess: Captain Watkiss was going to prove a most difficult man, one who seemed, curiously, to have even the admiral in awe of him. That could spell connections in high places, though Halfhyde knew of no Watkiss within the Admiralty. At all events, Sir John Willard passed over the angry words by restating that it would be the sole decision of Captain Watkiss. Then he began to outline the details of the forthcoming operation.

"Word has reached me from the Board of Admiralty," he said, "that a British merchantman, the full-rigged ship *Falls of Dochart,* registered in the port of Liverpool—"

"A ship under sail, sir?"

"Yes, Captain Watkiss. The *Falls of Dochart* was on passage from the Mersey to Alexandria when she was apparently apprehended by a Russian warship and escorted into the Black Sea—to Sevastopol in the Crimea peninsula."

"For what purpose, sir?"

"I have not been informed, and it's possible the reason is not known at the Admiralty—their intelligence came from the Foreign Office, who will no doubt have their own reasons for withholding information."

"And her cargo?"

"In ballast, Captain Watkiss. She was to have taken aboard a cargo of raw cotton for Liverpool when she reached Alexandria."

"And my flotilla?"

The admiral said, "I am in receipt of orders that the *Falls of Dochart* is to be cut out, and I am despatching the Fourth TBD Flotilla in execution of those orders. This is not to be a Fleet operation—the Mediterranean Fleet, as you will know, is due to sail west shortly for Gibraltar and the manoeuvres with the Atlantic Fleet, and the Admiralty appears to feel that to detach ships from the main Fleet at sea in the Mediterranean would be to give the incident an undue prominence and thus make it harder of solution—"

"Stuff-and-nonsense!" Captain Watkiss interrupted with a snap.

"I beg your pardon, Captain Watkiss?" Sir John's face was formidable, and he held his anger in check with obvious difficulty. "Both you and I must observe the edicts of the Admiralty, must we not, whatever our private feelings? You will prepare your ships for sea, Captain Watkiss, and be in all respects ready to proceed out of harbour at first light on Tuesday next. You will make your requirements for coal, stores, water, and ammunition known as soon as possible to my secretary, and they will be met in full."

Returning aboard the *Lord Cochrane* to supervise the packing of his gear for transfer to HMS *Vendetta,* Halfhyde reflected on the consternation that had gripped the officers in the admiral's study: for warships to enter Russian waters was tantamount to an act of war—it was perhaps not surprising that the Admiralty did not wish to involve the commander-in-chief and the main Mediterranean Fleet—and should a war in fact be provoked, then Captain Watkiss could find his career in jeopardy, and never mind that the orders had come from the Admiralty itself. It was always possible for blame to be shifted to the Commanding Officer on the spot: strict orders were frequently exceeded in the heat of an awkward moment, when a hard decision had to be made in seconds, and such excesses could be, and often had been in the past, turned against the simple seagoing commander. However, this time, Sir John had said, the British Government appeared to have accepted the inherent risks, and there would be no backtracking afterwards.

"I don't believe it, sir," Captain Watkiss had stated flatly. "I've a mind to refuse the orders."

"And stand accused of cowardice, Captain?"

"Have a care, Sir John. I'm no coward and you know it. A career in the Navy presupposes war and we all accept it, indeed welcome it. That is fact—I said it. But I dislike any possibility of being made a whipping-boy or a—"

"You shall not be, and you will obey the orders. Her Majesty's

Government has apparently decided that the risk attendant upon turning the other cheek to an unlawful arrest upon the high seas is much less acceptable than that attendant upon decisive action being taken. I agree with that, and so should any Briton worth his salt. The orders stand, but will be executed sensibly and with restraint—"

"There's the rub!" Watkiss said loudly.

"—which is to say that you are to provoke nothing and you are not to be the first to open fire if it should come to that. You will keep the British nose as clean before the world as possible, so that the Russian action is seen for what it is. In the first instance, upon arrival off the Dardanelles, you are to *request* entry. If it is refused by the Turkish authorities, as it may well be, you are nevertheless to steam through into the Sea of Marmara. Whitehall considers it highly doubtful that the Turks will impede you physically and equally doubtful that the Russians will open fire in the Bosporus and thereby risk war with Turkey." The admiral paused. "The difficulty, in my own view, will be to lay alongside the *Falls of Dochart*. At that, the Russians may stick. There has been no admission from St Petersburg of an arrest—word came through trading sources only. They will attempt to cover up. And that is where Mr Halfhyde comes in."

Halfhyde stared, "I, sir?"

"You, sir," the admiral answered crisply. "You have detailed personal knowledge of the Russian Navy—of Sevastopol, and more importantly of Admiral Prince Gorsinski, currently commanding the whole Black Sea naval area."

Halfhyde had felt his heart thump at the mention of Prince Gorsinski, related by blood to the Czar himself. Keeping his voice level he had said, "If I should meet Prince Gorsinski again, it's my death warrant, sir."

The admiral met his eye. "In Her Majesty's Service, Mr Halfhyde, death is always a possibility that must be accepted."

Crossing the Grand Harbour in a *dghaisa*, behind the baleful eyes of Osiris painted on either bow—a device used by the ancient Phoenicians to ward off evil—Halfhyde thought with bitterness of a wasted day of politeness towards Miss Mildred Willard. It was not an escort for his daughter—or, God forbid, a son-in-law—that Sir John had wanted, but a corpse to salvage British honour. Although his personal orders had not yet been passed in full, to Halfhyde in his present mood it was plain: give Gorsinski his revenge on Lieutenant St Vincent Halfhyde and he would release the *Falls of Dochart* with alacrity!

Chapter 3

HALFHYDE'S NIGHT was a mainly sleepless one disturbed by his doubts and fears; when sleep came it was filled with nightmare. Admiral Prince Gorsinski loomed, black-bearded and savage. Once, Gorsinski had had Halfhyde, then a midshipman, in his hands after a débâcle outside the Bosporus: taken prisoner to Sevastopol, Mr Midshipman Halfhyde had impressed Gorsinski, at that time port admiral, with his self-possession, courage, and bearing; and, when later he had been sent to Siberia, Gorsinski had secured his release from that Godforsaken place and his return to more civilized conditions in Sevastopol. A kind of friendship had developed between admiral and midshipman, and Halfhyde had learned a good deal about Russia and her Navy. He had steadfastly refused to give his parole, and after more than a year had managed to escape via Turkey and make his way back to England. Twice more since those distant days he had encountered the Russian aristocrat, and each time had caused nautical disaster to him and his ships. Any friendship had vanished; all Gorsinski wanted now was the death of the British officer who had three times made a fool of him.

To put himself back within Gorsinski's orbit was madness: yet the alternative was to refuse his orders, and the name for that was mutiny. Mutiny was punishable by death; and worse by far than death would be the attached disgrace, the charge of cowardice. At the very least—if he could disguise a refusal of orders tactfully, and achieve withdrawal by less direct means— he would all too likely be relegated once again from active service to half-pay, and his memories of that kind of half-life were still all too recent and vivid: lodgings in Camden Town with the good Mrs Mavitty, his nights disturbed by Mavitty's hacking cough coming to him through the thin walls; days of walking the streets, of preserving one good suit of clothes against better times, one uniform cleaned and pressed against a call to the Admiralty for appointment—days of keeping to the sleazier parts of London in case, in the acceptable parts, he should meet old friends and acquaintances who would press him to accept the drink or the meal which he could not afford to return; weeks that became months when he would not visit his father's farm in distant Wensleydale in case he should appear to scrounge. St Vincent Halfhyde valued his independence and his pride.

He would not go back to all that: he would not, could not possibly, refuse his orders. But his distaste for Vice-Admiral Sir John Willard grew large: the admiral knew the facts about Gorsinski—Halfhyde himself, across the world in Hong Kong, had given him all the details. Yet now, here in Malta, Willard had made his personal choice of Halfhyde above all the other lieutenants available to take the vacant command. And that single fact stank to heaven.

The torpedo-boat destroyer *Vendetta* was lying in Sliema Creek. Halfhyde, after taking his leave of Bassinghorn, made his way in the steam picket-boat to join his command, and was piped over the side as a Commanding Officer for the first time in his career. Somehow the shrill notes of the bosun's call, rising and falling as he descended the Lord Cochrane's ladder to the waiting boat, failed to strike the response they should have done. Halfhyde had no fear of war, of roaring gunfire, of the high responsibilities of command. No man entered Her Majesty's Service for the easy life. But for Halfhyde the magic moment of a first command had been spoiled by the strong feelings of chicanery, of deviousness in the reasons behind his appointment; and he knew that he was about to suffer the same kind of inner anxiety that had for so long dogged Henry Bassinghorn: the knowledge that captains were as expendable as their ships' companies and that every Commanding Officer was by virtue of his position most handily placed to be the scapegoat of high authority when high authority had overplayed its hand and was likely to be called to account.

Nevertheless Halfhyde found his heart begin to lighten as he crossed the deep blue waters of the Grand Harbour. It was a sparkling morning of sun and fresh blue sky, before the real heat of the day had struck. All around him the Mediterranean Fleet was refurbishing itself: clean water streamed from hawse-pipes and washports as the seamen divisions hosed down and scrubbed the already gleaming decks, bell-bottoms rolled up and feet bare. From the flag decks a signal exercise was being conducted with the Lascaris station; in the middle of it the Fleet flagship, HMS *Ramillies,* a battleship wearing the St George's Cross of Admiral Sir Michael Culme-Seymour, the commander-in-chief, at the main truck, made the Dress of the Day signal: *general from the Flag, dress of the day for officers Number Ten negative swords* . . . From Fort St Angelo came the sounds of a military band, the drums and fifes of an infantry battalion marching on the parade-ground below the age-old walls, sounds that echoed across the water and came back again from the climbing clusters of sandstone buildings along the waterfront. Emerging through the Grand Harbour entrance into the open Mediterranean, the steam picket-boat turned westerly for Sliema, and within minutes, as he came into the creek's anchorage, Halfhyde saw the TBD flotilla lying in line behind the *Venomous,* which was wearing the pennant of Captain Watkiss. First was the *Vortex,* then *Venus,* then *Venture,* and last of all the junior ship, Halfhyde's own *Vendetta.* As the steam picket-boat headed towards *Vendetta's* quarterdeck ladder, Halfhyde looked at the small vessel proprietorially. He liked the look of her: her lines were good and clean, her upperworks—bridge, funnels, guns, searchlight platform—all were nicely in proportion, and she looked well-kept, with fresh paintwork, sure sign of an efficient and conscientious first lieutenant, the man who would be Halfhyde's executive officer and second-in-command. As the new captain's boat was brought alongside, her bowman and stern-sheetsman standing with boathooks held smartly aloft, that first lieutenant was waiting at the head of the ladder with the officer of the day and his gangway staff.

Piped aboard, Halfhyde climbed to his quarterdeck and returned the salutes. "Good morning, Mr Prebble," he said to the first lieutenant.

"Good morning, sir. Welcome aboard, sir."

"Thank you." Halfhyde smiled, and held out a hand. The first lieutenant was of the same rank as himself, but Halfhyde was the captain and as such was entitled to the "sir." "Have my gear brought aboard, if you please, Mr Prebble, and stowed."

"Aye, aye, sir—"

"And while that's being done I'll lose no time. I'd like to be taken round the ship, Mr Prebble."

"Yes, sir."

"And," Halfhyde said, letting a degree of frost enter his voice, "I do not like to see lines hanging judas." He pointed to a rope's-end that had strayed from a coil otherwise neatly cheesed down and was dangling a little way over the ship's side. "See to that, Mr Prebble, if you please."

"Yes, sir."

"It turns the ship into a shambles," Halfhyde said loudly, and Prebble flushed. Halfhyde hid a grin; he was being unfair and he knew it; but the word would now spread like wildfire through the ship that the new captain had the eye of a hawk and made no bones about issuing reprimands. Halfhyde also knew something else: very likely Prebble had seen to it personally that the rope's-end had been a small degree untidy; a test for a new captain to sound him out, and also to give him a trifle to draw his thunder and something to complain about from the word go: all captains liked an excuse to let off steam! If that was the case, then Prebble was a good man and a sensible one . . . Some rapport having thus been established, Halfhyde followed his first lieutenant round the ship. He probed into everything; guns—the *Vendetta* carried a main armament of three 12-pounder guns and two torpedo-tubes—storerooms, cable locker, mess decks and cabins, engine spaces and boiler-room. The vessel was in good shape. Back on the upper deck again, Halfhyde looked aft from the turtle-decked fo'c'sle with pride, down past the bridge and the four funnels and the boats neatly griped-in to the davit-heads. Two hundred and forty tons displacement, and capable of some twenty-seven knots . . . not at all a bad command.

"I congratulate you on a smart ship, Mr Prebble."

"Thank you, sir."

Halfhyde looked back at him: Prebble was in fact a year or two his senior in age, though not in naval seniority. He stood stiffly at attention when addressed, perhaps more stiffly than would many officers of the same rank as their captain. He was a pleasant-looking man, with an open face and ready smile, and thick-growing red hair, of medium height and stockily built, with powerful shoulders. The face was freckled, as were the backs of the hands, which were large and strong, toughened from hauling upon ropes . . . Halfhyde said, "We shall go to my cabin, Mr Prebble."

"Aye, aye, sir."

Halfhyde led the way aft, moving along the flying-bridge to the compass platform, and along the main deck to the after hatch. Clattering down the ladder he entered his cabin, a small compartment with two ports, a low deckhead that would prove uncomfortable for his six feet, the narrow space filled to capacity with bunk, desk, washing cabinet and wardrobe. There was just room for two hard upright chairs: a compartment never to be compared with the palatial accommodation afforded the captains of Her Majesty's battleships and cruisers. By the door, Halfhyde's new servant hovered with a cloth over his arm.

"Your name?" Halfhyde asked.

"Bodger, sir. Able Seaman, sir."

"Very well, Bodger. You may perform your first task for me. A bottle of whisky. And one of gin, if Mr Prebble prefers?"

"Thank you, but no, sir. That's if you'll excuse me, sir."

"Of course," Halfhyde said with indifference. "It's as you wish. Are you teetotal, Mr Prebble?"

"No, sir. Only I never take any until evening."

Halfhyde smiled. "Wise and commendable, but I'll not follow your example myself today. Break your own rule, Mr Prebble, and drink to my first command!"

"Oh—well, yes, thank you, sir." Prebble seemed confused, embarrassed: he should perhaps have realized his captain's desire without having it underlined. Halfhyde put him at his ease as Bodger went off to procure liquor.

"I do not expect you to read minds, my dear Prebble. And I genuinely appreciate an abstemious first lieutenant. You'll not find me less so—except upon occasion! For one thing," he added with a smile, "the habit becomes expensive, and I live chiefly upon my pay."

"You do, sir?" Prebble seemed surprised.

"I do. And so, I think, do you."

"Yes, sir. But I'm—"

"From the lower deck, via the rank of mate—I'm aware of that. Let us get one thing straight: I have but one naval ancestor myself, who had the honour of sailing under Nelson and was present at Trafalgar."

"Yes, sir?"

"Daniel Halfhyde, gunner's mate in the *Temeraire*. Lower deck . . . and I'm immensely proud of him. Do I make myself clear, Mr Prebble?"

There was gratitude in Prebble's smile, and warmth as well. "Aye, you do, sir. And thank you."

"We shall get on well, I truly believe, and there's no need for thanks." Bodger came in with whisky and gin, and brought sparkling clean glasses and a jug of fresh water from a small cupboard fixed to the bulkhead above the roll-top desk. He poured the drinks, and left the officers alone. Halfhyde asked, "You know the orders, no doubt?"

"The Dardanelles, sir."

"And the purpose?"

"I don't know that, sir."

Halfhyde nodded. "As I thought. Well, you'll not be left long in ignorance—" He broke off; a signalman was standing in the open doorway, holding a board with a signal form clipped to it.

"Yes?"

"Captain, sir, a signal from the leader, sir."

Halfhyde took the board and read: Vendetta *from* Venomous. *You are to repair aboard immediately.* Halfhyde handed the signal back. "Thank you. I'll not send a reply. The message seems not to call for one."

"Aye, aye, sir." The signalman turned about and disappeared.

"A little peremptory," Halfhyde murmured, his eyes glinting, "and not addressed generally. It's me alone he wants." He paused, rubbing a hand across his long jaw and staring reflectively at his first lieutenant. It was in his mind to enquire of Prebble what was the view generally held in the flotilla of Captain Watkiss; but the answer was surely so clear as to make the question superfluous, and Halfhyde had no wish to subvert the flotilla's discipline by encouraging insubordinate utterances. He got to his feet. "Call away my galley, if you please, First Lieutenant," he said, then added less formally and with a smile, "I trust I shall survive Captain Watkiss, and have the pleasure afterwards of meeting you again!"

•   •   •

The accommodation in the flotilla leader was superior to that in the junior ships: Captain Watkiss, in a sense a species of flag officer, at least in his own estimation, was provided with an office in addition to a cabin that was twice the size of Halfhyde's. To achieve this latter, as Prebble had told Halfhyde before the new Commanding Officer had left, Captain Watkiss had had a bulkhead removed by the dockyard, thus taking in his first lieutenant's cabin. Selfishness had rippled down the line, resulting in the sub-lieutenant being relegated to a hammock in the cabin flat. Another item of news from Prebble went some way to explaining Captain Watkiss's cavalier attitude towards the vice-admiral: Captain Watkiss had two sisters. One was married to the First Sea Lord, the other to the Permanent Secretary to the Treasury, the man who was regarded as the Head of the Civil Service and who held the purse-strings of government. Such a combination of marriages made Captain Watkiss formidable indeed.

And this morning he looked it.

His face was redder than before and his lower lip protruded, giving him the aspect of a bulldog. There appeared to be no particular reason why Captain Watkiss should be in a foul temper, and Halfhyde had a shrewd suspicion it was being put on for his benefit, a preliminary show of strength as it were to impress the new lieutenant-in-command with the immense power of four gold rings and a brace of good marriages against two and none.

"Took your time," Captain Watkiss snapped.

"I beg to—"

"Hold your tongue." Watkiss flourished a copy of the sum-moning signal. "Time of origin, nineteen minutes ago—*nineteen minutes!* Should have been here in ten at the most."

"Had I wings," Halfhyde said tartly, "I would have been."

"Don't be impertinent with me. Be so again and I'll break you. I said, you took your time. That's fact—I said it. *Hold your tongue, sir!*" Captain Watkiss appeared to vibrate in his chair; his stomach, impacting against his desk, set off a reaction: a pen in a silver ink-stand tinkled gently. Halfhyde sighed and decided on non-provocation: it was early days. Although he realized full well that as few words as "Pompous old fool; and that's fact—I said it" would undoubtedly preserve him against Admiral Prince Gorsinski, Halfhyde's fighting spirit—*vis-à-vis* both the enemy and Captain Watkiss—would not now let him back out: this thing must be seen through. Captain Watkiss pro-ceeded to tell Halfhyde why he had sent for him.

"Your orders, your *personal* orders. I am instructed by the vice-admiral to pass them, and I now do so." He did; the orders were brief, pointed, and dangerous: if it was not found possi-ble to lay alongside the arrested *Falls of Dochart* and sail her out either under her own canvas or under tow, then the con-duct of the operation was to devolve upon Halfhyde. He was to pass his command to Lieutenant Prebble, and himself to pro-ceed ashore in plain clothes—in other words, as Halfhyde elicited, in disguise. Since Britain and Russia were not at war, he could scarcely be treated as a spy by virtue of his not, as a serving officer, wearing uniform.

"With respect, sir, you don't know Gorsinski. And suppose—by that time—we *are* at war?"

"This risk is to be taken nevertheless. Once ashore, you will first locate the *Falls of Dochart* if her position has not already been seen from the flotilla. You will then reconnoitre the state of affairs—we have no information as to whether or not the master and crew are still aboard or imprisoned ashore. You shall find that out. You'll also establish the reason for the arrest—the given reason, and the *real* reason. Then you'll return to the flotilla—to my ship, to me, to report. Upon your report will depend my decision as to the next move. That's all."

"Why me, sir?"

Captain Watkiss raised his eyebrows and his colour deepened. "Why *not* you, sir? Why anybody? Are you trying to shift your orders onto someone else, and to evade danger yourself?"

"No, I'm not!" Halfhyde snapped, his own face dangerous now. "What's more, you know I'm not, sir. My question was a serious one, and I repeat it: why me? In all the past circumstances—which perhaps you know about, or perhaps—"

"The past," Watkiss interrupted, "is the key to the future. *Your* past has been made known to me. You are being sent for the very reason that you have been in the Black Sea, in Sevastopol itself, before. No other officer in my flotilla has. You speak Russian. No other officer in my flotilla does. You have personal knowledge of this Gorsinski—again, no-one else has. You will know how his mind works, what he is likely to do in face of the entry of my flotilla into his area of command . . . I think you understand very well and I need not elaborate."

"With respect, I do not—"

"Hold your tongue. You may go back now to your own ship." Captain Watkiss waved a dismissive hand, exhibiting his colourful tattoo.

• • •

Watkiss remained in his cabin, disdaining to see a junior captain over the side. As Halfhyde waited for the recall of his galley, which was lying off some few cables'-lengths away from the leader, he pondered on something he had seen when he had come aboard: all the visible starboard-side ladders in the ship— quarterdeck to superstructure, superstructure to compass platform as well as that leading up from the cabin flat—bore painted notices, red lettering on white backgrounds: CAPTAIN ONLY. Halfhyde gave a wintry smile: when the *Venomous* cleared for action, it was much to be hoped that Captain Watkiss would permit less exalted feet than his own to double to their stations by the fastest route! Leaving by the port-side ladder, Halfhyde gave thanks to God for his own command; to be first lieutenant to Captain Watkiss would be penal servitude! Back aboard the *Vendetta,* he was met punctiliously at the head of the ladder by Lieutenant Prebble, standing at the salute as the bosun's call piped Halfhyde up the side.

"Are there fresh orders, sir?" Prebble asked.

"No, Mr Prebble, but I would suggest you bring me your lists of requirements for stores and ammunition immediately. I have no doubt Captain Watkiss will wish to have them some hours ago."

Prebble gaped, then gave a sudden smile of understanding at Halfhyde's retreating back. The requisition lists were in fact almost ready; and within the next half hour both the first lieutenant's and the engineer's stores lists had been approved by Halfhyde and on their way by boat to the flotilla leader for onward transmission to the dockyard. That afternoon Halfhyde made another tour of his command, this time unaccompanied, familiarizing himself with all aspects of the TBD's construction and capabilities, visualizing in his mind's eye the likely effects of hostile gunfire upon an essentially frail craft, formulating ahead of the event what action he could take to minimize and control damage. This was a captain's prime task—to take due account of all possibilities and to prepare plans for dealing with them as and when they occurred; thus might lives and precious minutes be saved. On his rounds Halfhyde spoke to many of his ship's company: the torpedo-coxswain, who in a small vessel took the place of a master-at-arms and acted as quarter-master when in action and when entering and leaving harbour; the torpedo-gunner's mate; the chief bosun's mate, commonly known as "the buffer"; the chief engine-room artificer who acted as engineer officer; the supply petty officer, Jack Dusty to his shipmates—and many others. He asked questions, some of them purely for information, some of them awkward and prob-ing ones designed to show up inefficiency or inattentiveness to duty and to make the men think ahead, as he did, to danger.

In the late afternoon Halfhyde changed into civilian clothes, had his boat called away, and proceeded ashore to Sliema. He took himself for a long walk, and later, as night began to fall, circled back around Sliema Creek into Valletta and its teeming hordes of libertymen from the ships of the Mediterranean Fleet and of soldiers from the various barracks on the island, rois-tering men in various stages of drink, singing their way along the narrow streets, streets so steep that most of them had been cut into steps. Dark-skinned women hung from windows, look-ing down on the mixture of goats and men, smiling, inviting with words and gestures. From some of the windows soft music came, and there was a curious smell, composed of heavy scent, goat droppings, sweat, and beer, the almost magical smell of foreign service for Her Majesty. At one moment Halfhyde was passed by a strange sight: a member of the Confraternity of the Holy Rosary, a brotherhood attached to the Dominican order, a man dressed all in white, even to his wide-brimmed hat, and with a white mask covering his features: this man was collecting alms to pay for mass to be said for the soul of a man who had committed the crime of murder, rare in Malta. Stalking past the white-clad holy man after dropping alms into the proffered box, Halfhyde glanced at the names on the seamen's cap-ribbons; names that in many cases were patriotically—or shrewdly—repeated above the fronts of the overflowing bars: the Warrior Bar, the Aurora Bar, the Inflexible Bar—the Maltese were excellent traders. And in Valletta every other establishment seemed to be a bar or a brothel, or sometimes both combined. The temptations were many; Halfhyde resisted them, thirsting for drink and women though he was, for notwithstanding plain clothes a naval officer was always unmistakable, and it would not do for a newly-appointed captain to find himself mixed up, willy-nilly, in one of the brawls that nightly shook the Malta bars; and there were his private reservations also about the importunate whores who called down to him from the clustered windows. Instead, with a set face, Halfhyde made his way along Strada Reale towards the total respectability of the Royal Naval Club where, along with a mixed crowd of officers from the Fleet, he drank a large whisky. Seated in a leather armchair, he flipped the pages of the *Times of Malta,* reflecting dourly that old Daniel Halfhyde, gunner's mate under Lord Nelson, had probably managed a much more vigorous stay in Malta . . .

•   •   •

At first light on the Tuesday morning the TBD flotilla lay with steam for immediate notice and the ships' companies roused out to fall in for leaving harbour. From the leader Captain Watkiss hoisted his sailing signal and requested permission to proceed; and the moment permission came from the Queen's harbourmaster, the order went out to all ships to weigh anchor. On the bridge of the *Vendetta* St Vincent Halfhyde felt a thrill, which he did his best to conceal from his officers, as he watched the links of his shortened-in cable come home along the fo'c'sle to leave the anchor at the waterline, ready for letting go if required whilst in the harbour's constriction. To be taking his own ship to sea for the first time was a landmark in any officer's career, a moment of great pride and satisfaction, to be savoured. One by one behind the leader the long, slim shapes moved out beneath the lightening sky, the *Vendetta* bringing up the rear. Once outside the harbour, Halfhyde turned for a backward look at the sand-coloured island and the fighting-tops of the great battleships still visible over the thickly-clustered buildings of Senglea. In addition to the thrill of command he was now beginning to feel a slow surge of excitement in his orders: he had never shirked a fight. Yet over all there lay the terrible shadow of Admiral Prince Gorsinski and his immense personal power inside Russia and its territorial waters: excitement in danger or not, Halfhyde could very well have done without the element of spying and intrigue.

He caught Prebble's eye as the latter looked aft from his station in the eyes of the ship. "Secure the anchors, if you please, Mr Prebble."

"Aye, aye, sir."

"Ship's company fall out to cruising stations," Halfhyde said to the officer of the watch, a sub-lieutenant. "I shall be in my cabin, Mr Sawbridge. I'm to be informed at once of any signal from the leader or if any other ship is sighted."

"Aye, aye, sir."

"In the meantime, maintain course and speed—and watch your next ahead, Mr Sawbridge, taking care to remain in station." Halfhyde turned aft to go down the ladder, then paused, astonished: coming through the harbour entrance was the great squat bulk of a monitor, with its huge turreted guns trained smartly to the fore-and-aft line and a string of flags at the starboard fore upper yard—the *Lord Cochrane,* directing her course towards the tail of the line of torpedo-boat destroyers and cleaving a broad white swathe through the deep Mediterranean blue.

"What the devil," Halfhyde muttered; then saw the signal lamp winking from the *Lord Cochrane's* bridge. He read off a signal addressed to the flotilla leader: *I am ordered to accompany you independently, detaching to lie off outside the Dardanelles.* That was all. There must have been a last-minute change of mind about employing units of the Mediterranean Fleet. The use of the word "independently" would mean that Captain Watkiss remained in command of his flotilla, however; neither he nor Bassinghorn would be in a position to give orders to the other— in Halfhyde's view, an unsatisfactory state of affairs. He was nevertheless grateful enough for the tacit promise of support, at any rate outside the narrows at the Dardanelles, from the *Lord Cochrane's* massive fire power.

Chapter 4

"MR PREBBLE!"

Prebble turned to face his captain. "Sir?"

"I wish lower deck cleared at four bells, if you please, Mr Prebble, when I shall inform all hands of our orders."

Prebble coughed. "Beg pardon, sir. You said Captain Watkiss didn't wish—"

"Thank you, Mr Prebble, that will be all."

"Yes, sir."

Halfhyde strode the bridge for a while in silence, then beckoned his first lieutenant to follow him down the ladder and thence to the quarterdeck. Once there, he said, "I regret to say, my dear Prebble, that Captain Watkiss's wishes elude me—I'm a forgetful man at times." He put a friendly hand on Prebble's shoulder. "Forgive me for snapping at you just now. I think you'll understand what I'm getting at?"

"A disregard of—"

"Say it not, Mr Prebble, say it not. Some things are the better for not being put into words. But you have the idea."

Having spoken fully at four bells in the forenoon watch, Halfhyde dismissed from his mind all thoughts of the reaction to be expected in due course from Captain Watkiss; once a decision had been made and acted upon, a post mortem was best left until a higher authority demanded one, and Halfhyde had a fair idea anyway that he would get support from Sir John Willard, who, though clearly he had been steering to windward of Captain Watkiss during the issuing of his orders, could not have attained flag rank had he not been possessed of a mind of his own. But he was not going to be allowed to forget his indiscretion so quickly. As the men were fallen out, a signal was received from the leader: Captain Watkiss, it appeared, had had his telescope trained upon his ships. *Why,* the signal demanded, *have you cleared lower deck?*

Halfhyde called, "Mr Prebble?"

"Sir?"

Halfhyde handed him the signal form. "Think of an answer, Mr Prebble!"

Prebble appeared to be racking his brains and achieving no result; he was not, it seemed, an officer of much imagination. Halfhyde said, "Never mind. Yeoman?"

"Yessir."

"Make to the leader: *I have been airing mess decks and flats.*"

There was a grin on the yeoman of signals' face. "Aye, aye, sir!" Barefoot, he ran off, swift and nimble, and the signal was made. There was no response; Halfhyde sensed huffiness aboard the leader and guessed that he would be made to suffer later for flippancy and insubordination. Nevertheless, he was content enough. He had sensed something else: a stirring of the men's minds as he had talked to them, briefly giving them the facts about the arrest of the *Falls of Dochart* beyond the Dardanelles and the Bosporus. Such indignities should not happen to British ships and their crews, and when they did all other British seamen felt themselves slighted. The response coming back from the men to their captain was none the less clear for being word-less; a ripple, a murmur had gone through the massed ratings that meant they were solidly behind the orders and looked forward to a slice of adventure. Malta was all very well; drink and women and the freedom of shore leave were always welcome, but were the more appreciated when something had been achieved. And Halfhyde knew he had a good ship's company.

The remainder of the day passed uneventfully except for sundry signals sent down the line by Captain Watkiss: *Venture*, out of station, was ordered to report the name of her officer of the watch. *Vendetta* was to trim her guns more closely to the fore-and-aft line. Exercises were ordered so as to improve the speed with which each ship closed-up her guns' crews for action, and the times taken were to be signalled back to the leader. Ill-tempered rebukes for slowness came to all ships until, after many repeats, Captain Watkiss brought the business to a close. As the sun sank in the sky behind them, the sea became ruffled with a light but steadily-blowing wind from the east, and *Vendetta* began to plunge her sharp bows through increasing waves, to send spray flinging back over the bridge personnel. As the last of the light went, a lamp flashed again from the dark shape that was the leader: Captain Watkiss warned of bad weather ahead and adjured his captains, unnecessarily, to see their commands battened-down against it.

Halfhyde went below for dinner in the small wardroom, his thoughts projecting ahead to their arrival in the Dardanelles passage when there would be much toing and froing between Captain Watkiss and the Turkish authorities, at any rate by signal. The Gallipoli Strait was of immense strategic importance, commanding as it did the entrance from the Mediterranean to Constantinople; and both sides were heavily fortified. Since the treaty of 1841 no foreign warship had been permitted to pass through the Dardanelles without Turkish authority; but as the years went by their approval had frequently been given for vessels to use the passage and strict interpretation of the treaty was weakening. Gorsinski must clearly have obtained permission to bring in the *Falls of Dochart* and her naval escort. It remained to be seen what the reaction to the British would be—but Sir John Willard's orders were clear enough: if necessary, the passage must be forced. And of that passage there were no less than some thirty-three miles from Kum Kalesi to Gallipoli before the ships could emerge into the wide waters of the Sea of Marmara. It could very well prove a suicide mission, though, as the vice-admiral had said, it was unlikely that either the Turks or the Russians would wish to provoke a war with the British Empire.

Dinner finished, Halfhyde went back to the bridge. The wind was freshening still, and the motion of the *Vendetta* was uneasy in the rising sea, a thrusting twist of steel into heavy waves, a motion against which it was at times difficult to keep one's feet. But Prebble had done a good job of securing the ship for bad weather; the anchors and their cables were nicely firmed down by the slips and cable-clenches and the hawse-pipes had been plugged against the sea's inrush, while from below there was a welcome absence of any sound of shifting stores or ammunition. Only the coal, heaving about in the bunkers, gave internal evidence of movement: Halfhyde spared a thought for the black gang, the sweating stokers wielding the great, shining shovels, feeding the furnace-mouths and sliding dangerously across steel deckplates as the vessel rolled and pitched and corkscrewed.

"Mr Prebble?"

"Sir?"

"I shall take a couple of hours' sleep in my sea cabin. I'm to be roused out immediately if the weather worsens or upon any signal from the leader."

In the darkness, Prebble saluted, hand against the brim of his sou'-wester. "Aye, aye, sir." There was pleasure in his voice, and Halfhyde's action in leaving the bridge had been deliberate: it was well for his first lieutenant to know he was trusted, that his captain did not intend to be breathing constantly down his neck. Nevertheless, Halfhyde had done no more than tear off collar and tie before his voice-pipe shrilled at him and he heard Prebble's tones as he ripped back the polished brass cover.

"Captain, sir, the leader's dropping astern and seems to be pulling across to starboard—"

"I'll be with you directly." Halfhyde slammed back the cover, pulled his oilskin on again, and ran the few steps to the bridge. He trained his telescope ahead, made out *Venomous* plunging away to the south and causing chaos in the line as she dropped back on its starboard beam, dangerously close to the ships in the middle. Halfhyde ordered *Vendetta's* wheel put hard over to starboard. She answered quickly, her head swinging round to port to carry her clear of the leader. As she came round in a tight circle, Captain Watkiss's masthead lamp began signalling, and Halfhyde read off the message for himself before his yeoman of signals had reported: *am not under control owing to engine failure.* Halfhyde ordered the helm eased to ten degrees of starboard wheel as he neared the end of his circling movement, and with the easing of the wheel came an easing in the angle of her list. With the ship's head coming back into the wind and sea as Halfhyde steered to place her ahead of the leader, there was a decrease in the weight of water coming aboard from the beam.

"Captain, sir." Halfhyde turned to find the yeoman of signals at his elbow. "From the leader, sir: *what are you doing?*"

"What am I doing?" Halfhyde gave a loud laugh and dashed seawater from his face. "Tell Captain Watkiss I am manoeuvring to place myself in position for passing a tow. I shall be streaming a grass line astern shortly and I suggest he does not— repeat, not—break cable."

"Aye, aye, sir."

"Mr Prebble, kindly make ready as fast as possible to tow aft. I shall not lead my cable aft—I shall tow with a hawser, with the intention of keeping Captain Watkiss's head to sea and giving him some steerage way pending repairs, rather than a long tow. When *Venomous* has the grass line, you may pass the towing hawser—and see that it carries a spring."

"Aye, aye, sir—"

"And one thing more," Halfhyde added, expecting a stream of messages of advice emanating from the leader. "You are to remember that I, not Captain Watkiss, am commanding *Vendetta*. Do I make myself clear, Mr Prebble?"

Prebble hid an understanding smile. "Clear enough, sir."

"Then carry on, if you please."

The first lieutenant went off at the run, passing his orders to the bosun's mates, whose pipes began shrilling throughout the ship, rousing out the watch below to back up the hands on deck in running out the wires and ropes. From the bridge, keeping his ship at a safe distance ahead of the floundering

Venomous, Halfhyde watched closely. The searchlights of both *Vendetta* and *Venomous* were now lighting the spray-capped water between the ships, while the stern of Halfhyde's vessel, and the bows of Captain Watkiss's leader, were brilliantly lit as well. Prebble was everywhere, urging, praising, hazing when necessary; and in a remarkably short time the heavy grass line was going out from the fairleads in *Vendetta's* stern, floating on the water and being carried down in a wide swathe by the wind towards the bows of the leader, a heaving-line attached to the eye held aboard *Vendetta,* where a leading-seaman stood ready to cast his end of the heaving-line to the *Venomous* as soon as the distance had been suitably shortened.

A hail came from the first lieutenant, who was using a megaphone: "All ready aft, sir!"

Halfhyde raised his arm in acknowledgement and called to the yeoman. "Make to the leader: *am ready to pass the tow and will close you now.* Mr Sawbridge?"

"Sir?"

"Have you been on the bridge before when a tow was passed?"

The sub-lieutenant shook his head. "No, sir—"

"Then now's your chance to gain experience. Carry on, Mr Sawbridge. Allow the ship to fall back to within half a cable's-length, but be ready to take avoiding action immediately. What do you do first?"

Sawbridge seemed irresolute. Briskly Halfhyde said, "You inform the engine-room that you are about to close. Engines are dirty things, offensive to any seaman, but they have been with us for a long time now and must not be neglected."

"Yes, sir." As Sawbridge bent to the engine-room voice-pipe,

Halfhyde hid a grin. Sawbridge was young, but would grow accustomed to that most difficult of things to master: the showing of initiative and decision when under the eye of potentially critical experience as represented by the captain. Halfhyde, himself ready to act upon the instant his ship should appear to be standing into danger, spared a moment to study the leader's bows through his telescope. As he had expected, Captain Watkiss was in the eyes of his ship, leaping up and down energetically and obviously shouting—and equally obviously placing his thick, squat body where it was most likely to impede the towing operation. Halfhyde watched Captain Watkiss raise a megaphone to his lips, and heard his name bellowed in a mighty shout against the wind; and he lifted his own to reply.

"Are you addressing me, sir?"

"I damn well am! Don't you know how to pass a tow, Mr Halfhyde?"

"I am passing one now, sir, as I have already informed you, and I am dropping astern for the purpose of passing it."

"Why the devil are you not leading your anchor cable aft?"

Halfhyde scowled. "Because I am not, sir. I have already advised you accordingly that you should not veer your own. I am merely passing a steadying tow to keep you out of danger and to prevent drift. I do not propose towing you to the Dardanelles."

"Damn you to hell! My engines—"

"Engines can be repaired, sir, and the *Lord Cochrane* astern has an excellent engineer officer and staff. I suggest you take my towing hawser to your fore bitts and make fast, after which I shall maintain steerage way only to keep us both head to the wind."

Halfhyde laid down his megaphone ostentatiously, and

turned to his officer of the watch. "Close enough, Mr Sawbridge, and well done." Taking up the megaphone again, he called aft. "Stand by now, Mr Prebble."

Prebble acknowledged, and nodded at the leading-seaman with the heaving-line. As the weighted monkey's fist at its end sped with true aim towards the leader's bows, Halfhyde took a quick look around at the other ships of the flotilla. They were standing clear on safe bearings, but no doubt ready to come in with assistance if required. Halfhyde directed his attention astern again, watching the leader; and was in time to see something that, had it not held a risk of extreme danger to life and to his own career, would have been funny enough: Captain Watkiss, who was still standing determinedly in the way, frustrating any attempt to catch the flung heaving-line, took upon his own forehead the full weight and impact of the lead weight in the monkey's fist. He lurched, fell flat, scrabbled on the sloping metal of the turtle-deck, and then, arms flailing, slid, rolled, and bounced down the side and into the heaving darkness of the sea.

Halfhyde reacted instantly. Through his megaphone he roared, "Away sea-boat's crew and lowerers . . . Mr Prebble! Send the sea-boat away aft, then come to the bridge. Mr Sawbridge, remain in charge until the first lieutenant arrives." Halfhyde was already stripping off his oilskins and monkey-jacket, dropping them on the bridge deck as he went for the rail. He dived straight in, taking the water clean, going deep. Surfacing, he dashed the sea from his eyes and saw his own sea-boat being manned at the davits and beginning to drop down for slipping, saw the men clustered at the bows of the leader, staring down into the water, one of them tending a heaving-line to which was attached a lifebuoy.

Then he saw Captain Watkiss, lying half submerged and face down, the air trapped in his oilskins keeping him just afloat. He appeared to be unconscious . . . striking out powerfully, Halfhyde swam towards the drowning man. He reached him and gave him support, waving up at the bows of the lurching flotilla leader and shouting. In a moment another lifebuoy came down and Halfhyde grabbed for it. With difficulty he struggled to get Captain Watkiss into the safety of the lifebuoy; a man dived in from the *Venomous* to help. As soon as Captain Watkiss was secured, the line was hove in; he impacted dangerously against the ship's side-plating, but, helped from below by his rescuers, he was dragged slowly back onto the deck, and more lines were sent down to bring up Halfhyde and the other man.

Dripping water, Halfhyde spoke to the leader's first lieutenant. "I suggest you signal the *Lord Cochrane* for a doctor—and then put me back aboard my own ship before Captain Watkiss is fully capable of expression. We shall then make another attempt to pass a tow, and this time we shall succeed."

The *Lord Cochrane's* Fleet engineer had accompanied the doctor, along with some engine-room ratings: by daybreak both Captain Watkiss and his engines were back to life and the flotilla was proceeding in an orderly manner through a restless sea under a bright blue sky flecked with hurrying white cloud, and the tow long since cast off. Halfhyde, catching up on lost sleep in his sea cabin, was woken by the whistle of his voice-pipe.

"Captain here."

"First lieutenant, sir. A signal from Captain Watkiss."

"Well?"

"He says that last night's manoeuvre was carried out in an unseamanlike manner, sir."

"By whom?" Halfhyde asked sharply.

There was an understanding chuckle. "By us, sir. He adds that the leading-seaman who cast the heaving-line is to be placed in your report and disrated."

"I see." Halfhyde's jaw came out dangerously and he sat up in his bunk. "Reply: Venomous *from* Vendetta: *if you seek scape-goats I shall report to Vice-Admiral Inshore Squadron that you impeded your ship's company and caused danger to life.*"

"Yes, sir." There was doubt in Prebble's voice. "Sir, will this be seen as tactful by Captain Watkiss?"

Halfhyde grinned tightly at his bulkhead. "I doubt it. But I'm not a tactful man, Mr Prebble. You will have the signal sent at once, if you please." He banged back the voice-pipe cover decisively. He was furiously angry that any officer should seek to vent his ill-temper on the lower deck. Nothing had happened to Watkiss beyond a wetting and a certain loss of dignity: it would be hard to take, but it had to be accepted. If the leading-seaman were to be disrated, a thing that Watkiss had no right to order in any case, then his whole future would be affected, from the moment the disrating warrant was executed until the day of his death; for his pension as well as his pay would be reduced, along with his reduction in rank. Halfhyde simmered, unable to sleep further. Watkiss had not even had the common decency to express his thanks for his rescue. All that day Halfhyde was minute-by-minute expectant of further signals of reproof, of damnation, of sheer fury; but the signal lamps remained quiet apart from sundry references to better station keeping, to ensigns foul of their staffs for more than half a minute, to the emission of too much smoke, and to six inches of codline hanging judas from *Vendetta's* outswung sea-boat. Acidly Halfhyde reflected, though he refrained from mentioning it to his first lieutenant, that Captain Watkiss must be studying him through a microscope.

Making twenty knots until the leader's engine failure and twenty-three to make up lost time after casting off the tow, the flotilla, with the *Lord Cochrane* still in company astern, was heading into the Sea of Crete by noon of the second day out from the Malta base. Course was set through the Kithira Strait between the islands of Kithira and Andikithira to leave Crete to the southwest as the ships proceeded across a sea that was now a flat calm blue. They steamed towards the Cyclades whose many islands had appeared to the ancients to be set with divine purpose around Delos, the birthplace of Apollo and of Artemis; according to Greek legend, Delos had been raised from the sea by Poseidon and had floated free until Zeus had fastened it to the bottom, that it might be a secure place for such illustrious births. Past the now fixed isles of the Cyclades the flotilla would come up into the Aegean, towards Cape Helles and Cape Yen Shehr at the entry to the Dardanelles passage.

Halfhyde, walking up and down his narrow quarterdeck with hands clasped behind his back, was preoccupied; Prebble, realizing the captain wished to be alone, kept out of the way. He knew something of Halfhyde's past; St Vincent Halfhyde, though he seldom spoke of his exploits, was on the way to becoming a legend in the Navy. Prebble, a man of limited horizons as compared with Halfhyde, could only shake his head in wonder at what his new captain had got away with, at his impetuous challenging of powerful men: in the Pacific he had caused a Russian cruiser squadron to become land-locked, when the eruption of a volcanic island had sealed them for all time into what had been a lagoon; in West Africa he had caused Russian ships to collide and become stranded, preventing an attempt by the Czar to establish a base; and more recently, again in Africa, had brought confusion and damage to the German Special Service Squadron. It was an imposing list of achievements for anyone of lieutenant's rank; and perhaps gave Halfhyde weight enough to withstand the enmity of Captain Watkiss.

Halfhyde's thoughts, as he paced beneath the hot blue sky, were also of the past, and of the threat for the future posed by the presence of Admiral Prince Gorsinski in the Black Sea. On the face of it, their mission seemed doomed to failure; there must be more in their orders than Captain Watkiss or the vice-admiral had revealed, and in that lay the threat of intrigue. A kind of diplomacy, rather than any act of war, was clearly envis-aged—yet how did one, diplomatically, force an entry to the Black Sea! What was behind it; were they all, Watkiss included, to be sacrificed to some politician's whim? Certainly a British ship had to be extricated from unlawful arrest, but there surely had to be better ways of achieving that. The flotilla was not especially powerful and could scarcely be expected to take on Russian battleships or heavy cruisers; and the role of the *Lord Cochrane* was as yet far from clear. In Halfhyde's view, if the Admiralty really wished to cut out the *Falls of Dochart* from Sevastopol, then it would in fact have been more appropriate to have sent the main Mediterranean Fleet with its heavily-gunned ships into the Dardanelles, to blast the protecting fortresses out of existence.

At ten that night the flotilla was past Andros and clear of the Cyclades; and with a little under a hundred and fifty miles to go to Cape Helles, Captain Watkiss ordered the speed to be brought down to seventeen knots for a dawn arrival. In the *Vendetta* there was tension throughout the mess decks: Halfhyde, informed of this by Able Seaman Bodger—and being sensitive enough to his ship's company's reaction to note it for himself—regretted the fool's paradise that would be prevailing in the other ships. Captain Watkiss, it seemed, took the view that the Navy was always ready for action and that no particular notice was required, that exercises alone were sufficient to ensure a speedy reaction to the unexpected. This was a view that was perfectly tenable, of course, and indeed was held by perhaps the majority of senior naval officers, though not by Sir John Willard. For his part, Halfhyde had no regrets about disobeying the order from the leader. The other ships might well be caught napping, but not the *Vendetta*. Halfhyde turned in shortly after midnight, handy in his sea cabin if required on the bridge. The ship proceeded smoothly through the night-bound Aegean, past the occasional lights of fishing craft. As the sky lightened into dawn, the masthead lookout reported the once-every-minute flash of the light from Cape Helles ahead, and the officer of the morning watch gave orders for the captain to be wakened.

Chapter 5

THE WEATHER was perfect; land and sea appeared covered with a golden haze, behind which there was colour and freshness everywhere, the kind of early morning when simply to be alive was pleasure. St Vincent Halfhyde walked out onto the bridge, dressed in a newly-starched white uniform brought by his servant.

"Good morning, Mr Prebble." He looked astern. "Where's the *Lord Cochrane,* may I ask?"

"She detached, sir, half an hour before first light."

"Why was I not informed?" Halfhyde's voice was cold.

"I'm sorry, sir. Her signals were only to Captain Watkiss, and I thought—"

"Of my sleep? In future, kindly do not. And do not *think—* thinking, First Lieutenant, is stinking. I expect my officers to *know.* And know this, if you please: I am always to be informed of all developments, even detachments."

"Yes, sir."

Halfhyde took a turn or two up and down the bridge to restore his good humour. Then he asked, "Where did she detach to, Mr Prebble?"

"She appeared merely to reduce speed, sir, leaving the rest of us to gain sea-way ahead."

Halfhyde nodded, and moved to the forward rail of the

bridge, looking out towards the land as the flotilla closed in towards the high, whitish promontory of Cape Helles with its fortified castle, visible to mariners from many miles away, marking the entry to the Dardanelles passage, that sinuous thirty-three mile strait varying in width from one to four miles and leading from south-west to north-east into the Sea of Marmara. To the north-east of Cape Helles on the European side of the entry loomed Tree Peak, 750 feet above sea level, and opposite Cape Helles stood the fortress on Cape Yen Shehr to complement that on Helles. There were fishing boats around on the open sea; and coastal shipping, sailing vessels trading between the islands or down into the Mediterranean, lofted white canvas above the blue.

The last time Halfhyde had entered these waters had been under sail—and as Mr Midshipman Halfhyde of Her Majesty's sloop-of-war *Cloud,* last of the sail-rigged steamers to serve in the British Fleet, he had shortly afterwards found himself under fire from a Russian warship. Sinking had been followed by rescue and his period of captivity in Gorsinski's area of command . . . Forcing Gorsinski from his mind, Halfhyde turned his telescope on the vessels under sail: in them lay sheer beauty, unsullied by coal-dust and the throb of engines. The passing of sail had been the Navy's loss, and by now there were few sail-trained men left at sea; one of this diminishing species was Captain Henry Bassinghorn, now somewhere in the Aegean behind the flotilla, a man as different from Captain Watkiss as was chalk from cheese . . .

Halfhyde became aware that Captain Watkiss was now communicating with his ships: a flag hoist had crept to the flotilla

leader's starboard upper yard-arm. Halfhyde, using his telescope, recognized it as a speed signal. Captain Watkiss was
ordering a reduction to seven knots. Not wanting to interfere
with the proper routine, Halfhyde waited until the officer of the
watch, Sawbridge, who was also the *Vendetta's* navigating officer, reported formally; then he nodded his assent. "Make it so,
if you please, Mr Sawbridge."

Sawbridge bent to the voice-pipe connecting bridge to
engine-room and passed the order. As he was doing so more
signals came from the leader: *prepare to anchor in line ahead.*
Halfhyde left the rail and walked to the magnetic compass in
its binnacle. "See to your pilotage, Mr Sawbridge. I shall take
the ship from now."

"Aye, aye, sir." The sub-lieutenant went aft to his chart-table
and occupied himself with taking bearings and memorizing
depths of water in preparation for anchoring. Halfhyde passed
the order, via the bosun's mates, for the cable party and side
party to muster; in fact the anchors had been cleared away for
letting go all the way from the Kithira Strait, and the chains
had been continuously manned by the leadsmen, for the island-
dotted Aegean was a shallow and dangerous sea for navigation.
Halfhyde once again studied the land through his telescope,
then moved back to look at Sawbridge's chart and the small
pencilled triangle that marked the ship's last observed position.
There was more than enough water ahead to ensure safety,
Halfhyde was glad to note: Captain Watkiss was evidently prudent enough when it came to guarding against the possibility
of shoaling water. Half an hour later the leader's preparatory
signal was hauled down, signifying the executive order, and

with admirable precision the ships of the flotilla let go their anchors and simultaneously swung out their booms and ladders as one.

Halfhyde called down to the fo'c'sle, raising his voice through his megaphone over the roar of the outgoing cable. "Third shackle on deck, Mr Prebble."

"Aye, aye, sir." The cable's rattle stopped and all was peace. The ships lay sleepily beneath the heat of the climbing sun, and Halfhyde sent the hands to breakfast when no further signals came from the leader. "We may wait all day, Mr Prebble," he said, sounding restless.

"Yes, sir. What do you suppose will happen next?"

"Captain Watkiss will ask permission to enter, of course, Mr Prebble, and I can only wish he would get on with it and—" He broke off. "I spoke too soon. Our leader is calling the shore station now, I fancy." A signal was being flashed from the *Venomous* and was being acknowledged word by word from the fortress on Cape Yen Shehr. Another period of inactivity followed the exchange of signals, and Halfhyde grew more and more impatient, angry that Watkiss should keep his Commanding Officers ignorant of what was going on. But after some two hours had passed with infuriating and frustrating slowness, a black-painted boat with a gleaming brass bell-mouthed funnel, not unlike a British steam picket-boat, was seen approaching the flotilla leader. Halfhyde's telescope showed, sitting in the stern-sheets, two superbly uniformed officers and a small, dark-skinned man dressed in funereal black.

Halfhyde snapped his telescope shut. "An admiral and a general, I fancy, and a much more dangerous civilian! We are being honoured, Mr Prebble—but I confess I don't like it."

"Why not, sir?"

"Because I'd not expect a simple permission to enter to be conveyed so ceremoniously—and if we enter as ordered *without* permission, the Dardanelles will enfold us like a rat in a trap."

Prebble nodded but offered no comment. The boat went alongside the *Venomous,* where Captain Watkiss was standing at the head of the ladder, complete with sword and a white helmet with a blue puggaree, the sun glinting on the four gold stripes of a post captain on either shoulder of his white uniform. The shrilling of the bosun's calls sounded across to the waiting ships, and the officers vanished below to Captain Watkiss's cabin. A little more than an hour later, they emerged again and went with Watkiss back to the ladder where the boat awaited them. Once again, there was full ceremony, with Captain Watkiss standing pompously at the salute. As the admiral, the general, and the civilian embarked and the boat turned away with them, Halfhyde's telescope caught Captain Watkiss in the unfriendly act of shaking his fist vigorously at their retreating backs. He glanced at his first lieutenant. "The signs are not propitious, Mr Prebble," he said. And he was not surprised when Watkiss made a general sign, ordering his Commanding Officers to repair aboard the leader at once.

"A flat refusal!" Watkiss said, his face radiating heat and anger. "Damn dagoes! I dare say you can still smell 'em, gentlemen! I tell you something else, too—I took damn good care to keep my backside to a bulkhead—never know, with dagoes. But this refusal . . ." He drummed his fingers on his opened roll-top desk. "You all know the orders, of course, and they stand. Has anyone any questions to ask? Yes, Mr Halfhyde?"

"The reason for the refusal, sir. Did they give one?"

"No."

Halfhyde raised an eyebrow. "They spent an hour, sir, saying no?"

"That's impertinent. Re-phrase it." Drumming away, Captain Watkiss stared out through a port, his head lifted superciliously.

"Very well, sir. You were talking for an hour, and no reason for the refusal emerged?"

"Correct."

"But surely—"

"There is no 'but surely,' Mr Halfhyde. I said they gave no reason; that's fact—I said it. The dagoes talked in circles, evading with their damn wiliness every point I tried to make!"

"I see, sir. May I ask, sir, with respect, what those points were?"

"You may. I have no reason to hide them, Mr Halfhyde. I pointed out the immense power of the British Mediterranean Fleet at my command, should I decide to call upon it—"

"How would you call upon it, sir?"

Captain Watkiss stared belligerently. "Have the goodness not to damn well interrupt your seniors, Mr Halfhyde. I would call upon it by despatching the junior boat back to Malta. *Your* boat, Mr Halfhyde. May I proceed?"

Halfhyde gave a small, ironic bow. "By all means, sir."

"Thank you!" Watkiss snapped. "I have to confess the dagoes were unmoved. I then pointed out that Her Majesty would resent very strongly any slight to one of her post captains, would resent it very strongly indeed. I pointed out that the British lion had strong claws when its tail was . . . was not allowed to wave freely."

"Indeed, sir. And the result?"

Watkiss snapped, "No damn result! Whereupon I informed the dagoes that I intended entering the Dardanelles for the Sea of Marmara within the hour—and that, gentlemen, we shall do."

"And what," Halfhyde asked, "do you expect the Turkish reaction to be?"

"I've no idea, but we shall no doubt find out soon."

"And you've no idea, sir, no personal notion, why they refused permission—you were not able to read between the lines as it were, and—"

"Hold your tongue, sir!" Captain Watkiss smote his desk peremptorily, his red face dripping with sweat. "I am tired of being questioned like some damn wart! *I* am the post captain, *you* are merely a lieutenant-in-command! You will do as you're told without question."

Proceeding back to his command over a sea of deepest blue, despite the shallows, a sea that was so crystal clear that the bottom could be clearly seen, Halfhyde's mood was a bitter one. His parting with Captain Watkiss had been an appalling affair of shouting and bad temper; Watkiss had been in such a rage that momentarily, Halfhyde believed, he had taken leave of his senses. Before dismissing his commanders, Watkiss had once again issued the firm order, in response to a query from the senior lieutenant commanding HMS *Vortex,* that none of the ships' companies were to be told the true facts; whereupon Halfhyde, never one to live a lie by concealing the truth, had informed Captain Watkiss that he had already taken it upon himself to make his ship's company aware of the situation; and Watkiss had blown up like a torpedo striking the hull of a battleship. After ranting and raving for some minutes, during which he restrained himself only with an obvious effort from striking Halfhyde, Watkiss had announced a decision.

"Since your damn ship's company know what they should not know, thanks to you, then your damn ship shall lead the flotilla in and take the enemy's first reaction!"

"With you also leading, I take it, sir, but from behind?"

"Hold your tongue! You shall lead in, weighing upon my signal. Afterwards, if you live, you shall face Court Martial for your damn disobedience. And if any of your ship's company should be killed, Mr Halfhyde, I shall see to it that you face charges of murder—murder—murder!" Captain Watkiss underlined each repetition with a heavy smiting of his desk, making its timbers shiver. "The flotilla will proceed in reverse order of seniority throughout, with *Venomous* bringing up the rear. Now get out of my sight."

Halfhyde had been unable to resist his final comment: "In that position, sir, your backside will be most vulnerable to the nastier Turkish aspirations, will it not?" Watkiss had appeared to be on the verge of a stroke, and Halfhyde had departed quickly for the upper deck and his own galley waiting off the ladder. Now, the sourness had caught up and was ready to overtake him. He had unwittingly placed his ship's company in more danger than might otherwise have been the case; and was mortified even further by something else that Captain Watkiss had thrown at him as a parting shot to speed him out of the cabin: if men who knew the full facts of a delicate situation should be captured either by the Turks or the Russians, then it would go hard for British diplomacy and themselves if they should be made to talk. Mentally, Halfhyde crucified himself:

he had had a duty to take that into account, and he had failed to do so. That was a bitter pill. His face grim and hard, he climbed the ladder to his quarterdeck and returned the salutes, meeting the query in Prebble's face.

"Prepare to weigh anchor, if you please, Mr Prebble. When you have given the orders, come to my cabin."

"Aye, aye, sir." Ten minutes later the first lieutenant knocked at Halfhyde's cabin door and was bidden to enter. Halfhyde's face was grey but his mouth was firm and his speech crisp.

"We enter in reverse order, Prebble. Captain Watkiss last, unless he changes his mind."

Prebble stared in astonishment. "Does he fear—"

"I think Captain Watkiss fears nothing! No, it's by no means cowardice. It's stupidity—on my part!" Halfhyde gave a full explanation, holding nothing back. Prebble made light of it, obviously concerned that his captain should not blame himself too much, indicating that he too, had been in total disagreement with Watkiss's order not to inform the lower deck. Halfhyde said, "You are a loyal first lieutenant, my dear Prebble, and I'm grateful, but the fault was mine alone, if fault there was. Now we must all do our best—that's all!"

"We shall, sir." Prebble hesitated. "Why do *you* think the Turks refused permission for entry?"

Halfhyde shrugged. "I don't know, really, that we need to seek a reason. The Dardanelles is within their jurisdiction, after all, and if they don't want us, then they don't. But a possible reason flickers through my mind, I confess!"

"And that is, sir?"

There was a gleam in Halfhyde's eye as he answered, "If

Captain Watkiss, whom the gods preserve, referred to the Turkish gentry, in their hearing, as 'damn dagoes' . . . then what should we expect?"

Within forty minutes of Halfhyde's rejoining his ship the signal came from Captain Watkiss to weigh anchor and proceed inwards, the ships' pennants being hoisted in reverse order of addressees—Watkiss was evidently in no mood to change his mind. With both her bower anchors veered to the waterline, ready for letting go if required, Halfhyde took the *Vendetta* out of the line and then ahead past the leader, saluting Captain Watkiss with the "still" on the bosun's call as he came abeam. The formal salute was punctiliously returned by *Venomous's* officer of the watch, but Watkiss pointedly turned his back as the junior ship went past. Halfhyde, on the verge of making a rude gesture at that broad, white-uniformed back, forbore when he saw Prebble's eyes on him. Whatever had happened, Watkiss was still the senior officer and the need for discipline was greater now than ever before. Halfhyde had no doubts that action in the Dardanelles was a strong possibility, and the men, if it came, must have confidence that there was no disagreement at command level.

As his ship steamed on to pass between the great, grey-brown fortresses whose massive guns looked out across the entrance to the narrows, Halfhyde tried to make some assessment of the chances one way or the other. It was fairly clear to him that the main reason for the refusal of permission to enter was simply fear of the Czar whose massive empire sat firmly on the back of the warlike but comparatively weak state of Turkey. The Turks would know that a British entry without

Russian approval could not but be unwelcome in St Petersburg, and it was also perfectly on the cards that the Turks knew all about the *Falls of Dochart*—indeed, since the sailing ship had herself passed through the Dardanelles, they could not be in ignorance of her physical presence in the Black Sea, even if they were unaware of the reason for her arrest by Russian warships.

As the flotilla closed in on the entrance Halfhyde could see soldiers behind the embrasures of the fortress on Cape Yen Shehr, armed with formidable long-barrelled rifles; and more soldiers behind the breech-blocks of the great guns that commanded the narrows. There was a curious silence as the line of ships moved inwards broken only by the sounds of the engines turning over at their slowest speed. Aboard the *Vendetta* every man on deck seemed to be holding his breath: Halfhyde glanced briefly at his first lieutenant. Prebble's face was shining with sweat and a muscle was doing a kind of St Vitus' dance at one corner of his mouth. No one was under any illusions now: if the fortress guns were ordered into action to protect the entrance, the leading ship at least would be shattered into flying fragments of metal. As *Vendetta* came closer to the land, Halfhyde found himself staring into the gun-barrels as the batteries were depressed to bear upon his bridge. Then, from a landing stage below the fortress walls, a boat came off with another high-ranking officer in its stern-sheets. This boat made for the *Vendetta,* and as it came abeam the Turkish officer stood up and waved his arms at Halfhyde, and called out in a poor attempt at English.

"Stop ze sheeps, Capitano!" There was more urgent arm-waving. "No stop, ze guns—bang!"

Halfhyde glanced down at the fo'c'sle and met Prebble's eye.

"A music-hall general, I fancy, Mr Prebble," he called.

"I think he should be taken seriously, sir. He believes us to be the leader."

"Undoubtedly! But I do not truthfully believe his guns will bang." Halfhyde took up a megaphone and called down to the gold-encrusted Turk. "In the kingdom of Captain Watkiss, the last shall be first," he shouted. Over his shoulder he said, "Engines to full ahead, Mr Sawbridge," then spoke again to the officer in the boat, pointing astern with his telescope. "My flotilla commander—last of the line. It is to him you must speak, and I wish you luck." Handing the megaphone to the boy seaman acting as bridge messenger, he closed his telescope with a snap.

Already the boat with its high-ranking occupant was dropping astern as the *Vendetta* gathered way, the water beginning to cream back from her knifing bows. They came abeam of the fortress batteries, right under the massive muzzles of the guns; Halfhyde, conning his ship in through the narrows, was aware of consternation and indecision among the guns' crews. Well ahead of the rest of the flotilla now, he swept past the fortress, his wash swilling up against its massive walls, his heart in his mouth as he prayed that sheer speed would not send his stern down to touch bottom in the shallow waters and render him helpless, stuck like a duck in the mouth of the channel. A moment later, with the *Vendetta* still safely under way though moving recklessly, dangerously fast, he was through and leaving the guns unable to bear upon his ship. But a split-second later the guns roared into action with a sound and a blast of heat that seemed to herald the approaching end of the world.

Chapter 6

"MAINTAIN FULL SPEED, Mr Sawbridge, a while longer yet."
Halfhyde was looking astern, feeling his very eyebrows singed
by the close discharge of the heavy guns. Outside the entrance,
the water was in torment, discoloured by the sand dredged-up
by the explosions of the shells. The air itself was filled with
flung spray, and through its curtain Halfhyde could see the
remaining ships, all of them out of line and in a disorderly
back-tracking manoeuvre, but all of them safely still afloat. The
signalling projector from the leader was furiously in action,
transmitting a stream of messages from Captain Watkiss.
Grinning, Halfhyde turned his back. He had a strong feeling
that Watkiss would now consider discretion to be paramount,
and would not follow through. They had all had a narrow
escape, and Watkiss would not want to push his luck too far.
Halfhyde stepped to the forward rail of his bridge as a report
came of another fortress ahead, being brought fast abeam by
the *Vendetta's* speed. Halfhyde's reading of the Admiralty Sailing
Directions for the Dardanelles had told him this was New Castle
of Asia at Koum Kaleh, a little over a mile from Cape Yen Shehr,
a strongpoint mounting sixty-four guns of heavy calibre, but of
some antiquity: a number of them threw nothing more lethal
than stone. Halfhyde's ship swept past before the ancient battery could respond to his passing.

"Mr Prebble?"

"Sir?"

Halfhyde rubbed his hands together. "We're the one that got away. Away from Captain Watkiss. We're on our own, Mr Prebble. I am now the senior officer, though without a flotilla to command!"

"Yes, sir. And the orders?"

"There is no change in the orders, Mr Prebble. The *Falls of Dochart* remains in Russian hands, and still has to be cut out."

"You mean we continue into the Black Sea, sir?"

"If the enemy permits. Would you have it otherwise, Mr Prebble?"

Prebble grinned, his face almost boyish. "I would not!"

"As I thought. Keep the men at their stations, Mr Prebble. Mr Sawbridge, bring down the speed to eight knots." Halfhyde paused. "We needn't worry about attack until we approach the next fortress, which is ten miles ahead by the chart. At that time I shall pipe for action. But for now, some small reward for excellent discipline whilst under heavy and somewhat sudden fire."

"Sir?"

"Rum, Mr Prebble! With Captain Watkiss well astern, I shall run my own routine. Pipe the hands of the messes to muster for rum at once, if you please, and inform the coxswain to break out for issue accordingly."

The order was received with much pleasure: neat spirit in the case of the chief and petty officers, three-water grog for the junior ratings, was consumed at stations, the novelty adding to the enjoyment; and a spontaneous toast was drunk to the captain. From the bridge, Halfhyde gravely bowed his acknowledgement, then turned his attention back to more weighty matters. Watkiss would, probably literally, be dancing with rage. As Halfhyde had remarked earlier, Watkiss was no coward, and he would be furious at the misfiring of his anti-Halfhyde stratagem, with its result in depriving him personally of the chance of action and glory—and promotion to boot. God alone could tell what reports would subsequently be sent to the vice-admiral and Whitehall as to Halfhyde's conduct in general and his impudent and risky forcing of the narrows without permission.

Halfhyde spoke of this to his first lieutenant. "But," Prebble said, "you were under orders to enter, sir. I don't see how Captain Watkiss can deny that."

"Ah, but the circumstances had changed! It's going to be said that I should have waited for fresh orders—but never mind, my dear Prebble, we have other things to concern ourselves with now."

"Yes, sir." Prebble hesitated, looking astern through eyes narrowed against the glare from the sunlight. "What do you suppose the *Lord Cochrane* will do? They'll have heard the gunfire, that's certain."

"Yes. I fancy Captain Bassinghorn will close the narrows, at least."

"And his guns could shatter the fortress."

"If he fired them. We mustn't forget the overall orders, which are that this affair must be handled with diplomacy and not gunfire."

Prebble nodded. "We didn't enter with diplomacy!" he said.

"Nor with gunfire, Mr Prebble. It was the Turks who opened fire!" Halfhyde lifted his telescope and studied the banks close on either side ahead. "We have the next of the forts in sight now." He turned to the officer of the watch. "Mr Sawbridge, sound for action, if you please."

"Aye, aye, sir." Sawbridge passed the orders to the bosun's mates and within moments the pipe sounded throughout the ship. Men left their harbour stations and moved at the double for the guns and torpedo-tubes, or the ammunition hoists.

Halfhyde kept his telescope trained on the fort, a smaller strongpoint than the main fortified castles at the entrance to the narrows but potentially a more effective one than Koum Kaleh and its museum-piece guns. The guns ahead were modern, and heavy enough to make Halfhyde's own twelve-pounders look like nursery toys and his mission suicidal. Halfhyde pondered, weighing the chances: clearly, his popguns would have no effect other than upon the gunners behind the batteries, men who would be immediately replaceable. The guns themselves would remain intact, as would the structure of the fort, the walls of which came right down below the water. But there was an alternative to the use of his twelve-pounders: his two torpedo-tubes were so sited that they could bear through an arc from dead astern to two points on either bow. With luck and a true aim he could strike the fort below the guns, and blow the lot to kingdom come . . . but to do so would scarcely accord with the spirit of diplomacy. Halfhyde frowned; it had to be one or the other, and the implications of either were far-reaching. To shatter diplomacy so early in the game might be of no help to the imprisoned *Falls of Dochart,* while to turn the other cheek might be to lose his ship and its company. The men looked to him alone for the decision: so did the crew of the arrested vessel, and so did Whitehall. Halfhyde had never underestimated the mental agonies of command; now they had struck him personally with their full force.

He paced the bridge, back and forth, the decision growing more urgent with every turn of the *Vendetta's* main engines, his tall angular body seeming bent with the weight of responsibility, his face creased into lines of sheer worry. Right or wrong . . . lives or the delicate balance of power . . . another ship's crew against his own, and overall the delicately-drawn hair-line of duty. Heads of state apart, there was perhaps no man on God's earth who carried the enormous responsibilities of the captain of a ship at sea.

He swung, his mouth hard. "Mr Sawbridge, the torpedo-gunner's mate to the bridge instantly."

Speed had been reduced so as to give more time for things to develop. Halfhyde, as his ship crept nearer, felt the sweat pour down his body, bringing dark patches to his white uniform. He kept his hands clasped firmly behind his back in case anyone should notice that they were shaking. His orders to the torpedo-gunner's mate had been clear, allowing no possibility of dispute afterwards: himself always opposed to authority's mealy-mouthed and circumlocutory ambivalence, he strove to make his own orders incapable of misinterpretation. Unless the negative came from the bridge, the torpedo-gunner's mate, who would be watching his bearings closely, with his tubes trained as far ahead as possible, would fire one torpedo in the instant that his sights bore upon the fort. There was no margin for delay when that moment came, no time for second thoughts: once they were past the bearing it would be too late. If the bearing drew aft it would put the ship too close to the explosion for her own safety and the firing would become a pointless, two-edged sword. Halfhyde's final decision had now to be made within minutes, and his silence would give the executive order to the torpedo-tubes. His quandary was still a desperate one: his orders from the vice-admiral still stood, but to shatter the fort could render those orders impossible of execution. The news would spread fast, and the end might come in the Sea of Marmara, where heavy ships could be deployed against him . . .

"Captain, sir." Sawbridge's voice was urgent. "The fort's guns are swinging to bear, sir."

Halfhyde's telescope came up, steadied on the fort: he was almost close enough now to read the expressions on the faces of the gunners, and he fancied he saw solid determination on that of the artillery officer behind the battery.

"Read off the bearing, Mr Sawbridge. How far to go?"

"Three degrees, sir."

"Within a hair's-breadth," Halfhyde said softly. Then he saw the officer lift his arm, and in that instant the ship came onto its action bearing. Halfhyde kept his lips firmly shut, and the Turkish officer's arm came down in a rapid, vicious-looking movement. There was a crash of gunfire, and a single shell whined close above *Vendetta's* bridge. Instinctively the bridge personnel ducked; the wind of the shell's passage could be felt, and so could something else: the slight tremor as the torpedo-gunner's mate pressed his firing switch and the "tin fish" dropped into the water on its errand of death and destruction, its controls set to minimum depth. For an instant everything seemed to stand still: then there was an appalling roar and a tremendous flash of brilliant flame, and as all the men on the upper deck threw themselves behind such cover as they could find, the fort blew up. One explosion followed another in a succession of mighty bursts as the magazines themselves caught.

Halfhyde yelled out to Sawbridge, "Engines emergency full astern, and watch your wheel!"

Broken masonry and chunks of earth were falling all around, smashing into the decks and dappling the water with spouts of spray, and bodies were falling in fragments. Down upon the bridge as the way came off the ship fell a human segment, a shoulder still bearing a blood-splattered gilded epaulette, with half the chest attached. As the *Vendetta* moved astern, the explosions seemed to go on and on; and when at last they ceased and the curtain of dust cleared, the fort had vanished entirely, not one stone left standing upon another, not one man appearing still alive.

Halfhyde, looking down with horror as once again the main engines were put to slow ahead, found the first lieutenant at his side. Prebble whispered, "They opened first, sir. They opened first—not us."

"And are dead. Dead, Mr Prebble—all of them. So who's to say when the question's asked?"

Prebble didn't answer. Diplomacy was now obviously at an end. But other things were not: as the *Vendetta* left the grisly and still-smoking remains behind a shout came down from the masthead lookout.

"Captain, sir! Ships coming through astern, sir."

"What ships?"

"It looks like the flotilla, sir."

Halfhyde took a deep breath and blew it out again. He trained his telescope astern. In the far distance he saw a succession of masts and smoke-belching funnels. As he watched, the leading ship began sending a signal, which was read off by the yeoman on Halfhyde's bridge.

"From the leader, sir, you are to heave-to."

Halfhyde caught Prebble's eye. "My overall command didn't last long," he observed evenly. "Stop engines, Mr Sawbridge."

"Aye, aye, sir." The telegraph bells rang as the handles were pulled over, and were repeated below in the engine-room. The *Vendetta* slowed, drifting to a stop in the fairway. Up astern came Captain Watkiss, who had evidently resumed the head of the line and was signalling again.

"From the leader to *Vendetta,* sir, you are to repair aboard immediately."

"Thank you, Yeoman. Mr Prebble, my galley, if you please."

Captain Watkiss lifted a shaking hand towards the burning area where the fort had stood. The tail of the tattooed snake waved as if with life of its own. "Did you do that, Mr Halfhyde?"

"I did, sir."

"May you be forever damned, Mr Halfhyde."

"No doubt I shall be, sir."

"And don't be impertinent. Your full report, here and now. You'll follow it up in writing and sign it in my presence, in my office, witnessed by my clerk."

"I shall do no such thing, sir."

Captain Watkiss gaped, his face scarlet, his eyeglass dangling on a silken cord down the front of his uniform. "Do you damn well *dare*—"

"You exceed your authority, sir."

"A post captain can never exceed his authority! It is virtually that of God!"

"But I have my own ship to command, sir. My report is my affair, and must be made in a conscientious manner, and after due and proper thought, and—"

"Hold your tongue, sir! You do not deny that your action destroyed a Turkish fort. You have already admitted as much."

"Yes, sir. I regret the necessity, and I regret the Turkish deaths—"

"Damn the Turkish deaths, Mr Halfhyde, Turks are but dagoes. It's not them as such that I'm concerned about—" Watkiss broke off and eyed Halfhyde sharply. "Have you casualties of your own to report?"

"Cuts and bruises and abrasions from falling stones and rubble, sir, no more than that I'm glad to say."

"And I am glad to hear it. The Turks, however—I care nothing for the fact of their deaths, but another fact remains: you have very probably brought about a state of war, Mr Halfhyde! Do you realize that, or are you too damn stupid to consider the results of your actions?"

"No, sir. But in my judgement I had no option. The fort had already opened upon us, and I was not prepared to see my ship and crew blown out of the water for want of explosive retaliation. My written report, when ready, will repeat that."

"And will also indicate clearly that you had no orders from me to blow up anything at all!"

"Yes indeed, sir. The orders were not yours, but the vice-admiral's . . . orders, that is, by implication. We were instructed, if you remember, sir, that if entry was refused, then the passage was to be forced. The use of the word forced, sir—"

"Yes, yes. I need no lessons in the use of English, Mr Halfhyde." Captain Watkiss turned away and began to strut up and down his quarterdeck: he had changed into a very curious rig, a kind of semi-uniform apparently of his own devising—a white number ten tunic with shoulder-straps and medal ribbons, sitting upon a pair of short white trousers, such as might be worn by a school-boy, but of a curious length that carried them below the knee and of a voluminous width that gave them the appearance of a short skirt, or kilt. The combination of helmet, eyeglass, tunic, and kilted rump upon the squat pomposity of Captain Watkiss produced a comic enough effect, one indeed that verged upon the ridiculous, and had the situation been less serious Halfhyde would have had difficulty in keeping a straight face. After some half-dozen turns of the deck, Watkiss came to a stop in front of Halfhyde; his initial violent anger appeared to have dissipated itself and he spoke more reasonably.

"I've referred to the results of your action, Mr Halfhyde. That is what we have now to cope with. My first consideration is my orders and their execution, which you have made considerably more difficult, blast you!"

"I apologize, sir. But may I ask how you yourself managed to enter the narrows, if it was not by force?"

"By the exercise of imaginative strategy," Watkiss replied promptly. "After the fortress opened, I persuaded Captain Bassinghorn to bring the *Lord Cochrane* to a position where—"

"The *Lord Cochrane*, sir? But she had detached—"

"*Don't interrupt your betters.* The monitor had not *far* detached, being ordered merely to keep out of sight from the narrows in the hope of a peaceful entry. When gunfire was heard, Captain Bassinghorn very properly closed at maximum revolutions. As I was saying: I persuaded him to bring his ship to a position where he could blow the fortress to smithereens with his bombardment battery. Captain Bassinghorn moved in with his drums and bugles sounding for quarters, and his turrets manned and trained upon the fortress." Captain Watkiss rubbed his hands together, his eyes gleaming. "Hey presto, Mr Halfhyde—hey presto!"

"Very imaginative, sir. Where is the *Lord Cochrane* now?"

"Lying off to seaward."

"And ourselves, sir? Are we to proceed into the Sea of Marmara?"

"That is what I have had to reconsider, with the damn politicians in mind. All these damn socialists too, stumping the country and undermining the loyalties of the common people to the whole concept of the Empire and British supremacy." Captain Watkiss raised his telescope and prodded Halfhyde's chest with it. "I'm no politician, though, and no damn socialist either, I need scarcely add. I'm a simple sailor who knows his duty and damn well does it!"

Halfhyde gave a cough into his hand. "You mean, sir, we proceed in execution of previous orders?"

"Yes! Yes, we proceed! Into the Sea of Marmara and then to the Bosporus. All ships closed up at action stations, Mr Halfhyde—and the devil take the damn dagoes!" Captain Watkiss turned upon his heel and strutted for'ard, his shorts flapping about his calves.

Once again, on his way back to the *Vendetta,* Halfhyde reflected upon Captain Watkiss's obvious physical courage, his undoubted keenness to see action. Something, however, underlay that personal and physical courage, and Halfhyde suspected that the underlying factor could be a lack of moral courage: Captain Watkiss had failed to give the order that in the circumstances he might have been expected to give—the unequivocal order to Halfhyde that no fort or vessel was to be engaged without express permission. The inference was that Watkiss had no wish to have to issue a firing order himself or even to have to give permission: it was better to suffer Halfhyde's impetuosity. And if this was so, then Halfhyde might well need to stand from under later on, and that was not a reassuring thought.

Stepping upon his quarterdeck, Halfhyde returned Prebble's salute. "We proceed as ordered, Mr Prebble, but no longer in our present isolation nor as first of the line. Captain Watkiss will steam past followed by the other ships, and we resume the rear position. Be sure that Captain Watkiss is most smartly saluted."

"Aye, aye, sir."

"And the ship's company to remain at action stations until fallen out by signal from the leader." Halfhyde turned forward and stalked to the bridge, hands behind his long back. There was still his written report to be considered and compiled, but that would have to wait. From the bridge he watched Captain Watkiss move past; the *Vendetta* saluted the leader by sounding the "still"—all hands on the upper deck coming to attention and facing to starboard, Halfhyde and his officers lifting their arms to the salute—which this time was pompously if absent-mindedly returned by the squat, arrogant figure on the leader's bridge. A sudden flash of sunlight reflected off Captain Watkiss's eyeglass and was a moment later followed by *Vendetta's* call-sign from a signalling projector. *Your decks are littered with rubble,* said the signal, *and are to be cleared and hosed down immediately.*

Halfhyde sighed, and sent the bridge messenger for the first lieutenant. Minutes later *Vendetta* was under way again, water streaming from her washports and her armament unmanned as her seamen wielded hoses, brooms, and squeegees.

• • •

Two more forts were passed without incident. No doubt, Halfhyde thought, the land telegraph lines had been busy, and their commanders had been ordered to preserve the fortresses intact.

"And in that, Mr Prebble," he said, "lies foreboding!"

"A trap ahead, sir?"

"Russian warships in the Sea of Marmara—a pound to a penny!"

"Would the Turks permit that, sir?"

"Gladly enough, I suspect, after what happened this morning."

"They'll have informed the Russians?"

"I don't know, Mr Prebble, but it seems likely enough to me. In any case, if the waiting ships aren't Russian, they'll be Turkish, and the prospect of action equally to be faced. A nice headache for Captain Watkiss!"

"What d'you think he'll do, sir?"

Halfhyde laughed. "I have a strange feeling, Mr Prebble, that he'll be hoping for the intervention of the Almighty!"

Prebble shook his head, lips pursed. "I don't know, sir. I've never known Captain Watkiss to be a religious man."

Halfhyde moved his shoulders irritably and stared ahead through his telescope: once again, he found in Prebble a lack of imagination, and a tendency to take things too literally. He said, "I meant to convey that Captain Watkiss will be hoping to have a decision made for him rather than be faced with the potentially dangerous and arguable decision to shoot first. And the time is almost upon him: I have the defences of Gallipoli in my view—and there is a boat heading for the *Venomous,* with a number of passengers aboard." He lowered his glass. "Warn all hands, if you please, Mr Prebble, that action may be imminent."

Chapter 7

THEY MOVED ON through the water, coming up in the mid-afternoon's stillness towards Gallipoli and the Sea of Marmara. The town, with its castle in its centre, was colourful with proliferating gardens and cypress trees, and was dotted with tall minarets; but the message of the minarets was contradicted by that of the heavy guns ahead. Those guns could be seen now from both the decks and the bridges of the flotilla, long menacing fingers pointing down towards the approaching British warships. There was an expectancy in the air, a feeling that at any moment those guns might open to send down their high-explosive to blast the intruders from the water. There was also, to Halfhyde, a sense almost of unreality about it all. Apart from those gun-batteries everything had an aura of peace and tranquility; it seemed impossible that the broody peace, the sun, and the colour could all be shattered into blood by one man's command, and the resulting pressure on the firing-levers that would discharge the guns.

He heard the voice of the yeoman of signals: "Leader's calling, sir. General signal." There was a pause, then: "*Reduce speed to four knots,* sir."

"Acknowledge, if you please. Mr Sawbridge, bring down the revolutions to four knots."

"Aye, aye, sir."

The way came off the ship; they seemed to do no more than drift ahead. The boat from the shore neared the leader, and from it a man in much-gilded uniform called up, apparently to Captain Watkiss. The boat headed alongside the *Venomous* and was lost to sight from Halfhyde's bridge. Within half a minute the signal lamp started up again, this time ordering the flotilla to heave-to, using their engines only as and when necessary to maintain their positions in safety.

Halfhyde lifted an eyebrow at Prebble. "Discretion has been decided upon, I fancy! But we shall see. I'd not expect Captain Watkiss to back down now, and retreat."

"No more would I, sir. Captain Watkiss is not . . . Captain Watkiss tends to be a bellicose officer in my experience."

Halfhyde kept a straight face. "Quite, Mr Prebble." He stalked the bridge, waiting for further word. All along the line the crews remained at action stations, with guns ready to fire if ordered. In Halfhyde's view Watkiss had made his task the harder by heaving-to—harder, that was, if he still intended to enter the Sea of Marmara. Had Halfhyde been in command, his preference would have been to pass the Gallipoli batteries at speed and make a bold Nelson-like dash for the sea beyond. He stalked back and forth impatiently as the afternoon wore slowly on; he tried, and not unnaturally failed, to make some assessment of what might be going on aboard the leader. Whatever the bargaining, it seemed to be hard. Crowds had gathered along the banks now, staring curiously, but no further boats approached the ships other than the one that had already gone alongside the leader and was now lying off at a distance.

"Lepers, Mr Prebble—or the batteries want a nice, clear field of fire!"

"Yes, sir. It's touch and go."

"Touch and go indeed, Mr Prebble, and I wish Captain Watkiss would make up his mind to go and be done with it." Halfhyde frowned. "There is still the Almighty to be considered."

Lieutenant Prebble gaped, his honest round face puzzled. "The Almighty, sir?"

"God, Mr Prebble—as I remarked earlier, Captain Watkiss may wish for intervention. I make no claims to be God, but it's just possible I might jog a divine elbow." He put a hand on the first lieutenant's shoulder and drew him towards the starboard rail of the bridge. "A word in your ear, my dear Prebble."

"Sir?"

"I have a stratagem," Halfhyde said solemnly. "It will need your cooperation. I have been thinking. Captain Watkiss's visitors can, I believe, be considered of some importance, or they would by now have been ejected . . . and the shore authorities would not have sent men of straw to conduct negotiations, that's clear enough. Do you follow me, Mr Prebble?"

Prebble shook his head. "No, sir, I'm sorry, but I don't."

"A hostage, Mr Prebble! With their negotiators on board, I have my doubts that the local generals and admirals will sanction the firing of the batteries—what say you?"

"Well, it's likely not, I suppose, but . . ."

"But what?"

Prebble rubbed at his jaw. "Well, sir, we're in no position to make Captain Watkiss go to sea!"

"That," Halfhyde said, "is where the stratagem comes in, Mr Prebble. We're not at anchor, we're only hove-to. A shift to sea can be very quickly accomplished once ordered. Listen, and you shall learn . . ."

The order was passed from the first lieutenant via the bosun's mates: "Secure from action stations. Hands to dance and skylark on the fo'c'sle. Clear lower deck . . . All hands move for'ard at the double."

Halfhyde beamed down from the bridge; the ship's company entered with gusto into the spirit of the stratagem. For the great majority it was the first time they had heard the strange but well-precedented pipe the purpose of which was to vibrate the fore part of a ship that had grounded aft and to give it an up-and-down motion, as well as to bring as much weight as possible forward of the centre line. And the hands, obeying the order to the letter, danced and skylarked with happy abandon. A concertina was brought up from below; then a banjo. Riotous songs and shouts of laughter swept down towards the frowning batteries of Gallipoli. Men watched in astonishment from the other ships of the flotilla; soon the proceedings were further enlivened by a Scottish stoker petty officer who emerged from his mess with a full set of bagpipes. The strident strains of Scotland shrilled out over the water; and within three minutes the apoplectic signal came from Captain Watkiss: *Vendetta from Venomous, kindly explain at once what is taking place.*

Halfhyde rubbed his hands. "Yeoman, make to the leader: *I have touched bottom aft and am attempting to shake loose.*"

"Aye, aye, sir." The yeoman clattered out the message on his shutters. On the fo'c'sle, dancing and skylarking continued, as did the warlike strains of the pipes. Suddenly, however, on the word from the first lieutenant, the riotous noises stopped. There was silence; and into this silence dropped once again the clack-clack of Halfhyde's signal lamp calling Captain Watkiss. *I am proceeding to sea*, ran Halfhyde's tongue-in-cheek signal, *and advise you order all ships to follow with utmost despatch. Torpedo firing mechanism inadvertantly tripped and faulty torpedo limping beneath flotilla towards you.*

Prebble was clearly anxious. "Do you think he'll believe it, sir?" he asked.

"No, Mr Prebble, but he'll not be chancing it all the same! I shall make my peace with him later. Mr Sawbridge, watch your helm. Make up to starboard of Captain Watkiss, and lead out to sea. Engines to full ahead, if you please."

"Aye, aye, sir." The sub-lieutenant passed the order to the engine-room. There was every evidence, should Captain Watkiss have his glass trained upon his junior ship, of immense haste to clear the narrows. The *Vendetta* surged ahead, coming up fast abeam of her senior sisters and rocking them with her wash. A string of coloured bunting was climbing rapidly to the leader's upper yard-arm to starboard ordering his flotilla out, and within seconds the ships' propellers were turning over. Coming up towards the *Venomous*, Halfhyde noted Captain Watkiss on the bridge, eyeglass flashing in the late afternoon sun as his ship began moving ahead. Off the leader's quarter was the boat from the shore, empty of important persons, its crew showing signs of panic and of disagreement amongst themselves. This disagreement appeared to be resolved just as Halfhyde steamed past and almost upset the boat with the turbulence of his wash: backs were bent to oars and the craft made with all possible speed towards the Gallipoli forts. Halfhyde became aware of a shout from his port side. Turning his head, he saw Captain Watkiss hailing him through his megaphone.

"Torpedoes, Mr Halfhyde, have to be damn well *paid for* when misfired!"

"Then we had better clear away before it goes up in price as well as in fact, sir." Halfhyde disregarded the next shouted comment and turned his attention to the safe handling of his ship. He had no fear now that the shore batteries would open fire: it was clear enough that Captain Watkiss had, in the interest of getting himself quickly out to sea, refrained from putting his visitors ashore—he would no doubt have considered it safer for the Turks themselves to remain aboard rather than face a misfired torpedo from an open boat. As he swept past below the batteries, Halfhyde raised his hand in a mocking salute, then turned to find his first lieutenant also staring towards the batteries, but with a glum face.

"You look unhappy, Mr Prebble."

"Yes, sir."

"Without reason that I can see. We're through, are we not?"

"Almost, sir. But those guns . . . now we're the other side of them, they're blocking the way out again."

Halfhyde laughed. "You have a trapped feel, Mr Prebble?"

"Well, yes, sir, I have."

"Then cast it aside. Traps open as well as shut, as many a hunter can testify." Halfhyde raised his telescope as the ship, moving fast beyond the last of the defensive positions on Gallipoli, began to approach the wider waters of the land-locked Sea of Marmara, that led through the Bosporus into the Black Sea. Before any report had reached him from the lookouts or from the yeoman of signals, he had seen the mastheads and fighting-tops of heavy warships looming over an arm of the land. "This was not unexpected, Mr Prebble. Warn the guns' crews, if you please. Yeoman, make to Captain Watkiss: *ships ahead believed to be Russian. Do you intend to resume the lead?*"

"Aye, aye, sir." The yeoman hesitated. "Sir, will Captain Watkiss take offence at the wording?"

Halfhyde raised an eyebrow, then chuckled. "The *double entendre* was unintentional, and you're quite right. Negative the second sentence—Captain Watkiss will no doubt make his intentions known without being prodded."

"Aye, aye, sir." The yeoman padded off to send the signal. Halfhyde, maintaining his speed, swept around the last of the land into the open sea. About three miles clear of the narrows, four heavy cruisers lay hove-to, the thick black smoke beginning to stream from their funnels in apparent indication that they were banking fires ready to get under way as the British flotilla came in sight. Once into open water, signals began flying from Captain Watkiss, ordering Halfhyde to take station astern. The leader altered course to starboard and swept importantly up the line, and as she came into position a signal lamp began winking from the Russian flagship, a signal in English that Halfhyde's yeoman read off. He reported, "From the *Nikolayev,* sir, addressed to the leader: *you are in violation of international agreements. Heave-to at once.*"

Halfhyde nodded. "Thank you, Yeoman."

The tension growing, all hands waited. To Halfhyde it seemed to be touch and go once again: all now depended, surely, on the importance attaching to the involuntary guests on board the

Venomous. Captain Watkiss at all events seemed to have no doubts in his mind: he was maintaining his course and speed, signalling to the Russian flagship as he went—Halfhyde saw the acknowledging flashes from the Russian's flag deck, though he was unable to read Watkiss's signals from his position astern. In line ahead the flotilla steamed directly towards the Russian ships, Captain Watkiss making to pass to starboard of the *Nikolayev*, whose squadron was lying disposed to port of their flagship. Halfhyde had identified the ships: with the *Nikolayev*, which was wearing the flag of a rear-admiral, were the heavy cruisers *Poltava*, *Mohilev* and *Bariatinski*. Their combined armament was formidable, and their strength seemed underlined by a sudden change in the weather as the light began to fade. A gusty wind sprang up out of the east, furrowing the sea's surface, chilling the men in their white uniforms, sending the ensigns stiffly out from their halliards and spreading the smoke from the Russian funnels, so that it wreathed and twisted around the guns and the decks. The small British force steamed impudently under the massive guns, whose turrets swung to bear upon them as they moved past the line.

There was no other reaction from the Russians—none, that was, until Halfhyde's ship had cleared the line by some half a mile; then the flagship swung round to starboard and steadied on Halfhyde's stern, a string of flags going up from her flag deck. In obedience to the disposition signal, the other cruisers moved ahead and took up station, one on either beam and one astern of the flotilla, while the *Nikolayev*, increasing speed, moved ahead past *Venomous* to take up her position in the lead.

"An escort," Halfhyde murmured, frowning. "Curious . . . a

premeditated look about it, as though the order to heave-to was
no more than a formality."

"A bigger trap than ever, sir," Prebble said.

"The bigger the trap . . . do you know, Mr Prebble, I have
a feeling the Russians may have overdone the trap."

"Sir?"

"Arresting a merchantman on a charge that may or may not
be genuine according to the circumstances, is one thing. To capture an entire British flotilla from Her Majesty is quite another."

"Even though a Turkish fort has been destroyed, sir?"

Halfhyde frowned. "You think of nothing but the difficulties, my dear Prebble! Turkish fort or no, Her Majesty is sure
to make her annoyance felt in the highest places. Do not forget Her Majesty's widespread marriage alliances, Mr Prebble.
Her granddaughter Princess Alix has recently become the wife
of Czar Nicholas, has she not?"

"Yes, that's true, sir. But will the Czar's counsels be guided—"

"Mr Prebble, the marriage bed, I stress, is but recent."

There was no answer from Prebble, but Halfhyde saw the
stiffness in his first lieutenant's face before the last of the
daylight went. He had offended the good Prebble: it was
unseemly to speak of such things in connection with the Queen's
family . . . Halfhyde smiled to himself, reflecting that it was a
slender thread upon which to hang the safety of the flotilla but
nonetheless a possible one. Even Czars had their human urges,
and even Czarinas, presumably, their right of refusal. And though
the hectoring strictures that would go speedily from Her Majesty
at Windsor to St Petersburg might not be explicit, they would
most certainly be peremptory and difficult to ignore.

•   •   •

The hundred-odd miles across the Sea of Marmara from Gallipoli
to Constantinople was made in seven hours, at the Russian's
maximum speed of seventeen knots. A seaman's first sight of
the old city at the junction of the Bosporus and the Sea of
Marmara was normally breathtaking, but on this occasion the
approach was made under night's cover, darkness that hid the
five-mile stretch of ancient battlements from Seraglio Point to
the Seven Towers, hid the hundreds of domes and minarets,
hid the romantic splendour of the Golden Horn between
Stamboul and Pera-Galata with Scutari in Asia clinging to the
slopes of Bulgurlu, hid the matchless beauty of the entry to the
Bosporus itself and the palatial mansions, gardens, and ceme-
teries of Pera on its high ridge, aristocratic quarter of a teeming, cosmopolitan city. Halfhyde, who had been this way before,
was in any case more concerned with his command and his
future than with scenic delights; in the event the navigation of
the Bosporus was made without incident, and the twenty-mile
passage to Fener Keui was completed by dawn. Emerging from
the Bosporus and standing clear of a line of marker buoys
guarding an area of shallow water, remarkable enough in the
Black Sea, produced by a geological disturbance of the bottom,
the ships set their courses for Sevastopol in the Crimea.

At eight-thirty that evening the British flotilla, still under
escort of the heavy cruisers, arrived off the port and was directed
into Quarantine Bay, where an otherwise empty anchorage was
commanded by a heavy-gun battery on the shore. The Russian
flagship remained in the river outside the anchorage as guard-
ship, and shortly after the flotilla's anchors had rattled out on

their cables a steam picket-boat was seen coming inwards from the *Nikolayev* and heading towards the leader. There was a verbal exchange between ship and boat but no one boarded the *Venomous*. However, within ten minutes of the boat's arrival alongside, a number of persons, clearly visible in the bright light thrown by the leader's gangway lamps, came up from below to the quarterdeck: Captain Watkiss, two resplendently uniformed Turkish officers, four soldiers—and a Russian. A Russian naval officer, a full admiral, heavily bearded . . . Halfhyde, watching closely through his telescope, recognized Prince Gorsinski, recognized him beyond all doubt. It was certain that Gorsinski had not gone aboard the *Venomous* from the picket-boat: Gorsinski, by the look of it, had been aboard the leader all the way from Gallipoli. No wonder the escort had had that premeditated look! Halfhyde, as Captain Watkiss saw the Russian and the Turks over the side of his ship into the picket-boat, snapped shut his telescope, his mouth set into a tight line. As soon as the boat bearing Gorsinski had passed his ship to head out of the anchorage towards the *Nikolayev,* Halfhyde was bidden by signal to repair immediately aboard the leader. Upon arrival his first question concerned Prince Gorsinski, but he was sharply interrupted.

"First, that torpedo." Watkiss's voice held accusation but astonishingly little anger. "I heard no damn explosion, Mr Halfhyde?"

"There was no damn torpedo, sir."

"I thought as much." Surprisingly, something like a grin lurked round the corners of Captain Watkiss's mouth. "What was the idea? To put a charge of dynamite up my backside?"

Tactfully Halfhyde said, "I would not myself have put it like that, sir."

"I should damn well hope not," Watkiss said energetically, "since it would have been impertinent. As impertinent as your damn invention of a misfired torpedo, which any fool could have seen through!"

"Yes, sir. Nevertheless, it had its effect. You went to sea— with your visitors as hostages."

"But not as a result of your stupid torpedo!" Captain Watkiss snapped, his body bouncing in the chair. "I had already decided to do that anyway." The eyes, pale blue, stared over Halfhyde's head towards the curtain over his cabin door. "Now more decisions have to be made."

"Yes, sir. And Prince Gorsinski? May I ask where he came from, and why?"

"You may. Gorsinski was paying an official diplomatic visit to Gallipoli, having taken passage in the cruiser squadron for the purpose. When he heard about the fort in the Dardanelles Strait, and about your action, he boarded me to demand reparations and my withdrawal."

"*He* demanded, sir? Surely, as a Russian—"

"Oh, very well, if you wish to be pedantic, he came aboard to back the Turkish demand. Naturally, I refused to concede anything, and insisted upon the handing over of the arrested British ship."

"And Prince Gorsinski, sir?"

Watkiss snapped: "He denied all knowledge of the *Falls of Dochart*. And at that time he did not say that a Russian squadron was waiting outside the narrows. I make the assumption that

the shoreside dagoes passed information to the Russians by signal, telling them we had Gorsinski and their own damn negotiators."

"No doubt, sir." Halfhyde paused. "Does Gorsinski know
I'm here?"

"No. But I believe he may suspect. He asked for the names
of all the officers of my flotilla—I refused to give him such
information, of course." Captain Watkiss stared straight at
Halfhyde. "*Could* he suspect, do you suppose?"

Halfhyde shrugged. "I doubt it, sir. Certainly he has good
reason to follow my career with interest, and he may be aware
of the Admiralty appointments, but—"

"Your present appointment was made locally, and would not
be in the Admiralty lists."

"Exactly, sir. He may simply be hopeful, rather than expectant."

"Let us hope so, Mr Halfhyde, for your sake." Watkiss
brought out a large handkerchief and blew his nose vigorously.
"You'll have to stand with more than your backside to a bulkhead from now on."

"I take your point, sir, but would make one of my own as
well: these are Russians, not Turks."

"Oh, all damn foreigners are the same," Watkiss said dis-
missingly, waving a hand. "Meanwhile, I'd like your views on
what we should do next. Of all my officers, you're the only one
who knows Sevastopol—and Gorsinski. Which is why you were
appointed, of course. This is where your special duties start, Mr
Halfhyde. Well?"

"I think, sir, for the moment at any rate, we should display
a masterly inactivity."

"What?" Watkiss stared. "You mean do damn all? Just wait?"

"Yes, sir. Everything comes to him who waits."

Watkiss shifted irritably. "Oh, fiddlesticks! I don't want any damn platitudes. I dislike waiting, I dislike inactivity. Dislike it intensely."

"So does Prince Gorsinski, sir."

"What? Oh—you mean we wait for *him* to lose his patience and start something? Is that it?"

"That's it exactly, sir. I feel we shall not have to wait long. But the ball is in Gorsinski's court now, and we must wait for him to play it. When we see which way it goes, then we can reach decisions." Halfhyde paused. "What were his orders to you, sir, regarding the flotilla?"

Watkiss looked angry. "Gorsinski doesn't give me orders. He made *suggestions*. My boats are free to communicate from ship to ship, but he's against anyone going ashore."

"And if they should do so?"

"They'll be shot!" Watkiss snapped.

"An extreme suggestion, sir."

"Hold your tongue—don't be impertinent to me!"

"No, sir."

"In the circumstances, I am stopping any shore leave for both officers and men."

"I see, sir. And did Prince Gorsinski make any . . . suggestion that you should not weigh and go to sea, sir?"

"Yes, he did."

Halfhyde went back in his boat, reflecting sourly that it looked a *fait accompli,* a whole British squadron at the mercy of the Sevastopol batteries and of Admiral Prince Gorsinski. All stood against them. The very waters of the anchorage, night-dark now, were dangerous: across them searchlights played at intervals, picking out this ship, then that, finding and holding Halfhyde's boat as it headed for the *Vendetta*. From each ship of the anchored line, came the routine challenge from the quartermaster: "What ship?"

"Passing," Halfhyde's stern-sheetsman replied. Halfhyde, dazzled by the searchlights, hoped fervently that Gorsinski was not lurking upon the waters, studying lit-up faces . . . but reason told him that there was absolutely no reason for Gorsinski to suspect that his old enemy might have come back to the Crimea. Gorsinski would *not* be expecting him; Captain Watkiss, who, with his perennial impatience with foreigners, considered them all dagoes and persons of doubtful sexual practices, could not be considered an infallible guide to Gorsinski's inner thoughts. Nevertheless, it was clearly sensible that he, Halfhyde, should keep himself concealed as much as possible. Back aboard his own ship, absorbed in naval routine and surrounded by his officers and men, Halfhyde could laugh at his fears. They seemed totally unreal, as indeed did the whole situation in which the flotilla had found itself. In his cabin, Halfhyde, after dismissing his servant, poured himself a generous whisky and turned into his bunk. The day had been long, as had the day before; the whisky compounded his weariness and he was soon sleeping deeply. Halfhyde was not aware of the sounds on deck, of something bumping its way along the ship's side, nor of the hasty entry of the gangway messenger to his cabin. But it took little time for the boy seaman's urgent voice to penetrate the layers of sleep: Halfhyde came awake with a jump.

"What is it?"

"Captain, sir—"

"Out with it!"

"A man making his way to the ladder, sir, on a baulk of timber. He's been brought aboard, sir. He says he's the second mate of the *Falls of Dochart,* sir."

James MacAllister, second mate of the *Falls of Dochart,* was a strongly-built Scot from Fort William in Invernessshire, a man in his early twenties and not long out of his apprenticeship. His level eyes and his bearing impressed Halfhyde, as did his direct manner.

"A passenger was embarked at Palermo in Sicily," MacAllister told Halfhyde. "Only the captain knows the details, but I'm of the opinion the passenger was a Russian, and a man of some importance—"

"His name?"

"I don't know. Again, only the master knows, I believe. I'm judging from his looks and his dress as much as anything— that, and the few words I heard him speak. He spoke in English, but I fancy the accent was Russian."

"And he was bound where, Mr MacAllister?"

"Alexandria, I imagine. I heard nothing of any *en route* port of call after Palermo."

"And your ship—"

"Was intercepted a little to the sou'west of Masara Bay."

"In Crete. And you think this passenger may have been the reason?"

MacAllister nodded. "I do. There's no other reason that comes to mind, anyhow. And the man's actions upon the Russian warship's approach tend to the same view: he went to his cabin, brought out a revolver and shot himself. The Russians put a party aboard, and searched the ship. They arrested us to stop the word spreading, I've no doubt. And you'll see the implications of that, Mr Halfhyde: they'll not be letting us go again—ever."

"They would be foolish to bank upon it! And now you—your escape's going to be noticed before long. Did you cause any loss of life in the course of it?"

"No loss of life. A gangway guard sent down a companion ladder, with concussion and likely a broken leg, that's all. My idea was to reach one of the warships—we'd heard rumours you'd come in, you see—before tomorrow."

"Tomorrow?"

"Tomorrow the crew's being removed to the Karnakol gaol. They say it's escape-proof. I dare say it is. I had to get the word through."

"Which you have done, and done well." Halfhyde got to his feet and paced the small cabin, two steps one way, two the other. Another problem had arisen, and a highly dangerous one for him personally: when tomorrow came, at the latest, MacAllister's escape would be discovered by the Russians. The first place to look for him would clearly be the British ships in the anchorage. The search would be most thorough, and in the course of it Halfhyde's identity might well become known.

Chapter 8

CAPTAIN WATKISS, who had not yet breakfasted, stared balefully through his port towards the Russian harbour installations. Finding no inspiration there, he swung back upon his early-morning visitor. "Why did you not report to me at once, Mr Halfhyde?"

"I decided, sir, that too much boat activity during the night hours might attract the Russians' attention."

"H'm." Captain Watkiss screwed his eyeglass in more firmly. "What do we do with this man, this second mate?"

"I suggest we dress him in naval uniform, sir—"

"Tricky, that. Suppose he's recognized? Where does that leave us?"

Halfhyde shrugged. "We're fully entitled to take our own nationals aboard without Russian permission, sir. So far as I can see, they can do nothing about it. The danger lies in the simple fact of the search."

"Danger for whom?" Watkiss's eyebrows went up.

Halfhyde gave a small, ironic bow. "Myself, sir. If you remember—"

"Oh. Of course. Yes, I take your point, Mr Halfhyde. Well?"

"Are you going to permit the Russian authorities to board the flotilla, sir?"

Watkiss blew out a long breath. "I believe I may have no

option. We are in their hands. I shall protest, you may be sure, and do what I can to prevent boarding—short of force, that is. Force, in the circumstances, would be pointless, quite pointless. Naturally, I shall make very strong representations to the vice-admiral for transmission to Whitehall."

"When will you do that, sir?" Halfhyde asked politely.

"Why, when we return to Malta."

"I see. You don't think, sir, that that will be rather too late?"

Watkiss stared blankly. "Too late for what?"

"For me, sir."

"Don't harp, Mr Halfhyde. You've already mentioned your skin. Be assured I have it well in mind."

"I'm glad to hear it, sir. In that case, may I suggest that when Mr MacAllister is dressed in naval uniform, he be sent across to you?"

"Why?"

"I would assume you'll wish to question him, sir." Halfhyde paused. "There is also—if I may harp again—the matter of my skin. If MacAllister should be found, it would be better if he were not found aboard *my* ship."

"You mean, you might become the subject of a special interrogation? What about me?"

"You have nothing to hide, sir."

"True." Watkiss pursed his lips and rubbed reflectively at his nose. "Very well then, have Mr MacAllister put into uniform and sent across. By the way," he added, "this passenger in the *Falls of Dochart*. Have you any ideas as to who he might have been, Mr Halfhyde?"

"None at all, sir, though I fancy he could have been a political refugee."

"Yes, quite! Probably one of these blasted socialists one hears about in Russia." Captain Watkiss narrowed his eyes in thought. "Who was that German feller?"

"Karl Marx, sir?"

"That's right, that's right!" Watkiss waved his telescope threateningly, as though he had Karl Marx within range. "May have been one of *his* damn confederates! Not surprising he was wanted by St Petersburg if that's the case."

MacAllister, now dressed anonymously as a naval rating and briefly instructed by Prebble in such aspects of warship procedures as could be learned in the time available, went across to the *Venomous* in the galley within an hour of Halfhyde's return—and not a moment too soon. Shortly after he had disappeared from the deck of the leader on his way to Captain Watkiss's cabin, five boats were seen approaching the anchorage from the naval dockyard, each of them containing armed military personnel. One for each of the flotilla: a comprehensive search indeed! Quickly, Halfhyde had the word passed to all hands that his name was not to be revealed to the inquisitors: if asked the question direct, they should answer that it was Smith. When the boat detailed for the *Vendetta* came alongside, Halfhyde stood back; and his first lieutenant formally returned the salute of the Russian officer in charge as the latter set foot upon the upper grating of the ladder.

"Good morning," the officer said in good English. "I have the permission to embark, please?"

"You may come aboard," Prebble answered.

The officer pointed down to the waiting boat-load at the foot of the ladder. "My soldiers too."

Prebble was blunt but polite, "May I ask why this is necessary, sir?"

"You may. It is to inspect."

"Inspect what, sir?"

"For contraband."

"I must ask my captain first," Prebble said, and turned about, marching up to Halfhyde and saluting smartly. "Sir—"

"I heard, Mr Prebble," Halfhyde broke in, keeping his voice low. "Contraband my backside—that's just an excuse. They're making no admissions, any more than Gorsinski did. We shall let them board." He walked up to the Russian officer. "I am the captain of this ship. You may bring your troops aboard, but a protest will be made through my senior officer the moment I reach a British port."

The Russian inclined his head. "I am sorry for such intrusion, but I have orders, you understand." He hesitated. "Your name, please, Captain?"

"Not necessary," Halfhyde said in a cold voice. "Aboard this ship you will have the goodness to address me as *sir.*" He turned away and strode to the after end of the quarterdeck, his telescope under his arm, a captain of a warship who had no desire to watch the humiliation of his command. The Russian officer shrugged, glancing at Prebble's stony face, and called down to his NCO in the boat. The soldiers filed up the ladder and the search started immediately, with a request from the officer that the ship's company be mustered on the upper deck, every man of them. Prebble passed the order to the bosun's mate to clear lower deck, and himself accompanied the search below, while the hands mustered in the waist. The search of stores, engine

spaces, mess decks and flats was thorough, but was clearly conducted with an eye to concealed persons rather than contraband, the nature of which had in any case not been stated. After
this the soldiers passed down the lines of men on deck, care-
fully scrutinizing each one individually and making a brief personal search, a mere running over of hands so as to keep up
the contraband charade. His duty completed, the Russian
politely saluted Prebble, and withdrew his men to the boat,
offering no further comment.

Together Halfhyde and Prebble watched the boat head back
towards the dockyard. "A clean bill of health, then, Mr Prebble?"
Halfhyde asked sarcastically.

"Yes, sir."

"I trust Captain Watkiss will have fared as well," Halfhyde
said. He wondered what would be Watkiss's reaction if the
Russians were to recognize MacAllister and try to remove him
from the ship. If Watkiss resisted, as was likely enough, trouble would come to a head, and that might be no bad thing.
And there was something else to ponder: what reason would
the Russians offer for the arrest of a British subject, and what
would be the result of their natural—and correct—assumption
that MacAllister had already reported the facts about the *Falls
of Dochart?* Pacing the quarterdeck with his first lieutenant, pacing largely in silence, Halfhyde mulled over the possibilities in
his mind and was much relieved when he saw the last of the
troop-filled boats leave the leader's side, apparently without
MacAllister on board; and within the next few minutes his relief
was confirmed by a miniscule one-word signal from Captain
Watkiss: *negative.*

This was followed shortly after by a general signal bidding all Commanding Officers to wait upon Captain Watkiss immediately.

"Damn you to hell, Mr Halfhyde, it is perfectly clear! I have no intention *whatsoever* of regarding myself as a captive of any damn foreigners! Hence, as the officer in command of a visiting flotilla—I repeat, *a visiting flotilla*—I am *ex officio* Senior British Naval Officer Afloat." Captain Watkiss cleared his throat and allowed his eyeglass to fall to the end of its black silk toggle. "Further: when visiting a foreign naval port for what may be a long stay, it is customary to appoint a British Naval Liaison Officer. Since there is no one else to make such appointments, I have appointed myself. Is that not clear enough, Mr Halfhyde?"

"Quite clear, sir, but I have a difficulty in mind."

"What difficulty?" Watkiss snapped.

"The difficulty of your identity, sir. How are we to know, for instance, when you make a signal, which of your several capacities you are acting in?"

"God," Watkiss prayed, "give me strength. When I am acting as senior officer of the flotilla, any signals will be sent as usual—from *Venomous*. When I am acting as British Naval Liaison Officer, Sevastopol, signals will be sent from BNLO. In my third capacity, I shall send signals from SBNOA. All of you, gentlemen, are to ensure that your signal distributing offices maintain three quite distinct signal logs. Now to other matters . . ."

The "other matters" were, sensibly enough, concerned largely with keeping the ships' companies healthy and occupied, whilst swinging at anchor and confined aboard their ships. Among other things the British Naval Liaison Officer, Sevastopol—who seemed to have solved his own occupational problem satisfactorily, Halfhyde noted—would approach the Russian naval command for permission to land exercise parties daily; and would be making strong representations, no doubt doomed to failure, for permission to contact the British Ambassador in St Petersburg. When these and other matters had been dealt with, the Commanding Officers returned to their ships. As Halfhyde remarked to Prebble, Captain Watkiss was going to have difficulty in reconciling his attitudes: a guest—a visiting captain as he considered himself to be—did not normally ask permission to complain about his hosts.

"*Three* logs," Watkiss's chief yeoman of signals said to his leading signalman. "Easy if daft. *Venomous*—BNLO—SBNOA. There'll be triplication, of course, but it can't be bloody helped. Example: Captain Watkiss, 'e wants to nip ashore. 'E can't, not without asking permission of SBNOA. Permission granted, 'e 'as to let BNLO know, just for information, see? So 'e makes a signal from himself, to himself, repeated for information to himself. That's what I mean by three logs. Each self 'as to 'ave a separate file." He sighed and shifted a quid of tobacco from one side of his mouth to the other. "When I get back to Pompey, mate, they'll never bloody believe I served under the 'Oly Trinity."

"Captain, sir! Wake up, sir!"

Halfhyde was once again in deep sleep, and the voice failed to penetrate. In desperation the bosun's mate reached out and shook the sleeping man's shoulders. Halfhyde came awake, eyes wide and dangerous. "Don't you know the regulations, man?

Aboard a ship, sleepers are awakened by the voice alone, never the hand. Reason: sudden wakefulness brings bad temper, and a blow struck leads to Court Martial proceedings. Well, what d'you want?"

"I'm sorry, sir. It's urgent, sir." The bosun's mate was clearly shaken, and not by Halfhyde's angry words. "A Russian party has boarded, sir, and the officer is asking for you."

"For me?" Halfhyde sat up in his bunk and swung his legs down to the cabin deck. Sudden alarm struck him. "In what capacity—and by what name?"

"The Russian asked for Lieutenant Halfhyde, sir."

Halfhyde felt suddenly cold. "I see. Who's the officer of the watch?"

"Mr Sawbridge, sir."

"And his reply to this Russian?"

"That he didn't know the name, sir, but would inform the captain."

"Well, good for Mr Sawbridge, though I fear it's not going to work! Other measures are called for, I fancy. How many Russians are there?"

"Six, sir. And all armed, sir."

"I see." Halfhyde was pulling on shoes and trousers. "Then arm yourself, lad, from the rifle rack outside my cabin." He reached into a drawer of his desk and brought out a loaded revolver. "Then go to the foot of the ladder and call up to Mr Sawbridge that I'd like the Russians sent down. You and I shall take them when they reach the cabin flat. Off you go this instant. I'll be—"

He broke off, staring past the bosun's mate towards the doorway. The curtain had been hauled back, and two Russians stood there with drawn revolvers. Both were in naval uniform: one was a seaman, the other an officer, a youngish man, tall and elegant, with a disdainful look on his face. Heels together, he gave Halfhyde a small, stiff, ironic bow, over the barrel of the aimed revolver. From his shoulder swung gilded tassels, the aiguillettes of an admiral's personal staff—Halfhyde recognized him instantly.

"You are to come with me, please, Captain Halfhyde," Gorsinski's flag lieutenant stated distantly. "Admiral Prince Gorsinski waits." He gestured to the armed seaman beside him, and the man pushed through into the cabin and thrust his revolver into Halfhyde's flank. "To the quarterdeck and my boat, and quickly."

Halfhyde stared back frostily, not moving. "You have the impertinence to give me orders aboard my own ship, and to attempt to arrest me? A British naval officer, my friend, has the backing of the British Admiralty, the British Fleet, and—"

"Fine words," the flag lieutenant sneered, "and with no present meaning in Sevastopol. You are in the hands of Russia now."

"—and of his own ship's company, here present," Halfhyde went on calmly, disregarding the interruption. "You will meet a fine reception, I fancy, when you show yourself on my quarterdeck again!"

The Russian shook his head. "Not so, Captain Halfhyde. Your gangway personnel will have been given no opportunity of communication."

"I shall need only to raise my voice."

"To do so would be most foolish, as you will see. I suggest most earnestly that you remain silent, unless you wish all your men to suffer. Come now." The flag lieutenant spoke in Russian to his seaman, and the man prodded with his gun, urging Halfhyde from his cabin. Halfhyde walked out past the bosun's mate, who was ordered by the flag lieutenant to follow his captain.

Halfhyde climbed the ladder to the quarterdeck, emerging through the hatchway at the top into the menacing barrel of a Russian rifle. Sawbridge and the quartermaster were being held against the after screen by another armed seaman; and Halfhyde was about to lift his voice in a rousing shout when he became aware of the massive bulk looming through the darkness on his starboard beam. As his vision became night-accustomed he recognized the outline of the heavy cruiser *Nikolayev*, which had moved in from her guarding position outside the anchorage and had swung her guns to bear upon the *Vendetta*. There was other activity too: much inter-flotilla signalling had started, and Halfhyde spared a fleeting thought for Watkiss, whose three separate identities might well be busy asking each other unanswerable questions as to the intentions of the *Nikolayev*. In Halfhyde's eyes those intentions could very well be no more than bluff; but Russia was as ever a law unto herself, and the British ships were indisputably enclosed within Russian seas, cut off from all aid despite his own boasts about the Admiralty and the British Fleet. He made the only decision left open to him: he had to accept his own fate discreetly rather than take any risk of the *Vendetta* dissolving in a blast of flame and gunfire, that would shatter her to fragments within seconds.

Halfhyde stepped towards his accommodation-ladder. "Mr Sawbridge," he said formally. "I am proceeding ashore under duress. My compliments to Mr Prebble, if you please, and he is to inform Captain Watkiss that Admiral Prince Gorsinski has requested the pleasure of my company."

"Yes, sir."

"Goodnight, Mr Sawbridge."

"Goodnight, sir." Staring in bewilderment, Sawbridge saluted, and Halfhyde went down the ladder into the waiting boat, which at once cast off and headed inshore for the naval dockyard.

Chapter 9

"OH, BALLS and bang me arse, Mr Prebble!" Captain Watkiss shook his telescope violently at Vendetta's first lieutenant, attending as peremptorily instructed aboard the flotilla leader. "Are you a complete dolt?"

"No, sir."

"Hold your tongue and don't argue with me. I detest officers who answer back."

"With respect, sir," Prebble said doggedly, his cheeks flaming, "you asked a question—"

"No, I didn't! I made a statement, Mr Prebble, a *statement*. You're a dolt, a fool; that's fact—I said it. Hold your damn tongue, sir!" Watkiss held his telescope aloft as though about to strike. "Now let us calmly consider your ridiculous suggestion. Make it again."

"A landing-party, sir, to—"

"Yes, that was it. Landing-party!" Watkiss expressed scorn admirably in both voice and face. "To storm the Bastille, Mr Prebble, or perhaps to march with fixed bayonets upon the Winter Palace in wherever it is?"

"The Karnakol prison, sir—and I did not mean to attack, exactly, sir."

"We don't know if Mr Halfhyde's in the Karnakol prison— his bidding was to Gorsinski in person. Gorsinski's related to the Czar—he's bound to be a gentleman, and civilized. And if you don't suggest attack with your landing party, Mr Prebble, then, pray, what the devil *do* you suggest?" Watkiss's eyes gleamed. "Dance and skylark again, not upon your fo'c'sle this time, but in the streets of Sevastopol?"

"No, sir. But I thought—we all thought—the ship's company has a high regard for the captain, sir, and—"

"He's only been aboard a dog watch," Watkiss said huffily.

"Yes, sir. That's true, sir. All the same, sir, the point stands."

"A demonstration of loyalty—is that what you mean?"

"Well, yes, sir, in a way it is. A demonstration that might impress the Russians."

Watkiss lifted his face and scratched reflectively beneath his chin. "Well, it's a possibility. I might consider it," he said somewhat surprisingly. "Yet I doubt if they'd let us land, you know—and certainly not with arms."

"To make the attempt could of itself force the issue, sir, one way or the other. That's really what I meant to say," Prebble added.

"Then you should have said it. I don't like *timid* officers, Mr Prebble; they aren't command material as you'll discover if you aren't careful. In any case, I'm far from convinced that we should force the issue, whatever the issue may be. Mr Halfhyde himself spoke of masterly inactivity, and I may well decide upon that until some clarification emerges." Watkiss hove in his eyeglass and placed it in position. "Go back now to your ship, Mr Prebble. I shall let you know what I decide."

Currently, though in all probability not for very long, life was a thing of much comfort for St Vincent Halfhyde. He had been taken from the dockyard jetty, in a carriage with outriders, to the headquarters of the Black Sea naval command. Wearing nothing more than trousers into which his nightshirt was tucked, he felt at some sartorial disadvantage as he got down from the carriage and climbed a flight of shallow stone steps to an imposing entrance, above which was set the royal arms of the Czar. Inside, a sentry saluted the flag lieutenant, and a petty officer came forward, also saluting.

"A message to the admiral, Petty Officer Godin. Captain Halfhyde of the British Navy awaits his pleasure. Captain Halfhyde, follow me to your allotted quarters."

The flag lieutenant turned away and led Halfhyde, still under the guard of the armed seaman, along a sumptuous corridor and up a magnificent flight of marble stairs, carpeted in deepest red; never, Halfhyde reflected, had his feet stepped upon pile so thick. Gorsinski, now more senior than when Halfhyde had last been in the Crimea, appeared to live more regally than did Her Majesty Queen Victoria in Windsor Castle: after his last commission, when he had most decidedly reddened the face of the German Admiral von Merkatz in Plymouth Sound, Halfhyde had been summoned to Windsor to tell his story to an intrigued old lady in widow's weeds. He had been surprised to find many of the carpets there not only somewhat worn but also bearing traces of the misdeeds of Her Majesty's small pet dog, a testy beast that spent much of its time crouched suspiciously at the hem of Her Majesty's dress . . .

Halfhyde, proceeding along yet another splendid corridor, was halted by the flag lieutenant outside a massive door, which was opened for him by his armed escort. The flag lieutenant gave an order and the seaman went in ahead of Halfhyde, striking a match which he touched to a taper. From the ceiling hung a crystal chandelier. The seaman manipulated a kind of pulley-hauley system and the chandelier came down like a sea-boat on the falls; a tap was turned, gas hissed, the flame was applied and, fizzing and popping, the clumsy structure was hauled back into its position aloft, a long metal pipe disappearing upwards into a hole in the ceiling. Halfhyde found himself in a large, airy room containing comfortable arm chairs, a walnut writing-desk, a wash-stand with china basin and jug, and chamber-pot cupboard beneath, a vast four-poster bed with a gold and maroon canopy, a carpet as thick as that upon the great stair-case, and two huge windows covered by drawn maroon velvet curtains.

"You will, I think, be comfortable," the flag lieutenant said.

"For how long?"

There was a shrug. "I cannot say. Prince Gorsinski will send for you when he is ready. Do not try to escape. It is not possible, and the attempt would lead to death."

The flag lieutenant turned away and left the room, followed by the seaman. Halfhyde heard the turning of the lock and made a guess that an armed guard would be left on watch outside. He moved across to one of the windows and pulled the curtain aside. Stepping into the recess, he looked out. The windows gave onto the dockyard and beyond it the anchorage where the flotilla lay; Halfhyde was able to pick out the lights of his own ship and the others, gangway lights that were already dimming as the sun came up to expose the eastern sky, reflecting off the cold, flat waters of the Black Sea onto the cranes and stores, jetties and slipways and ropewalks of the dockyard. Halfhyde could see other things too, things much closer at hand: outside his windows ran a balcony, from which two bearded faces stared in, expressionless above cartridge belts and fixed bayonets.

Halfhyde gave them a mocking grin, and saluted them with thumb to nose and fingers spread fanwise. Then he jerked the velvet curtain across again, removed shoes and trousers and went to bed in his nightshirt.

After an early breakfast, Halfhyde received a visitor. To be confronted once again by Admiral Prince Gorsinski brought one of the more unpleasant of his life's encounters to Halfhyde; in fact his arrival produced in Halfhyde something not far from terror. Yet there was a touch of anti-climax about it: Gorsinski, bearded like the balcony guards, tall, well-built, still with little stomach to spoil the line of his immaculate uniform, was polite and even gracious. He could afford to be, Halfhyde thought sourly.

"You have breakfasted well, I trust, Captain Halfhyde?"

"Not 'captain,' sir. Lieutenant-in-Command—Lieutenant by rank still."

"Your pardon." Gorsinski bowed stiffly from the hips. "And the breakfast?"

"Excellent."

"I am glad. I would have come to you earlier, for the matter is urgent, only I was prevented by other duties. In the meantime I arranged for breakfast."

Halfhyde raised an eyebrow. "You're over-concerned about my breakfast, I think. The condemned man's last meal?"

"I hope not, my friend." Gorsinski sat down opposite Halfhyde in a brocaded chair. "You are by no means condemned."

"Why not?" Halfhyde asked coolly.

"Why should you be, Lieutenant Halfhyde?"

Halfhyde smiled. "Revenge, sir—simple revenge!"

"Oh, but no, no!" Gorsinski spread his hands, his face innocent of all such thoughts. "You put the *St Petersburg* ashore in the Bight of Benin, thus depriving me of one flagship. You cause the *Grand Duke Alexis* to smash into my ship. You imprison the *Ostrolenka* in the results of a volcanic upheaval, thus depriving me of another flagship. But I have no thought of revenge—no, none at all, my dear Halfhyde!" The Russian smiled again; Halfhyde fancied the smile was a trifle forced this time.

Halfhyde nodded. "You like being deprived of flagships? No doubt I can arrange for catastrophe to strike the *Nikolayev*—but I forgot, she's not your flagship, is she. You're land-bound now, are you not, Prince Gorsinski?"

"Yes, I am land-bound as you say." The admiral waved an arm around. "This, now, is my flagship, what you in the British Navy call, I think, a 'stone frigate'?"

"Yes," Halfhyde said innocently. "They can't sink, or be stranded. For some admirals, they're less demanding on the national purse."

"I think you are being rude," Gorsinski said in a stiff tone.

"And I think you're being naive—or you imagine I'm stupid. Revenge is starting from your very earholes, sir; you can't wait to watch me dangle from some other admiral's yard-arm, or perhaps you'll use the chimneys of your stone frigate! But before I die, there's something you want unless I'm very much mistaken. That accounts for the veneer." Halfhyde paused, watching Gorsinski's face. "Am I right?"

"Partly, only partly. I almost hanged you once, from my own main upper yard-arm—"

"I remember the occasion well."

"But I have had second thoughts since then. Oh, I have brooded—I admit!" Gorsinski smashed a fist into his palm. "You shall not hang, Lieutenant Halfhyde. For a man such as you, I believe lifelong imprisonment would be far worse!"

"Siberia again?"

Gorsinski nodded. "Siberia again, but this time with no friend at court to help you. Siberia is as cold as ever it was, and as swept by the east wind. The ice and the snow are still there, and waiting."

"I see. Well, we know where we are now, don't we? But I presume there's an 'unless' clause, is there not?"

"Yes, there is."

"What is it?"

Gorsinski gave no immediate answer: he got to his feet and crossed the room slowly towards one of the big windows, where for a while he remained staring out over the dockyard and the sea beyond. Then he came back towards Halfhyde and stood looming over him where he sat. "I know," he said softly, "why your ships have come to Sevastopol."

"Tell me."

"You seek the *Falls of Dochart.*"

"Correct. Do I take it I now have an admission, sir?"

Gorsinski nodded. "Yes. I arranged to have obstacles put in your way by the Turkish authorities, who were by no means disposed to let you through anyway, but these obstacles failed to—"

"Just a moment," Halfhyde interrupted. "You spoke of obstacles in *my* way. Did you know, then, that I was aboard the *Vendetta?*"

Gorsinski shook his head. "Your own advent—for which now I welcome the failure of the Turkish obstacles—was fortuitous, my dear Halfhyde. I had no idea you were steaming into my hands! Your name was quite innocently given to my military search party by another of the commanding lieutenants of your flotilla."

"I see. And the *Falls of Dochart?* How and where is she now?"

"All shipshape, though without her master and crew. She has been moved round to Balaklava, eight miles south-east of here."

"And the 'unless' clause, Prince Gorsinski . . . this has to do with the *Falls of Dochart?*"

Gorsinski nodded. "That is so, but in a sense indirectly. It is concerned rather with the master, and a passenger he was carrying from Naples."

It was on the tip of Halfhyde's tongue to correct this statement: MacAllister had said Palermo. He caught the word in time, and Gorinski somewhat grudgingly made his own correction; Halfhyde was left uncertain as to whether the slip had been intentional. But Gorsinski made no reference to the escape of the sailing ship's second mate. It was possible the search of the flotilla had satisfied him, and that his recovery efforts were now centred elsewhere. Gorsinski continued, "This passenger is now dead, and dead men cannot speak. We know who he was, but we do not know the names of his friends inside Russia, nor what they plan to do. It is considered necessary that we do know. I have orders, personal orders to this effect, from His Imperial Majesty himself—from my Czar. Do you understand?"

Halfhyde answered, "No. But I'm able to make the assumption that you expect me to find out what you seek. Am I right?"

"Indeed you are, my dear fellow." Gorsinski gave a syco-phantic smile.

"How?"

Gorsinski said, "There is one man who is very likely to know: the master of the *Falls of Dochart.*"

"Then why not ask him? Though—allow me to guess—you *have* asked him, and he's refused to speak?"

"Precisely."

"He doesn't fear death or Siberia—or both? I assume you've made the usual threats?"

Gorsinski lifted his arms in something like despair. "You are right. Threats are quite useless. The master—his name is Matthews—is a deeply religious man. This sometimes happens at sea in merchant ships, due perhaps to the long voyages. This old fool reads the Bible to his officers in the saloon each evening in a loud voice, and also quotes the scriptures before any man goes ashore to the temptations of the land. Captain Matthews refuses to put any person in jeopardy by testifying against him, believing this would come between himself and God. The threat of death means nothing to him, and for a particular reason, my dear Halfhyde."

"What reason?"

Gorsinski's answer was gloomy. "Captain Matthews will very shortly go before God in any case. He is sick of a fever, and the doctors say he is a dying man. He knows this and all that counts with him is his standing with God. I—Prince Gorsinski, related to the Czar of all the Russias—I make no impression."

Halfhyde sat in silence, pondering: it was true that the mas-ter of the *Falls of Dochart* would be likely to have information about his passenger, though the extent of it was a matter for conjecture; the second mate, MacAllister, had known nothing, but that was to be expected. Masters were not noted for taking second mates into their confidences. And it was clear enough to Halfhyde that Gorsinski was about to ask for assistance in extracting information from the sick Captain Matthews. He put the question, and Gorsinski nodded. "Just so, Lieutenant Halfhyde. That is why I had you brought here. You are not sick, and I think also it is true to say that you stand in no particular fear of God. Siberia you fear more—that is my opinion."

"I have a respect for God. I am a believer and a Christian."

"But not so committed as Captain Matthews. I think you would find it easier to obtain the information I require, and risk God, than to accept the sure and certain prospect, if you refuse, of Siberia." Gorsinski wagged a finger in his face. "Consider this, Lieutenant Halfhyde."

"Are you not forgetting one thing, sir?"

"What thing?"

"The conscience of Captain Matthews, and God as well so far as that goes. If Captain Matthews won't talk to you, why should he talk to me?"

Gorsinski smiled. "Because you are a Briton, and more—a British naval officer. You are to be trusted, are you not?"

Halfhyde said coldly, "I hope so indeed. And that is sound reason for not betraying any man's trust in me. I think you insult me, Prince Gorsinski."

"It is better to be insulted, Lieutenant Halfhyde, than to suf fer the long torment of the salt mines of Siberia. You will make up your mind quickly, please. Captain Matthews is close to death."

Chapter 10

SIBERIA was undeniably unpleasant: the then Mr Midshipman Halfhyde had suffered badly in the bitter cold of sub-zero temperatures, in barren landscapes cut by the knife of the east wind until a man's very blood seemed to freeze in his veins; and the only source of warmth was provided by the back-breaking work in the salt mines. It had been a time, thankfully short in Halfhyde's case, of terrible hardships and deprivation, of hunger and thirst and a total lack of all human dignity. He still held sharp images in his mind of the long-stay prisoners, gaunt men with sunken, colourless cheeks, skin hanging on their bones like clothes on hangers in a closet, men with no hope in their eyes, who looked forward with a desperate longing to the day when their troubles would end upon the death-heap that grew almost hourly.

Halfhyde acknowledged to himself, frankly, that all this was in his mind, and that the prospect was too appalling ever to be accepted again. Yet he was satisfied, when finally he agreed to talk to Captain Matthews, that he was not doing so out of disloyalty or cowardice: it was part of his mission to make contact with the *Falls of Dochart* and her crew, and now, quite fortuitously, the chance was being offered him on a plate by Admiral Prince Gorsinski himself: it could scarcely be turned away, and indeed to do so might well be considered dereliction of his appointed duty. When he had spoken to Captain Matthews would be the time to consider what he should report back to Gorsinski.

A boat from the dockyard attended upon HMS *Vendetta,* bearing a note in Halfhyde's handwriting addressed to the first lieutenant: in response to which Halfhyde's white uniform tunic and cap, with a clean pair of white trousers and other accoutrements, were handed to the boat's coxswain. Half an hour later Halfhyde was fully dressed in uniform and proceeding in a carriage with Prince Gorsinski towards the Karnakol prison.

"I shall speak to Captain Matthews alone," he said, glancing sideways at Gorsinski as the carriage swayed through the streets of Sevastopol, largely the streets of sailortown and with overtones of Portsmouth, Chatham, or Devonport. "I insist upon that, sir."

"You are in no position to insist, Lieutenant Halfhyde."

Halfhyde gave an acid smile. "I disagree. You say Captain Matthews will trust me. That remains to be seen. What is as sure as tomorrow's dawn is that he will not trust *you*—or any other Russian. Unless I am alone, sir, a pound to a penny he'll not open his mouth!"

Gorsinski muttered something in Russian, shifted angrily on the carriage leather, then snapped, "Very well then, you shall be alone. But take care, Lieutenant Halfhyde. Take much care."

"I shall indeed, sir." Halfhyde paused. "Am I to understand that Captain Matthews is in the hospital wing, or the sick quarters of the prison?"

"Neither," Gorsinski answered shortly. "The Karnakol gaol has neither hospital wing nor sick quarters. Prisoners are prisoners, Lieutenant Halfhyde, they are not sub-divided into sick and unsick." He laughed. "Do you not remember Siberia? Did not the sick work with the fit men, and did not the dying work with the merely sick?"

Halfhyde, feeling again that Siberian cold in his bones, gave no answer. The carriage rolled on along mean streets, whose inhabitants cringed back along greasy walls as the aristocrat passed by in comfort. Ahead of Gorsinski the coachman's whip cracked, ensuring clear passage from the pedestrians, now and again taking a man's or a woman's back to rip away the thin clothing when the unfortunate person, deaf perhaps or inattentive, had failed to leap aside soon enough. Halfhyde sat with a grim face, wondering, as he had wondered on his last enforced visit, how much longer the Russian peasantry and workers would put up with such treatment from their masters.

Arriving at the Karnakol gaol, the carriage pulled into a gateway set between high stone walls and surmounted by barbed spikes. A warder passed them through, bowing as he recognized the Prince; Gorsinski made no acknowledgement of the gesture but sat staring ahead as the carriage went on across a dirty courtyard sunk like a chasm beneath the high prison buildings. Little light seemed to penetrate; the sheer gloom was deadening to the spirit and over all there was a smell that increased a hundredfold when they got down from the carriage and entered a reception area: a foul stench of dirt and neglect, of urine, even an emanation as of human spiritual decay, overlaid by the astringent, cover-up smell of disinfectant. And there was noise everywhere: a coming and going of men, of working parties under shouting warders carrying truncheons which they used indiscriminately, a banging on cell bars, a ringing of feet on the metal stairways, and a clatter of pots and pans from the direction of the kitchens.

Gorsinski, in his uniform as an admiral of the Czar's Fleet, stood looking disdainful and flicking with a linen handkerchief at his sleeve as a senior warder approached, his face an unhealthy prison grey.

"Your Highness—"

"The captain of the British sailing ship."

"Yes, Your Highness."

"How is he?"

"There has been no change, Your Highness."

"He is not to die yet." Gorsinski indicated Halfhyde. "This is an officer from the British flotilla in the port. You will take him to Captain Matthews, and leave him. They will talk in private."

"Very good, Your Highness." The warder bowed obsequiously.

Gorsinski laid a hand on Halfhyde's shoulder. "Speak to good effect, my friend Halfhyde! And have a care for all I have said today."

"I shall, sir." Halfhyde turned away behind his guide. To his surprise, instead of being led up the maze of steel stairways to the catwalks onto which the barred cells opened, he was taken through a massive door at the back of the reception area and down a steep flight of dirty stone steps lit by a single guttering candle-lantern at the bottom. Here the stench was almost over-powering and Halfhyde found his stomach rising in bile to the back of his throat. With an effort he retained it, and spoke in Russian to his guide.

"What part of the gaol is this?"

"The old part." The man's voice seemed flattened, hemmed in by the closeness of the walls.

"The very old part, I shouldn't wonder! It has the feel of dungeons."

"Once they were dungeons, yes. The English captain is important and the orders were to separate him from other prisoners, so he is down here."

"In the sick dungeon," Halfhyde murmured. "Great God above us, why do you allow existence to such abominations as the Russian rulers?"

The guide turned his head. "Your pardon?"

"It was nothing. Merely a reflection upon the livestock, of which I feel there are plenty—and I mean feel."

"Fleas," the warder said off-handedly. "Also lice, and rats. They are to be found in all prisons." He walked on; behind him, Halfhyde was forced to bend his head so as not to bang against the low stone overhead. The passageway, more like a tunnel, was lit at intervals by more candle-lanterns, their flames flickering eerily in the cold draught and adding the smell of melting candle-grease to the others. Off this tunnel opened the dungeons, all of them empty as evidence of the modern Russian mercy. All empty but one: from some yards off, Halfhyde heard the loud groans of the sick Captain Matthews, sole and leprous occupant of this grisly place. Yellow light streamed from his dungeon, light from another of the lanterns set in a small hole cut into the stone to connect the dungeon with the tunnel. Alongside this hole was a thick door, metal-bound, its timbers damp and blackened and mildewed. The warder brought a key to bear upon the lock; it turned reluctantly, with a long-drawn sound like a scream. Ancient hinges creaked as the Russian pushed open the door.

Halfhyde went in: at the far side of the dungeon, on a raised wooden platform, lay an elderly man who had once been big, as was obvious from his frame, but now was shrivelled and reduced by sickness. The face was haunted, the eyes, staring from deep sockets, ghastly. The old mariner was heavily bearded, a grey outcropping thrust over the top of the thin blanket that covered his body, which was shivering with fever. Halfhyde turned towards the warder, and gave a jerk of his head towards the door.

"I have Prince Gorsinski's word that I am to be left alone with Captain Matthews. This you know. Now go."

The Russian nodded, swung round and left the dungeon, once again making the lock scream as he turned the key. Halfhyde walked towards the platform bed. Sombrely he looked down. "You are Captain Matthews, are you not, master of the ship *Falls of Dochart?*"

The lips parted, but there was no word, no sound beyond a bubbling of phlegm in the throat. Halfhyde began to doubt whether anything could penetrate the clouding mists that wreathed the sick man's mind. "My name," he said, "is St Vincent Halfhyde, a lieutenant of Her Majesty's Navy and presently commanding Her Majesty's torpedo-boat destroyer *Vendetta*. I come to your assistance. I ask you to trust me." He blew out a long breath of frustration and put his handkerchief to his nose: even the aroma of "pusser's Sunlight soap" was a better prospect than the stench of the Karnakol gaol's deep dungeons. "But something tells me I'm talking to a brick wall." He looked away, unable to meet the sick man's steady but apparently uncomprehending gaze.

At the foot of the wooden bed, lying on the floor in a heap, was a dark blue frock-coat with brass buttons, and on top of it a tall hat, indication of a shipmaster's status. Halfhyde felt immense sadness: this wreck of a man, this strong man brought

down by the insidious germs of fever, had so recently commanded a fine full-rigged ship, bowling easterly through the
Mediterranean. In his mind's eye Halfhyde could see Captain
Matthews upon his poop-deck on other voyages, on terrible
passages of Cape Horn, or running his easting down before the
westerlies in the high south latitudes, thrusting his command
through the turbulence of the Southern Ocean, from the Cape
of Good Hope to the Leeuwin before storming on across the
Great Australian Bight for the pilot off Sydney Heads. Days of
good clean wind and salt water that could keep a ship's lee rail
under for weeks on end, days when the thought of ending his
life in the stinking pit of a Sevastopol gaol would never have
occurred to a British master mariner in his wildest imaginings.
Halfhyde looked down again at Captain Matthews and spoke
almost to himself. "I'd be better employed offering prayers to
God for a soul about to slip his cable, rather than . . ."

His words died away; there had been a movement in the
sick man's face, a twisting of the lips into a faint smile, and
then, to Halfhyde's utter astonishment, the right eyelid came
down in a wink. Halfhyde gaped; this was totally unexpected.
In a low voice, weak certainly, but sounding far from death's
silencing grip, Captain Matthews said, "A word with Our Lord
is never wasted, Mister, never wasted. And I'm not so sick as
the Russkies believe me to be. The Lord is not yet ready for me
—I'll not be called aloft just yet."

"Well, I'm glad to hear it, sir."

"But the Russkies—*they're* not to know, d'ye hear me?"

Halfhyde nodded. "I hear indeed. For your part, Captain
Matthews, did you understand what I told you?"

"I did, Mr Halfhyde, I did. We'd had word that your flotilla had entered."

"And you'll trust me?"

The eyes narrowed a little and the grey bush of beard sprouted farther out from the blanket's cover. "You look what you say you are. The Queen's ships . . . they produce your stamp of man, Mr Halfhyde. You run true to form. The Royal Navy produces a type. We in the merchant ships are a race, a race of seaman. D'you understand me?"

"I think I do, Captain Matthews. I ask again, will you trust me?"

The old man closed his eyes and said, "Wait. I shall ask the Lord. In Him I trust. He will tell me about you."

Halfhyde gave a sigh of exasperation; the wait was a long one as it turned out, as though a very great deal in respect of Halfhyde had been recorded by the Lord, who was now engaged upon a considerable degree of research and was sorting out the good from the bad. While the lips of Captain Matthews moved in prayer, the Russian warder outside, and Prince Gorsinski in the fresher air above, might well be losing their patience. However, the report, when it came, was evidently satisfactory. Captain Matthews, his voice so low now that Halfhyde had to bend closer to hear, said, "I shall trust you, Mr Halfhyde. Tell me why you have come."

"I shall tell you," Halfhyde said, "and I shall tell you truly. Admiral Prince Gorsinski has sent me to ask questions of you."

"And the questions?"

"The facts about your passenger, the one who died, and about his friends, and their plans."

"I thought as much. I've already been asked that. What else, Mr Halfhyde?"

Halfhyde asked, "Do you confirm that your passenger was the sole reason for the arrest of your ship?"

"Yes. At any rate, I can conceive of no other reason, and no other reason has been offered to me. As to that, there will be trouble coming to the Russkies, Mr Halfhyde, once the Queen knows what they've done!"

"Yes, indeed. Therefore your passenger must have been worth the risk, a man of great importance to St Petersburg."

"Of course—I realize that. And I think trouble has already started for the Russians, has it not? I refer to the arrival of your flotilla."

Halfhyde gave a hard laugh. "Which is now also under arrest! Prince Gorsinski has a short way with opposition. Will you tell me about your passenger, Captain Matthews?"

"I will not."

"It will be safe with me. It will never be made known to Gorsinski. I shall report to him that I had no success."

The beard jutted a little farther. "I'll not say. The Russians use torture. I know my own strength but I do not know yours."

Halfhyde said angrily, "Then why not seek guidance again?"

"The Lord is not to be troubled every time the bell strikes, Mr Halfhyde. Even He can lose patience." The old man's eyes seemed brighter now as they stared directly into Halfhyde's face. "Why do you wish to know all this? What help would this be to you?"

"When I return to report to my senior officer, *all* information could be of use."

"You intend returning, when you have this information?"

Halfhyde laughed. "Intend! I have been frustrated in advance by Prince Gorsinski. Like you, Captain Matthews, I am under arrest and in the personal power of Gorsinski!"

"Well, that's honest, to be sure." The eyes stared harder, seemingly almost to bore into Halfhyde's mind with all the authority of the old captain's heavenly mentor and guide. "Do you intend to procure your release by naming names to Prince Gorsinski?"

Halfhyde felt his face flush, but gave his answer evenly: "I'm a man of honour, Captain Matthews, as I would judge God to have just informed you, since you said you'd trust me."

A glimmer of humour shone for a moment in the eyes. "God was not precise as it happens, but I have judgement to use also. I believe you to be a man of honour, Mr Halfhyde, have no fear about that."

"Then you'll tell me what I ask and tell me also—"

"No."

"But for God's sake—"

"Take not," Captain Matthews broke in sternly, "the name of the Lord thy God in vain. I said no, and I meant no. This means that you can go back to Prince Gorsinski with a clear conscience, telling him no less than the truth. It means something else as well."

"What else?" Halfhyde asked frigidly.

The captain chuckled. "I have no fear at all of death and I do not shrink from meeting the Lord. But I do not propose to go before my next owner smelling like every privy in Christendom—I shall go from the clean wind and a wet deck and with all sails set! I look into your face, Mr Halfhyde, and I see a man of intelligence and a degree of wiliness—enough,

I think, to ensure the escape of both of us from the Russkies'
arrest. I suggest you go and see to it at once."

Easier said than done: Halfhyde went back along the tunnel-
like passage feeling bitter. Gorsinski was a man of instant temper, a man who expected obedience to every whim, a man
whose wish was his command. Halfhyde grinned to himself
as he climbed behind the warder out of the dungeon area: even
Gorsinski's virtual order that Matthews was not to die appeared
to have been obeyed, thus seeming to indicate that God also
came under the orders of Prince Gorsinski, kinsman of the
Czar. Halfhyde reflected upon escape: on the face of it, it was
out of the question, at least for Captain Matthews. To extract
him from his dungeon in the well-guarded Karnakol prison
would require two battalions of infantry backed by the threat
of heavy guns such as the *Lord Cochrane* carried . . . and
Halfhyde would not consider getting away on his own and leaving the old mariner to rot his way to the death he so plainly
detested. Once again the sea visions came to mind: a ship towing out from the Mersey to come down the Irish Sea to the
Fastnet and the start of a 12,000-mile run through wind and
weather to Australia; or the haul through the Sunda Strait and
up the Java seas to China and its pirate-infested waters where
the *prahus* lurked for the kill as the great sailing ships stormed
past the Paracel and Pratas reefs. To meet death there was fit-
ting for a man like Captain Matthews with his patriarchal beard,
Bible in one hand and revolver in the other, his grey whiskers
streaming out before the wind and his mind already with his
God. Halfhyde grinned again as he followed the warder to the
Governor's room; it was now up to him to speed Captain

Matthews towards a worthier end! But the prospects of this appeared no closer when he entered the Governor's room and found Gorsinski pacing up and down impatiently, his eyes looking nearly as feverish as those of the sick man in the dungeon.

"Well, Lieutenant Halfhyde?"

"A nil report, sir. No result."

"Nothing, nothing at all?"

"Nothing at all. Captain Matthews spoke chiefly to God rather than to me. For him the end is near. As you said, he seems not to fear it." Halfhyde shrugged. "And who can blame him? His surroundings are an abomination, and death will come as no more than release—a point you have perhaps not considered, sir."

Gorsinski glowered, hands behind his back, face belligerent. "I have not considered it, no. Captain Matthews is a prisoner—so are you. I do not consider the feelings of prisoners, Lieutenant Halfhyde."

"Then you make a mistake, sir."

"I do not make mistakes!" Gorsinski snapped.

"Your pardon, sir." Halfhyde gave an ironic bow from the waist, his eye glittering. "Having but recently been in vicarious touch with God, I failed to realize that He was to be found in this very room—but no matter. Your mistake is this: if Captain Matthews were moved to more pleasant surroundings, I believe his attachment to life would be greater."

"You are talking nonsense—"

"No, sir." Halfhyde held up a hand and his voice grew harder. "I talk no nonsense, and I suggest you listen. I have a much closer knowledge than you of our British mariners and their often idiosyncratic characters. Put Captain Matthews closer to his own element, which is the sea, and he may not only recover but also regain the wish and the will to live—"

"And to answer questions, Lieutenant Halfhyde?"

Halfhyde shrugged. "As to that, I can't say. But I suggest you leave no stone unturned. It's you that want the answers, not I."

Gorsinski's eyes narrowed to dangerous slits. "You are suddenly cooperative, at least in your very kind suggestions! No doubt you have considered Siberia?"

"I've considered it," Halfhyde responded with an off-hand air. "But I'm not particularly set upon helping you, and I suggest removing Captain Matthews back to the *Falls of Dochart* on humanitarian grounds which may very well work for your advantage at the same time. I think you'd not be taking much of a risk—but, of course, it's up to you, isn't it?"

"Precisely, Lieutenant Halfhyde—"

"And your kinsman the Czar won't be pleased if you don't find that information before Captain Matthews dies."

Gorsinski retained his temper with a struggle: Halfhyde had the impression he might yet mull over the transfer of Captain Matthews; it would be no skin off his nose and he might well be persuaded to see this. A moment later, through the open window, strange and ominous sounds were heard—shouting, and confused noises of running men and horses and over all a weird and strangled sound like that of a pig in torment.

"The devil take it!" Gorsinski said irritably, and strode across to the window. As he gave an exclamation of surprise and anger, a loud knock came at the door behind him. A warder came in hurriedly. Gorsinski swung round, his face bleak.

Chapter 11

CAPTAIN WATKISS had reached his decision shortly after the departure of Prebble back to the *Vendetta*. After due consideration of Prebble's suggestion, Watkiss had seen virtue in it. Further consideration produced in him the conviction that it was all his own idea and he lost no time in sending for *Venomous's* first lieutenant.

"Have a signal made, Mr Beauchamp: *general to all ships from Senior British Naval Officer Afloat, Sevastopol, repeated British Naval Liaison Officer for information*. Ensure there's no damn balls-up in the Distributing Office . . . no, no, no," he added angrily as he saw the first lieutenant scribbling notes. "*That's* not the damn signal! Write *this* down: *intend landing an armed party at four bells. Each ship will provide one officer, one petty officer and twenty seamen to lay alongside* Venomous *at 9:45, armed with revolvers and rifles and one hundred rounds per man. Rig for officers Number Ten negative swords, ratings will wear white duck. Gaiters will be worn*. Understood, Mr Beauchamp?"

"Yes, sir—"

"Another signal, this time to *Vendetta* from, ah—*Venomous: bagpipes will be brought*. Pity we haven't any damn Marines—don't put that in the signal. Get on with it, Mr Beauchamp."

"You don't think, sir, that the Russians—"

"Russians, Russians. Damn foreigners, and I don't give a fish's tit for foreigners, Mr Beauchamp. Are we mice, or are we men?"

The question was obviously rhetorical and the first lieutenant asked, "Do you intend landing yourself, sir?"

Watkiss gave a vigorous nod. "Yes. I shall land and lead." He stared. "Well, get on with it, man, get on with it!"

Mr Beauchamp, a portly man with the half stripe of a senior lieutenant between the two thicker ones on his shoulders, stood his ground and tried again. "I'm not sure it's wise, sir—"

"Not sure, Mr Beauchamp? Did I hear you say, *not sure?*"

"You did, sir. The Russians will never allow a party to—"

"Not sure, Mr Beauchamp?" Captain Watkiss's eyeglass dropped to his ample chest, catching the sunlight coming through the port to sparkle at the first lieutenant. "There is no damn need for you to be sure of anything, Mr Beauchamp— sureness is *my* prerogative, and mine alone." He waved his arms, his face reddening dangerously. "Go away. Get out of my sight."

"Very good, sir." His teeth clenched against further verbal indiscretion, Mr Beauchamp turned away and was pursued along the alleyway by his captain's voice, adding wisdom to sureness in the list of his sole prerogatives.

On the last stroke of four bells in the forenoon watch the assembled boats of armed seamen, led by Captain Watkiss in his galley, left the leader's side and were pulled inshore by their crews. As they came abeam of the *Nikolayev,* a signal lamp flashed in their direction. Captain Watkiss, sitting importantly in the sternsheets of the galley with his arms folded and his expression truculent, snapped: "Yeoman!"

"Yessir. I see the signal, sir."

"What does it say?"

"*Where are you going,* sir."

"*Exercise.*"

The yeoman crinkled the skin around his eyes and looked at Captain Watkiss in puzzlement. "Beg pardon, sir?"

"*Exercise.* Are you deaf? The signal—take up your Aldis, damn you, and *make it!*"

"Just the one word, sir, like?"

"Yes!"

"Aye, aye, sir." The abrupt reply was flashed across the water and the procession of boats continued towards the shore behind Captain Watkiss. There was a bright sun gilding the blue water and striking golden fire from Captain Watkiss, who had added his sword to his strange rig of Number Ten tunic and long shorts, and had replaced his white helmet with his peaked cap rimmed with the gold oak leaves of his rank. There was a smirk upon his face now: he had the measure of the Russians and no mistake! They were flummoxed by his laconic signal; as ever, boldness had paid off. Even within the hostile confines of a Russian port, the Royal Navy stood supreme and was not to be trifled with by foreigners. The British flotilla—the Russian would be thinking—quite possibly had permission from Prince Gorsinski to land parties for exercise. Questions would no doubt be asked of the shore authorities by signal, but by the time they were answered he, Captain Watkiss, would have landed and would have his seamen fallen in and ready to march.

March upon what?

Captain Watkiss lifted a plump hand and rubbed reflectively at his chin. Shortly before leaving the leader, Mr Beauchamp had asked that very question, not of Captain Watkiss himself to be sure, but in a complaining undertone of no one in particular. Watkiss, whose ears were sharp, had taken it in; and upon their return aboard, Mr Beauchamp would find himself placed in open arrest for insubordinate impertinence. Meanwhile, however, the question remained hanging in the air and would have to be faced, but all in good time. Captain Watkiss was a firm believer in flexibility. It was, in his view, a mistake to form too comprehensive a picture of future events, for to do such inhibited one's powers of reappraisal when those events failed to turn out as expected.

Rounding the corner from the anchorage where his flotilla lay, Watkiss began to make his approach to the naval dockyard and its jetties. His seamen, hardy fellows all, pulled with a will and without tiring, though now and again a foot, heavily-booted for the march, slipped over a stretcher and almost capsized its owner: seamen were more accustomed to barefoot activity, and their toes were as good as fingers to them. As his boats made in towards the dockyard wall below a long, towering warehouse, Watkiss became aware of shoreside activity. Russians were gathering: dockyard workers, sailors, soldiers with rifles. A shout rang out across the narrowing gap of water.

"Take no notice," Watkiss said. He heaved himself to his feet and stood in the stern-sheets, rocking a little, and shouted back: "I'm putting my party ashore and to the devil with you!"

"Sir," Beauchamp said suddenly, "they're going to open fire!"

"Pray hold your tongue, Mr Beauchamp, they will *not* open fire. Such a dangerous decision can be made only in St Petersburg, not by the locals. We shall call their bluff." Anticipating the impact of his galley upon the dockyard wall, Watkiss sat down again. The boats came alongside, and from each, two men jumped out with lines which they made fast to the bollards set along the wall. The Russians stared in silence and made no move to stop the landing. Smiling triumphantly, Watkiss disembarked onto some stone steps and bounced up to the jetty, sword in hand. He called down to the boats.

"Mr Beauchamp, get the men ashore and fall them in." Thinking suddenly of his own remark to Mr Prebble, the Bastille came into his mind and he made his decision. "We shall march to the Karnakol gaol, Mr Beauchamp."

"That'll be dangerous, sir—"

"I think you are lily-livered, Mr Beauchamp." Watkiss turned away and strode towards the Russians, meeting their stares boldly. "Clear a gangway there! Clear the way for my men to muster! You shall not impede one of Her Majesty's post captains in the execution of his duty!"

"Curious," Halfhyde said, staring from the window. "But heartening, I find."

"It is your small, fat flotilla leader," Gorsinski said angrily. "With a pig's bladder ahead of him. I find his choice of instrument appropriate. And soon both shall be punctured. Your Captain Watkiss is a lunatic, Lieutenant Halfhyde!"

"But a brave one, I think."

"Pointless bravery is so stupid. It is not bravery. It is bravado, which is a different kettle of fish, as you would say." Gorsinski turned abruptly from the window, his face menacing. "Come below with me, Lieutenant Halfhyde, while I settle this ridiculous manifestation of British lunacy!" He paused, frowning. "Yet on second thoughts, no. You are better kept out of the way—"

"I suggest a third thought, sir. Allow me to come. I may be able to help."

Gorsinski scowled. "Help . . . you?"

"Help, I, sir. I believe your first concern is with finding out names. I believe you have no wish to provoke the British Government too far. Am I not right, sir?"

"Yes, you are right," Gorsinski said after a pause. "I could have your Captain Watkiss shot, but do not wish to do so."

"Quite. If I come with you, I may be able to persuade Captain Watkiss to withdraw his armed parties—and his bagpipes. A peaceful ending, sir, is what we both wish. Well, sir?"

Gorsinski pondered, frowning. "His purpose appears to be to cut you out, Lieutenant Halfhyde—"

"Perhaps, sir. But be assured I shall not allow myself to be cut out. We have unfinished business, you and I."

"I have your word?"

Halfhyde bowed. "You have, sir. And you may depend upon it. The last time I was here in Sevastopol, you remember, I never gave you my parole."

"That is true. What motivates you now?"

"As I have said, sir, unfinished business. The good Captain Matthews waits in filth and misery. I intend to stay until you shift him from his dungeon—for his good and yours."

Gorsinski, making up his mind, nodded. "Very well, so it shall be." He turned to the prison governor. "Colonel Kostavitch, look to your defences. The British seamen may try to force an entry. Come, Lieutenant Halfhyde." He stalked from the room, a tall and imposing figure in gold and blue, every inch the aristocrat and kinsman of the Czar, a figure to reduce the pompous flamboyance of Captain Watkiss to the level of the ridiculous.

• • •

"You, sir. Prince Gorsinski." As Halfhyde and Gorsinski emerged from the prison entrance, Captain Watkiss flourished his sword. Ridiculous he might be, with a wind now starting to flap his immense shorts around sun-red knees, but he had courage, Halfhyde reflected, with more than a touch of pride. He had much else, and so had the seamen: mud and filth, chucked along with jeers by the crowds of civilians, men and women less inhibited than the Russian soldiers and naval ratings. "Prince Gorsinski, I say! Do you hear me?"

"Yes, Captain Watkiss, I hear you."

"Then you should have had the common courtesy to damn well say so! I demand the handing back of Mr Halfhyde of my flotilla, and of the master and crew of the ship *Falls of Dochart*, illegally arrested by Russian vessels!"

"That is a mis-statement—"

"No it isn't; it's fact—I said it. Damn you to hell, sir. You are also illegally holding my own ships, and I demand free passage out to sea—"

"You are free to sail whenever you wish, but only at your peril, Captain Watkiss." Gorsinski smiled, and flicked a handkerchief over his uniform. "You will be fired upon by every gun that I can bring to bear."

"Piracy!" Captain Watkiss shouted, his face almost purple now. "I am a post captain in Her Majesty's Fleet, and as such the present representative of Her Majesty Queen Victoria—and I command you to release your prisoners into my custody—"

"You command no influence here, Captain Watkiss."

"I command men. I command rifles. One word, sir, and you could be dead, and so could many others. And then our countries will be at war—and your Czar, I fancy, none too pleased! Have a care, Prince Gorsinski." Watkiss, his eyes staring wildly with a hint almost of a crazed state of mind, lifted his drawn sword high above his head. "I shall give the order if provoked. When I bring down my sword—"

"A moment, sir." Halfhyde, recognizing beyond doubt that Captain Watkiss meant every word he had said, stepped forward with a hand raised. "A word, if you please."

"God damn you, Mr Halfhyde, be so good as to withdraw from my line of fire instantly."

"No, sir, I shall not."

"Then the instant you are released from Prince Gorsinski's custody, you disappear into *my* arrest—*close* arrest!"

"As you say, sir. But I am acting for the good of both countries. This must not be permitted to become a war, sir. I beg you to consider that Her Majesty would be as angry as the Czar—though, of course, should Prince Gorsinski overstep the mark further than he has, Her Majesty will make her displeasure known in the right quarters."

"You are a traitor, sir! A damn traitor!"

"No, sir. I am a peacemaker, that's all. And I am in personal touch with Captain Matthews of the *Falls of Dochart*."

There was a moment's silence; then Captain Watkiss said, "Oh. You are, are you?"

"I am indeed, sir, and I believe this affair can be settled with honour for all sides—"

"You do, do you?"

"Yes, sir, and in peace rather than war."

"Sounds like a namby-pamby counsel," Captain Watkiss said disagreeably, but he inclined his sword against his shoulder instead of bringing it right down. Halfhyde felt the sweat of sheer relief pour down his face. In one of his lightning changes of mood, Watkiss had rejected belligerency and for the moment the spark of danger had failed to ignite the charge. Halfhyde saw relief also in the eyes of the seamen and officers behind their captain: they had had no desire to face an unnecessary death. Halfhyde met the eyes of his own stolid, stocky Prebble, and of Beauchamp of the *Venomous,* both of them looking grateful for the reprieve.

Halfhyde followed up his advantage fast. "A wise decision on your part, sir, if I may be allowed to comment."

"I trust so, Mr Halfhyde, for your sake."

"Yes, sir. And may I also say that your presence here has been of much help." Halfhyde felt angry surprise emanating from Prince Gorsinski, and hurried on before the content of this curious statement could be analysed. "If I may be permitted, I shall continue my negotiations with His Highness Prince Gorsinski, who now knows—thanks to you, sir—that the British Lion is prepared to use his claws."

"Yes, indeed. And will do so if provoked further! Well, I'm glad to have been of some help, Mr Halfhyde." Watkiss paused. "But you, my dear fellow—what is to become of you? Have you considered that? Prince Gorsinski—"

"Yes, sir. I have considered it from time to time."

"And your conclusion?" Watkiss enquired keenly.

"Yet to be arrived at, sir, but I am well accustomed to looking after myself."

"I see. I wish you good fortune, Mr Halfhyde." Watkiss raised his voice. "Prince Gorsinski, I am about to return aboard my ship and I trust you'll not interfere or I shall be forced to open upon your men. And be so good as to instruct your damn civilian mob not to cast excrement at my landing-party. Good day to you, sir!"

Sheathing his sword, Watkiss turned about and made his way to the other end of the line, the end that would be in the lead for the return march. Halfhyde, watching his thick back moving away down the lines of seamen, guessed that in Watkiss's mind the march would be no retreat but a triumphal return after impressing the Russians with a show of strength that would cause them to think again. As the order to move was passed, the armed files stepped out with their rifles sloped, and in the rear the stoker petty officer blew air into his pipes. The British column moved away to the bold strains of "The Heroes of Vittoria," and Halfhyde felt Gorsinski's hand come down on his shoulder.

"The British," Gorsinski observed, "never cease to intrigue me, especially their naval captains. Have they all to be mad, Lieutenant Halfhyde?"

"I've not heard that it's an essential qualification, sir, but it's said to help."

They went back inside to the gloom of the Karnakol prison.

"Well, I call that most successful, Mr Beauchamp." Watkiss shaded his eyes from the high sun as his boats were pulled back to the anchorage. "The men were splendid, and I propose to splice the mainbrace throughout my flotilla. See to that, if you please."

"Aye, aye, sir."

Watkiss settled himself comfortably upon his thwart. "Yes, a success indeed. Though I'm somewhat worried about Halfhyde, I must confess."

"His safety, sir?"

"Well, yes. Gorsinski's said to want his guts for a necktie, but if you ask me . . ."

"Sir?"

"Halfhyde and Gorsinski," Captain Watkiss said in a sombre tone, "seemed to me *friendly*, Mr Beauchamp. Hatching some plot!"

"I think that's hardly likely, sir."

"I'm not aware that I asked for your disagreement, Mr Beauchamp. Halfhyde's a lone wolf, always has been so they say, and threats can undermine men's minds. I only hope to God he isn't a damn traitor, that's all." Watkiss stared out towards the *Nikolayev* as his boats were pulled past, then waved a hand towards the Russian cruiser. "Twisted their tails, Mr Beauchamp, that's what I've done. Not a flicker from their damn signal lamps this time! I hope you're damn well ashamed of your yellow streak as displayed this forenoon."

Chapter 12

BACK IN THE KARNAKOL PRISON, Gorsinski paced the room, frowning. Halfhyde watched, realizing that great decisions were being reached, and that his own fate, even if only indirectly, was involved in them. He had had similar thoughts back in Malta, when first apprised by the vice-admiral of his orders: the thoughts that told him chicanery might be afoot, that the release of the *Falls of Dochart* might be achieved by sacrificing him to Prince Gorsinski. But since then it had become obvious that much more was involved than a simple desire for revenge on Gorsinski's part. For some while now events of great moment had been stirring inside the huge Russian land-mass that straddled the world from China to Europe, events not unconnected with all that the Karnakol prison, and Gorsinski himself, stood for: the peasants and the workers were restive, anxious to throw off their yokes, and there was rumour that even the Russian Army and Navy had dissidents in their ranks—that the socialist ideas detested so much by Captain Watkiss were eating insidiously into the minds of the men, and that the rumbling discontent might one day erupt in bloody mutiny. Thus Admiral Gorsinski was going to leave no stone unturned in the rooting out of the persons who were spreading the seeds of rebellion and disaffection.

Gorsinski halted by the window and stood with his back to

Halfhyde, staring down into the mean street up which Captain Watkiss had marched his landing-party. After a long, brooding silence he said, "There can be more persuasion, Lieutenant Halfhyde."

"Torture?"

"Pain can be inflicted, yes."

"On Captain Matthews?"

Gorsinski nodded. "For whom death apparently holds no terrors. Or upon you."

"I know nothing, sir."

"How can I be sure of that?" Gorsinski swung round suddenly, his eyes hard. "You tell me your British merchant captain told you no names. How can I know this for certain, Lieutenant Halfhyde?"

"You have my word. I can offer no more than that. And you trusted me in the first place, did you not? There was an obvious indication that you would believe what I told you after I had spoken to Captain Matthews."

"Because of Siberia—yes!"

Halfhyde smiled acidly. "I dislike reminding you, sir, but Siberia is still there. The threat remains. I assure you, I have told you the truth."

Gorsinski muttered something in Russian, something that Halfhyde failed to catch, then, scowling, swung back to the window. After another lengthy deliberation he said over his shoulder, "Very well, Lieutenant Halfhyde, I shall agree to your suggestion. Colonel Kostavitch?"

"Your Highness?"

"The British merchant captain will be returned aboard his ship under guard. We shall see what it produces."

Halfhyde asked, "And I, sir?"

"You, Lieutenant Halfhyde? I do not know yet. For now you
and I shall return to my headquarters, my stone frigate as you
call it."

They went back again through the sleazy streets and alleys in
the sumptuous carriage, thrusting through the crowds. Those
crowds, after releasing some of their frustrations on the British
sailors, were now back to their normal level of cringing obse-
quiousness as the coach-whips of Prince Gorsinski flew above
their heads. On arrival at headquarters Halfhyde was returned
under escort to his palatial apartment, its balcony still strongly
guarded by armed men from the Russian Fleet. On that return
journey Gorsinski had been non-committal and mainly silent,
but Siberia had shone with a cold certainty in his hard eyes.
Halfhyde had no doubts left that that was to be his fate, but
believed it would not happen yet: not whilst Captain Matthews
lived and remained silent, at all events.

Pacing his room, disliking intensely the caged feeling,
Halfhyde pondered his present duty and tried to assess where
precisely it lay: which was the more important—the actual
cutting-out of the *Falls of Dochart,* or the life and honour of her
master and crew? To cut out the ship and sail her through the
Black Sea to the Bosporus and on to the Dardanelles was plainly
impossible in any case, in the face of the Russian guns; but if
Captain Matthews would answer Prince Gorsinski's questions it
was possible that the ship and the crew would be released, and
some diplomatic formula found to explain away, with apologies, all that had happened. Thus, if Matthews should eventually find his interest in life renewed by being back aboard his

ship, and if he should decide to tell Halfhyde what he knew,
then would Halfhyde be justified in placing the lives of unknown
Russian dissidents before those of British seamen?

On the face of it, Halfhyde knew very well, the answer was
a resounding no. Nevertheless, he was deeply reluctant to betray
Matthews's confidence, and to play Gorsinski's game for him.
He also had much sympathy with the oppressed common people of Russia. During his previous stay in the Crimea as well as
today in Gorsinski's carriage, he had seen enough to sicken any
decent man. Memory took him back to the port of Fishtown
in the Bight of Benin, where Gorsinski's flagship had suffered
mutiny by embittered men whose conditions of life and pun-
ishment were such that the chance to escape from them was
worth the risk of being swung as corpses from Prince Gorsinski's
yard-arms.

There had to be another way, a bolder and more honest way.
The way of the seaman . . . Halfhyde stopped in his restless
perambulation and faced a long wall mirror set at one end of
the room and stared thoughtfully at his reflection, a thing he
had seldom done before, considering himself too long and thin
and angular to form a rewarding subject for study. But now he
looked closely and with a difference in his attitude. It had often
been remarked in his family that from descriptions handed
down through the generations it appeared that he bore a resemblance to his ancestor Daniel Halfhyde, the gunner's mate. This
he took with a pinch of salt: word of mouth was an unreliable
yardstick, and old Daniel had not been of a class to have his
portrait painted, so of proof there was none.

"All the same, Great Grandfather," Halfhyde said aloud as
he stared into the mirror, "there could be something in it.

Gunner's mate in the fighting *Temeraire* under Lord Nelson's flag . . . by God, sir, you were no more a diplomat than I! And I have an idea what *you* would have done, had you held your King's commission as I now hold my Queen's."

Halfhyde turned away from the mirror, bolstered by the past. He gave a laugh, a sound of exultancy. It was damned impossible, but he was going to do it.

The rest of that day passed slowly, very slowly, and Halfhyde bit his nails with impatience. For what he had to do, night was essential: the force of the unexpected was always greater when it struck under cover of darkness—and also, of course, there were less men about. But the wait was hard upon his nerves, and every moment he expected to be sent for by Gorsinski, to be despatched either to the cells or to the bedside of Captain Matthews for another probing attempt to extract information. Relieved that as the hours passed he was not sent for—his sole visitation was to bring food and drink—he was yet surprised that his services were not being called upon. For all Gorsinski knew, Captain Matthews was on the very brink of death; thus some haste might reasonably be expected, and its absence might well indicate that other measures were now being applied to the old mariner.

Restlessly Halfhyde continued pacing his apartment, backwards and forwards as the day wore on towards dusk, when the harbour lights came up beyond the sentries marching their post on the balcony. As the dusk deepened, Halfhyde drew the curtains across the windows and operated the curious contraption that ignited the gas chandelier; and went on waiting and waiting until Gorsinski's headquarters lay silent and bedded down for the night; the only sounds to reach Halfhyde were now the footfalls of the sentries on the balcony, relieved at two-hourly intervals by means of an iron ladder from the ground outside. It was two hours past midnight when, judging the safest time to have come, he pulled on a bellrope hanging beside the massive fireplace, and waited again. Someone, somewhere in a guardroom below was sure to be awake; within five minutes of the summons, Halfhyde heard a man's voice speaking to the sentry at the door, and then heard the key turning in the lock.

The door opened and an armed petty officer said in Russian, "You rang. What do you want?"

"I want Prince Gorsinski. I wish to go to his room. I have important information for him."

"His Highness is sleeping, and is not to be disturbed."

"His Highness will be more disturbed by not being woken, I promise you. Tell me this: in what terms does His Highness frequently address his ratings?" When no answer came, Halfhyde answered his own question. "As dogs. You know this as well as I. And dogs are for shooting. If you value your skin, you will take me at once to Prince Gorsinski, or in the morning I shall ensure your death."

Halfhyde had spoken with peremptory harshness, in the tones of an officer accustomed to instant obedience to orders; and the petty officer's reaction to the tone and to the uniform of commissioned rank was precisely as Halfhyde had known it would be. He came to attention and said stiffly, "Then come and I will take you to His Highness." He stood to one side, allowing Halfhyde passage out into the corridor, then closed in behind him with his revolver nudging Halfhyde's backbone. He led the way to another wing of the building on the same level as Halfhyde's accommodation and halted outside a massive door, shut and guarded by a naval rating standing with his rifle in the "order" position.

"The British prisoner to see His Highness the Admiral," the petty officer said. The sentry opened the door, and Halfhyde walked ahead of his escort into the flag lieutenant's office and through it into a corridor, off which opened a number of doors. He was halted outside one of these and the petty officer knocked, looking scared to death as he did so. There was no response, and he knocked again, more loudly; this time an angry voice called, "What is it? Whoever it is, come in—and then go again quickly!"

The petty officer opened the door, his face white. "Your Highness, it is the British officer, the prisoner—"

"What does he want? Lieutenant Halfhyde, what—"

"A matter of urgency, sir." Halfhyde pushed past the petty officer unceremoniously, disregarding the revolver. "A matter of urgency and of much importance. I must speak to you alone." As he spoke, Halfhyde took in the disorder of Gorsinski's bed-chamber: glasses were lying on their sides on a mahogany table, and there were two empty vodka bottles, and Gorsinski himself had a bleary look about the eyes as he stared from his bed. "It is to do with Captain Matthews."

Gorsinski went on staring for a moment, then made a sweeping gesture at the petty officer. "Leave us. Remain outside."

"Yes, Your Highness." The Russian disappeared, thankful to be still alive, and the door was shut.

"Speak," Gorsinski said. "Be brief, Lieutenant Halfhyde."

"As brief as you wish, sir. We must go aboard the *Falls of Dochart*."

"We?"

"You and I."

"Are you mad, Lieutenant Halfhyde?"

"By no means, but perhaps I have been slow. During the day I put some fragments together and fancy I have made a whole, or at least a pattern of some kind."

"What fragments?"

"Fragments of Captain Matthews's confused speech, sir. When I reported to you, I had found no sense and the pieces seemed not worth mention. But now—"

"Now what?" Prince Gorsinski, nightcapped and night-shirted, sat up in his enormous four-poster bed. "Quickly!"

Halfhyde shrugged. "I could be wrong, sir."

"Tell me!" Gorsinski shouted. His voice was very slightly slurred from the vodka and Halfhyde fancied that this, quite fortuitously, could be working in his favour; his story might sound less full of holes to a man suffering some small befuddlement of his senses.

"I shall indeed tell you, sir." Halfhyde paused. "If I should be instrumental in bringing enemies of the Russian state to justice, then—"

"You will redeem yourself in my favour."

"I, and my flotilla, will be allowed to leave peacefully, and the *Falls of Dochart* also?"

"Yes! You have my word. Tell me what you have to say, and quickly!"

"Yes, sir. I believe there may be secret hiding places aboard the *Falls of Dochart*."

Gorsinski stared. "My good Halfhyde, she has been searched from truck to keelson. You talk nonsense!"

"With respect, sir, the search may not have been conducted with sufficient thoroughness. It is easy to miss secret stowages aboard a ship, and your men will not be accustomed to British merchant ships and the ways of British merchant seamen, who make a virtue of the crime of outwitting our good excisemen."

Gorsinski stared again at Halfhyde, murmured something into his beard, and sat up in his bed, heaving the sheets about. After a while of scowling thought he said, "There is some truth in what you have said, I agree. Some truth . . . more precisely, please, what is it you are suggesting?"

"That documents exist relative to passengers carried. There was mention of letters, and a dark place—or I fancy so. I repeat, it is a day's thought that tells me—"

"You made no mention earlier of letters or of dark places!"

"No, I agree, I did not, sir." Halfhyde's tongue was firmly in his cheek now. "My mind was attuned, perhaps, to more shipboard matters, and what I *thought* Captain Matthews referred to was letters of marque. If I may explain, letters of marque are a commission issued by a government, authorizing masters of merchant ships to capture prizes—"

"Yes, yes, yes! I know all this! And letters of marque were abolished by the Declaration of Paris in 1856!"

Halfhyde inclined his head. "As I realize—but Captain Matthews is an old man with a long and now confused recollection, and I believed him to be accusing you of piracy. And since that is what in fact you've committed, sir, you can scarcely find it surprising—"

"Have the goodness to keep to the point, Lieutenant Halfhyde. You are suggesting another search—for letters in a dark place!

This is nonsense, a figment of your stupid British imagination, I think."

"I've admitted I could be wrong, sir, but you would be foolish to dismiss what I say—"

"Well, if it satisfies you, I will order a further search of the ship. You may safely leave that in my hands."

"With respect, sir, I think you and I should go with the search party."

"Why so?"

"Because," Halfhyde said, giving a discreet cough, "there was mention of your name."

"In what connection?"

"Well, I believed originally it was to do with the accusation of piracy—the letters of marque. But reflection has made me unsure. Were I in your shoes, sir, I would find it safer and more prudent to be present at the fresh search. I think you will understand?"

Gorsinski, to whom intrigue came as second nature and who almost certainly had dirtied his hands from time to time in the interests of self, played smartly into Halfhyde's trap: he would do better, he announced, than accompany a search party. He and Halfhyde would carry out the search themselves, unattended—though this he did not stress—by any other eyes and mouths. Though still inclined to be sceptical, he was obviously worried, and came out speedily from his bed to don his uniform. When dressed, he led the way out of his room and along the corridor, stalking arrogantly ahead of Halfhyde through the flag lieutenant's office—usefully as well as arrogantly, for his turned back enabled Halfhyde, struck by a sudden thought for the future, to gather up some sheets of his official headed writing paper and some envelopes, which he thrust down the front of his white uniform before proceeding out past the sentry. The petty officer had already been despatched ahead to summon Prince Gorsinski's carriage, and now came hastening back to inform His Highness that the coachman waited. They embarked without delay and were driven fast from the dockyard out of Sevastopol towards Balaklava. The night was fine but cold; Halfhyde shivered in his thin white uniform. Gorsinski, who was wearing a boat-cloak, sat silent and withdrawn in his corner of the carriage as it swayed southwards through desolate countryside, scoured by a wind coming down across the Sea of Azov to the north-east. He seemed to have much on his mind; Halfhyde wondered what raw spot had been touched, what deviousness Gorsinski had been up to that he would prefer kept dark. There was also, he fancied, a degree of physical discomfort in the Russian owing to drink: Halfhyde felt a touch of sympathy. A sudden night awakening was always unwelcome after such indulgence . . .

In the small port of Balaklava the carriage rattled past grander buildings than those to be found in the purlieus of Sevastopol; Balaklava had something of a reputation as a health resort, and its inhabitants were well-lined. Halfhyde grinned to himself, reflecting that in a short space of time the rich convalescents might well have other things to think about than their state of health. The carriage headed on for the shore and a number of jetties extending from a hard beyond the town itself. A handful of vessels lay berthed, merchant vessels, coasters mainly; there was no warship in sight. At the last of the jetties Halfhyde saw the three tall masts, the slender poles of the ship *Falls of Dochart* with the lower sails furled on the yards. There was a lantern swinging at the head of the gangway, and an armed sentry marched his post on deck.

The carriage slowed, stopping at the shore end of the jetty, and the coachman jumped down from his box and opened the door. Followed by Halfhyde, Gorsinski got out. "Wait," he commanded. That was all; the coachman bowed low, and Gorsinski turned away, wrapping his boat-cloak tightly around his tall body, and strode along the jetty. Reaching the ship's side, he climbed the gangway, casting back the cloak to reveal his uniform.

"Admiral Prince Gorsinski," he announced to the sentry, who presented arms, "and Lieutenant Halfhyde. We are going below."

"Yes, Your Highness."

"No one else is to board the ship. And no one is to leave, unless by my own order."

"No, Your Highness."

"Where is the British captain, Captain Matthews?"

"In his cabin, Your Highness."

Gorsinski nodded. "Come, Lieutenant Halfhyde," he said, and turned away towards the after part of the ship. He pushed open a door leading below the raised poop-deck and went aft along a short alleyway to the saloon, and through this to another alleyway beyond. Two doors opened off; outside one stood another armed sentry, who came to attention as the gilded aristocrat approached. Gorsinski took no notice of him, but opened the door and went in, followed by Halfhyde. In a bunk lay Captain Matthews, apparently sleeping, and in a chair beside sat an old crone, dressed in black, nodding and swaying and also sleeping.

Gorsinski made a sound of impatience and prodded at the crone with a silver-headed cane. She came awake with a start, staring blearily, lips working over toothless gums, her skin puckered like a nut. There was a smell of drink.

"Who are you, old woman?" Gorsinski snapped.

The ancient eyes began to take in the uniform's splendour. She said, "I, I am the nurse—"

"And I am Prince Gorsinski. Get out."

"Your Highness—"

"Get out. Go into the saloon. Remain there until further orders. You leave at your peril. Go." When the old woman remained seated, staring up at him dumbly and clearly terrified, Gorsinski leaned forward and dragged her bodily from the chair, giving her a push towards the open door. She staggered and fell in a heap; Halfhyde went to her assistance and brought her upright, trying to close his nostrils against the combined smell of liquor and unwashed clothing.

"I'll take her to the saloon, sir," he said.

"As you wish." Gorsinski seemed indifferent, looking at the sick man on the bunk. After shutting the cabin door behind him, Halfhyde had almost to carry the ancient nurse along the alleyway and into the saloon, where he made her as comfortable as possible on a settee; then, searching around for matches, which he found on a shelf above the fireplace, he lit the oil lamp that swung in gimbals above the long, polished mahogany table in the centre of the compartment.

Then he went back towards the master's cabin. The Russian

sentry, his revolver holstered on a leather belt, watched his approach, without suspicion. Halfhyde decided that now was his opportunity: he smiled as he came up, and then, just as he appeared about to enter the cabin, he turned suddenly and, before the man could react, had reached out and gripped his throat, squeezing it tight and stopping all sound beyond a faint gurgling. The body struggled, the legs kicking out violently until Halfhyde wrapped himself around the man and held him fast, away from the cabin door. He kept up his vice-like pressure, forcing the adam's-apple up against the back of the neck until the gurgling stopped and the limbs were slack. Then, breathing hard himself, he held the man supported against a bulkhead, removed the revolver from his holster, thrust open the cabin door and sent the unconscious sentry rolling in towards Gorsinski, who was bent over the sick man.

Gorsinski swung round, and found his eyes staring into the muzzle of the revolver.

"Tear up a sheet, Prince Gorsinski," Halfhyde said. "Bind him, gag him . . . and shut him in the wardrobe. At once, please, or I shall shoot you."

"You would not dare—"

Halfhyde said stonily, "I have nothing to lose and all to gain, if I may insult you with a cliché. In all conscience, my dear sir, you have painted a black enough picture of my future in Siberia!"

Halfhyde had in fact meant precisely what he had said: Gorsinski would die. Gorsinski read the truth in his face, and was left with no doubts whatsoever. His face pale with fury and not a little fear, Gorsinski had obeyed orders. Firmly bound and gagged, the sentry was placed in the wardrobe, a space which would give him little room to move when he returned to consciousness.

"This will not last long for you, Lieutenant Halfhyde," Gorsinski said coldly. "You must see for yourself the impossibility of escape!"

"By no means. I am fully confident of success. You are now about to send orders for the crew of the *Falls of Dochart* to be released, and returned aboard."

Gorsinski laughed loudly, scornfully. "Pish!" he said.

"I assure you there is no pish about it." Halfhyde reached into his tunic and brought out the pilfered writing paper and envelopes, somewhat crumpled from his recent struggle with the sentry, but otherwise intact. With a sweep of his hand he indicated Captain Matthews's desk. "Pen and ink awaits your hand, sir. You will write to Colonel Kostavitch at the Karnakol gaol and order the release of the prisoners, as I have indicated. They are to be aboard this ship within three hours of the receipt of your orders. Bear in mind that I read Russian as well as speak it."

"You cannot get away with this, Lieutenant Halfhyde. When it is known I am not at my headquarters, that I have disappeared, I shall be looked for."

Halfhyde shook his head. "I think not, sir. You were known to leave peacefully of your own free will. There will be no questions asked in time—in time for you, that is." He placed the writing materials on the desk. "At once, if you please, Prince Gorsinski."

He brought up the revolver, aiming it at the Russian's head. Gorsinski glared, but sat down and wrote. When Halfhyde had read the orders, the sheet of paper was placed in an envelope and addressed in Gorsinski's handwriting to Colonel Kostavitch, marked "most urgent." Halfhyde was confident the orders would not be queried, but as a precaution he made Gorsinski write another, this time to his flag lieutenant, informing him of what was being done and instructing him to see to it that the prisoners were released with all despatch, and the sea area kept clear for the sailing of the *Falls of Dochart* back to Sevastopol once the crew were aboard.

"That is what you intend?" Gorsinski asked.

"My true intentions, sir, remain for the time being inside my head."

When the second letter had been written and passed by Halfhyde, Gorsinski, with raised eyebrows and a look of superior intelligence, asked, "How do you propose that these shall be delivered, pray?"

"Your coachman waits as ordered by you, sir. And, for a little while, so do we." He looked towards the bunk and its occupant. Captain Matthews was either in a sleep so deep that nothing of recent events had disturbed it, or he was unconscious: Halfhyde fancied the latter to be the case. His breathing was not good, and Matthews, who had originally appeared to him less ill than had been thought, could well have taken a turn for the worse. It was possible that the journey from Sevastopol had been too much for the old man, and the attentions of the dirty old crone less than that which would have been expected from a member of her profession in England. In any case, until a doctor could be brought to him, there was nothing to be done. Halfhyde thought of getting Gorsinski to make a request for a doctor, but decided against it with reluctance. The fewer the Russians they had aboard the *Falls of*

Dochart the better; and at least, if Captain Matthews was to die, he would not now be in Russian hands, in the filth of a Russian dungeon. For the moment Matthews could not be Halfhyde's principal concern: Gorsinski had to be watched with the eyes of a hawk; and although Halfhyde had a shrewd idea the Russian admiral would take no personal risks at this stage, preferring to rely on eventual rescue by *force majeure,* Halfhyde would take no chances. As they went on waiting, he kept the revolver aimed at Gorsinski, who grew more and more restive as time passed. But after half an hour Halfhyde heard the sounds he had been expecting outside: the footfalls of the man sent down to relieve the cabin sentry. Jerking his revolver at Gorsinski, he issued more orders.

"You will call the man into the cabin. When he enters, tell him the man he was to relieve has been despatched on a personal errand for you. You understand, sir?"

"Yes!" Gorsinski snapped.

"I hope so, for your sake. You will then hand him the envelopes and tell him to take them to the gangway, and to see that a man is sent with them to your coachman, with orders that he should break all records into Sevastopol. You understand this too? And remember—you are very close to death, Prince Gorsinski."

The footsteps stopped outside the cabin, then went somewhat hesitantly past, indicating a degree of puzzlement. Halfhyde whispered, "Now, and play for your life!"

Gorsinski scowled, but obeyed. He called out, "The sentry there—come in and report!"

Halfhyde put the revolver out of sight but ready to shoot.

The sentry came in, crashing to attention before the admiral's gold lace. "Your Highness!"

Holding out the letters, Gorsinski spoke precisely as ordered. "These envelopes are to reach their addresses with the utmost despatch. My coachman will take them. See to it."

"Yes, Your Highness." The man took the envelopes, saluted, and went off, closing the door behind him. Halfhyde let out a long breath of relief, and brought the revolver into sight again as a threatening reminder.

"And now what, may I ask?" Gorsinski enquired with icy politeness.

"Another wait, this time for the British crew," Halfhyde answered, "and I'd advise you to pray there are no slips, Prince Gorsinski!"

The Russian's lip curled. "Advice I might well return for your own consideration, Lieutenant Halfhyde," he said. "You would do well to remember that you are now inside Russia, and not upon the open sea."

Chapter 13

IT WAS DAYLIGHT NOW; by Halfhyde's estimate the very ear-
liest the British prisoners could arrive would be four hours after
the despatch of the orders to Colonel Kostavitch. Dawn had
already been breaking when those orders had gone, and
Halfhyde was becoming tired after a sleepless night and a lengthy
and close vigil upon Gorsinski. Gorsinski himself had dozed,
or had appeared to; Halfhyde felt that might well be a posture
to lower his guard. He had not moved even when Captain
Matthews had stirred in his bunk and groaned, lifting a hand
shakily to his head.

The old man was lathered in sweat; that, Halfhyde fancied,
could be the fever breaking. A good sign, perhaps—or possibly a bad one, indicating a worse fever. He was no medical man;
and even if he could leave the cabin to go for the ancient hag
in the saloon, he believed her knowledge would prove unequal
to a diagnosis. After a while, however, the signs did seem better: Captain Matthews opened his eyes and stared, blankly
enough, at the deckhead above his bunk. Soon he seemed to
register, a frown of bewilderment came to his face, and he
turned his head to meet Halfhyde's eye.

"I have seen you before," he said in a low, hoarse voice.
"Where am I, and who are you?"

Halfhyde told him; he shook his head slowly, his eyes

puzzled still. "I had a strange dream, very strange." He paused. "I was ascending to heaven . . . by way of the mizzen ratlines. At the mizzen truck stood an angel, beckoning me on. My instinct as a seaman held me back, for I knew there was no way beyond the truck of a mast." Once again he turned his head and saw Gorsinski. "Who is that?" he asked.

"Not an angel," Halfhyde said, "and at the end of a revolver rather than the truck. He is your tormentor, Captain Matthews— Admiral Prince Gorsinski, now himself my prisoner. Tell me, how do you feel now?"

"Not well, to be truthful, but I think better. I have a grip upon life." Suddenly the old eyes filled with tears. "To be back aboard my own ship . . . that is wonderful, Mr Halfhyde, wonderful. My mind is clear again."

Halfhyde smiled. "The truck-bound angel has weighed anchor?"

"I beg your pardon?"

"Never mind, my dear sir, you must forgive my frivolity, for which I apologize. I am more of a sinner than you, though like you I have been known to follow God."

"Follow God, Mister, and fear not. That's my motto. I believe God is leading us now." Captain Matthews paused, wiping the sweat from his forehead with a hand that still shook with weakness. "There is a quotation from the Scriptures that I find apt, one that I have often read to my own officers, and—"

"Your pardon, Captain Matthews. Another time, perhaps, if you'll be so good." Halfhyde got to his feet and poked at Gorsinski with his revolver, causing the Russian's eyes to open. "I hear marching feet along the jetty. From now on you must be very careful, Prince Gorsinski. Your circumstances, should they be revealed to anyone, will become so much the worse. A report will be made to you from the gangway when your former prisoners are alongside. When this is made, you will order them to be mustered on deck by the gangway. Captain Matthews, the prisoners I refer to are your crew."

"My crew, Mr Halfhyde?"

"All now to be released to rejoin your ship."

The old man shook his head in wonder. "The Lord be praised, and you as His instrument. That is good news indeed!"

"And should speed your recovery. But for the moment you must remain in your bunk, and appear still as if deadly sick." The march of men outside had stopped now; voices were heard, apparently an exchange between the gangway sentry and a warder from the Karnakol prison. There was tension in the cabin now: this was the moment, the first of many yet to come as Halfhyde knew, when his extravagant plan could go sadly astray and lead to the deaths of many men. Gorsinski was looking savage and expectant; he saw his own moment of revenge approaching, and was ready to strike back with the speed of a snake once he was given the smallest opportunity. The exchange of shouts between pier and gangway stopped, and a man clattered down the accommodation-ladder from the poop, spoke to the sentry outside the cabin, and knocked on the door. Bidden to enter, he reported to Gorsinski.

"The prisoners from Sevastopol, Your Highness."

Gorsinski hesitated, caught Halfhyde's eye and saw the threat. He said in a distant-sounding voice, "They are to be mustered on deck, by the gangway."

"Yes, Your Highness." The man left the cabin, shutting the

door behind him. Once more Halfhyde brought his revolver into sight, once more he cautioned the Russian.

"You'll be the first to die, Prince Gorsinski. We shall go on deck now. You shall keep close by me. I shall speak to the British seamen. You will remain silent. Do you understand?"

"To the devil with you, Lieutenant Halfhyde!" Gorsinski snapped.

"I take that as an indication that you understand very well, sir." Halfhyde had no fears that Gorsinski would give away any of the truth prematurely by his manner or by his silence: Gorsinski the cold aristocrat was not accustomed to speaking to the lower orders at any time other than to cast a command in their direction and watch for their instant obedience. Halfhyde looked across at Captain Matthews. "There's a bound and gagged Russian in your wardrobe, Captain. So far he has been silent, and is to remain so. If there is a noise, I shall rely upon you to cover it with some action of your own when the sentry opens the door." He added, "I'll not be long."

"Take your time, Mister, and God be with you."

Halfhyde nodded and glanced at Gorsinski. "Your boat-cloak, if you please, sir."

"Why?"

"I shall carry it for you—over my arm. An act of politeness of a lieutenant towards an admiral—the day is not cold."

Gorsinski scowled, but took off his boat-cloak and threw it contemptuously towards Halfhyde, who draped the garment over the revolver in his right hand. He urged Gorsinski towards the door, pushing it open for him. As they went past the sentry, the man slammed to attention and stood back against the bulkhead. They went through the saloon: the old crone was still there, slumped on the floor, with her head and one arm thrown across the settee and an empty bottle of liquor lying on its side. Gorsinski put his head in the air and looked the other way. From the alleyway beyond the saloon they emerged onto the open deck and found the vessel's crew, haggard, dirty, and unshaven, fallen in before the after cargo-hatch in two ranks.

Halfhyde, keeping a pace to the rear of Gorsinski, his concealed revolver within an inch of the Russian's spine, moved towards the British seamen. Taking a chance that the armed Russians on the gangway would have no English, he said, "My name is Halfhyde, a lieutenant of the Royal Navy. Prince Gorsinski has a gun in his back, gentlemen, and knows he will die instantly if there is difficulty. Now—Prince Gorsinski, you will call to the warders from the Karnakol prison to return at once to Sevastopol. That, and no more."

Haughtily Gorsinski called the order. The warders saluted and moved away towards the hard behind the jetties. When they were out of earshot, Halfhyde gave his next order to Gorsinski: "The sentries to go below to the saloon. At once, sir!" He nudged with the revolver, and after a further moment's hesitation Gorsinski gave that order as well. The sentries, possibly surprised but not daring to show it before His Highness the Prince, obeyed the order and vanished towards the saloon; and Halfhyde turned back to the ship's crew again.

"I know you're all tired and hungry," he said, "but you're on your feet and you're seamen, and you don't want to remain in Russia. Which of you is the first mate?"

A tall man lifted a hand. "I am."

"And your name?"

"Hawker."

Halfhyde nodded and said briskly, "Very well, Mr Hawker, make sail at once, if you please."

The first mate gaped. "Make sail, did you say?"

"I did, Mr Hawker. Your captain is below, still a sick man, but I have no doubt you have the experience to sail the ship to Sevastopol—am I right?"

"Aye, you're right enough—"

"As for me," Halfhyde said modestly, "I too have some knowledge of sail. I served as a midshipman in the Flying Squadron under Rear-Admiral the Earl of Clanwilliam. Mr Hawker, your masts are ready crossed with their yards and the sails furled, and all that is needed is to shake out the canvas. If I may suggest it, I think you will find a wind once a boat's crew has towed you out beyond the headland and the fortress."

Weary as they were, the prospect of freedom drove the hands to superhuman efforts. The lines from the shore were cast off, and a party of men thrust the *Falls of Dochart* away from the jetty using massive bearing-out spars; while more men manned the starboard lifeboat at the davits and were lowered into the water with a grass line, to begin the laborious tow out to sea, to where a wind could be found. When the ship had moved away from the jetty, the fore and main courses were shaken out and hauled up on the lifts, ready to take the wind. Then the upper and lower topsails were sent up on the foremast, watched by Gorsinski's surly eye: Halfhyde had kept him firmly stationed upon the poop, so that any passing boat's crew could see the Russian admiral in his full uniform, ostensibly in command of the ship. By this time Captain Matthews, Hawker, and the ship's bosun and carpenter were all armed with rifles taken from the Russian sentries in the saloon: this surrender of weapons had been made upon the personal orders of Prince Gorsinski, temporarily removed from the poop for the purpose, Halfhyde's revolver pressed close to his body. With the sole exception of Gorsinski himself all the Russians were now securely bound and locked into the bosun's store in the fore-peak, a smelly place of oil and tar, paint, grease, and tallow: their number did not include the original sentry from the wardrobe. When his wooden prison had been opened up, it had been found a coffin. The man was stone cold dead, which doubtless accounted for his total silence through the hours of waiting.

"I'm sorry," Halfhyde said to Gorsinski. "It's the fortune of war, but—"

"But it is not war, Lieutenant Halfhyde! You have killed and it is not war. You are a murderer. From now on you must have more of a care than ever."

"I shall, sir," Halfhyde said. "But allow me to express my regret for what had to be done—as a result of your own illegal actions. As it is, as soon as we are at sea, the man will have proper burial."

"At sea? What do you mean, at sea?"

Halfhyde laughed. "All in good time, sir. From now on you shall find life full of little surprises!" He moved to the starboard rail as the ship inched on behind the sweat and the brawny arms of the pullers in the lifeboat. Away ahead, beyond the bluff promontory with its fortress, there was a ruffling of the sea's surface, indicating a fair weight of wind, fully enough to fill their sails. Halfhyde was consumed with impatience now: they had a start and they had the initial advantage that no one ashore yet knew the truth of what had happened, but speed was vital in these early stages. Halfhyde willed the vessel on for the wind and the open sea, as did the earnest prayers of Captain Matthews, in current intercession with his Lord for swift winds and ocean spray. The old mariner's pleadings were far from silent: Halfhyde noticed the ears of Prince Gorsinski a-cockbill by the cabin skylight which stood just before the ship's wheel.

"What is it, sir?" he asked, grinning.

"It is the old madman, battering at the wits of his God."

"As you would like to batter at those of your Czar, I fancy, sir." Gorsinski snarled, "And yet shall do so!"

"You think so?" Halfhyde gave a loud laugh. "Not for a long time yet, my dear sir—look ahead there—do you see? We almost have the wind!"

Within the next fifteen minutes the sails had started to fill, the wind straining the canvas from the cringles as Hawker tacked the ship on a nor'-nor'-easterly course in accordance with Halfhyde's directions.

Captain Watkiss was at his luncheon, munching some fine slices of Aberdeen Angus beef—the best there was in his opinion— with fresh potatoes and some beetroot, the latter limper than it should have been, had the petty officer cook had his wits about him when it came to the proper management of the ice-box. As Watkiss pondered what to do about the petty officer cook upon his return to Malta, a knock came at his door, and the pulling aside of his curtain revealed the first lieutenant.

Watkiss stared. "I'm at luncheon, Mr Beauchamp."

"Yes, sir, but—"

"Well, since you're here. This damn beetroot." Watkiss prodded with a fork, lifting a flaccid red lump towards his first lieutenant. "Improperly frozen, damn it!"

"I think you're thinking of cucumber, sir—"

"I am *not* thinking of cucumber, Mr Beauchamp. I am thinking of beetroot, *limp* beetroot, Mr Beauchamp, and not liking what I am thinking. Will you kindly do something about it."

"Sir, beetroot shouldn't really be frozen—"

"Yes beetroot should! That's fact—I said it. Either I am properly fed or the petty officer cook goes into arrest. So do you, if you persist in arguing and answering back. I don't want a first lieutenant who answers back, sir!" Watkiss stared, protuberant blue eyes hostile. "Why the hell did you interrupt my luncheon anyway?"

"There's a ship, sir, entering—"

"Ship, ship! Why didn't you say so, instead of standing there dithering, Mr Beauchamp? Well, get on with it: *what* ship, and *where?*"

"Entering the anchorage, sir. The *Falls of Dochart*."

"The *Falls* . . . by God, Mr Beauchamp, you've taken leave of your senses. She's under arrest!" Captain Watkiss dabbed at his lips with his napkin, leaving traces of beetroot behind. "Or are the Russians handing her back after all, do you suppose? My march—my landing-parties!" He rubbed his hands together and beamed, ill-temper speedily forgotten in his hour of success. "One should always take the bull by the horns—remember that, my dear Beauchamp. It pays—it pays!" He bounded to his feet and clutched Beauchamp's arm. "I'll come up at once." He was out of his cabin and up the ladder in a twinkling, training his telescope on the *Falls of Dochart*, whose sails were now coming down in the lifts.

"Heaving-to, I fancy. Perhaps they'll send a boat with someone to apologize—the vice-admiral's going to be most delighted, most pleased." Watkiss clutched again at his first lieutenant's arm. "What a beautiful sight, my dear fellow. Nothing like sail, nothing like it at all. I always said—those damn filthy engineers—" He broke off. "She's signalling. Making semaphore. Read it, Mr Beauchamp, we'll not wait for the yeoman."

"Yes, sir." Using his own telescope, Beauchamp began reading the signal from the sailing ship's poop. "It's from Mr Halfhyde, sir."

"*Mr Halfhyde?*" Watkiss repeated incredulously.

"Yes, sir. His signal reads—"

"That—damn—Halfhyde! God Almighty, what's he up to now!" Captain Watkiss, his thunder seemingly stolen, looked furious, his face scarlet and fists clenched. "Well, what's the damn signal, then?"

"Mr Halfhyde has released the crew and is in control aboard the *Falls of Dochart*, sir."

"*Captured* her?"

"Yes, sir. And Prince Gorsinski too."

"Oh, damn it, Prince Gorsinski what, Mr Beauchamp?"

"Prince Gorsinski captured, sir. He's Mr Halfhyde's prisoner—"

"Good God above us!" Watkiss put his head in his hands. "What next!"

Beauchamp concentrated again and after a while reported, "Halfhyde suggests you make a signal in your official capacity to the shore authorities, informing them that you have Prince

Gorsinski in your hands and intend weighing for sea with
Gorsinski as your hostage, sir."

"That's what he suggests, is it?"

"Yes, sir—"

"Then he must think again!" Captain Watkiss lifted both
hands in the air, one of them clutching his telescope, and shook
them towards the *Falls of Dochart.* "I can't possibly do such a
thing! I can't possibly! Why, Gorsinski's related to the damn
Czar! It'd be like—it'd be like some damn froggy coming across
the Channel and capturing the Prince of Wales! Can't you imagine . . ." His voice trailed away with the sheer enormity of it
all. Then strength returned. "God damn Halfhyde, the man's a
threat to world peace and my damn sanity! Gorsinski must be
handed back—with apologies. Tell Halfhyde that, if you please,
Mr Beauchamp. He's to act upon it instantly on pain of arrest
and Court Martial!"

Chapter 14

ABOARD *VENOMOUS* there had been scenes of passion that had taken time to subside; that they had done so at all had been due to the unlikely intervention, bravely attempted, of Lieutenant Beauchamp. Halfhyde's reply to Captain Watkiss's signal had been brief and rude, consisting of the one word: *no.* His next signal had produced fuller details. He intended sailing the *Falls of Dochart* through the Black Sea, the Bosporus, the Sea of Marmara and the Dardanelles into the Aegean and the Mediterranean with Prince Gorsinski as his safeguard. The first sign of trouble would put Gorsinski's life at risk. As for the rest, Halfhyde was indifferent: Captain Watkiss could come if he chose; otherwise he could stay in Sevastopol and face the music.

Watkiss, at first speechless, eventually uttered at some length. Mr Beauchamp then produced his heaven-inspired balm. He said with a touch of desperation, "The bull, sir—"

"What bull?"

"By the horns, sir. It always pays. You said so yourself, sir."

"Yes. Yes, by jove, I did, didn't I?" Captain Watkiss planted his eyeglass firmly and stared at Beauchamp. "But am I to suppose you're suggesting I accompany Mr Halfhyde? Or that he is the bull to be grasped?"

"I think an escort, sir. The vice-admiral—"

"Yes, the vice-admiral indeed." Captain Watkiss turned away and paced his quarterdeck for a full minute, looking sage. Gorsinski's presence, certainly, would be bound to ensure a strong degree of safety: the Russians would never open fire upon such a personage, and the dirty, baggy-knickered Turk would be most unlikely to risk the wrath of the Russian bear by doing so. Gorsinski could be put ashore when they emerged from the Dardanelles, where with any luck Captain Bassinghorn would be still waiting; then the massive bombardment batteries of the *Lord Cochrane* could take over the protection of the frail hulls of the TBD flotilla. Yes . . . Captain Watkiss rubbed his hands together and his eyes shone.

"I have made up my mind, Mr Beauchamp. Most clearly, Mr Halfhyde will require an escort. I have decided to provide one."

"Yes, sir."

"Have him told so, if you please. The flotilla's still at immediate notice for steam, is it not?"

"It is, sir—"

"Then make the signal to weigh. Mr Beauchamp. My compliments to the navigating officer, and he is to lay off a course for the Bosporus—and then for Gallipoli."

"I have consent, Mr Hawker. Consent and an escort. And you have the wind on your port quarter, standing fair for the Bosporus. I suggest all sail, and a clean pair of heels."

The mate looked back at him sardonically. "You sound confident, I'll say that."

"I am confident. With a good wind and Prince Gorsinski, we're going to succeed. Tell me, Mr Hawker: is Captain Matthews a driver?"

Hawker pursed his lips, his eyes hard and shrewd in a thin, strong face. "Not a driver. A fine captain and a good man—too good, perhaps. But not a driver."

"Too much God?"

"Aye, maybe so."

Halfhyde cocked an eye at the mate. "And you, Mr Hawker?"

"God and I are far apart, I fear."

"And you're a driver."

"Of ship and men, Mr Halfhyde."

"Then drive both very hard to the Dardanelles." Halfhyde glanced aloft: the wind was good and was freshening, as though God were firmly on their side, or at least the side of Captain Matthews. "Your Captain seems stronger and wishes to command from his bunk. I shall persuade him that he is not in fact as well as he thinks he is. The ship's yours, Mr Hawker."

Hawker nodded, and followed Halfhyde's glance aloft. Then he raised his voice in a bellow. "All hands . . . all hands stand by, man the lee braces! Wear ship . . ."

The *Falls of Dochart* came round until she was headed out of the anchorage on a southerly course, and then all her remaining canvas was sent up to clothe her yards—topgallants, royals, skysails, all billowing from the cringles in a straining mass of white beneath the blue sky; Prince Gorsinski, still under guard, stared aft from the poop towards the dwindling port of Sevastopol. Behind her steamed Captain Watkiss's flotilla, smoke pouring in black clouds from the funnels of the torpedo-boat destroyers, as the stokers banked the fires with flung shovelfulls of coal. Captain Watkiss in the leader, steaming to overtake the *Falls of Dochart* and assume charge of the escort, cursed engineers in general and his own in particular: smoke was an abomination to paintwork and ship-cleanliness, and was also an obvious indication to the shore that the British ships were breaking out.

"They'll have seen our movement in any case, sir," the first lieutenant said, reasonably enough.

"That's not the point, Mr Beauchamp, thank you. Smoke is a give-away, smoke is unpleasant and I don't damn well like it. Tell the engine-room to stop making it instantly."

"Aye, aye, sir. And Mr Halfhyde's suggestion, sir—"

"Did he make one?"

Captain Watkiss seemed to have expropriated the whole manoeuvre, Beauchamp thought. He said, "In regard to telling the shore authorities that he has Prince Gorsinski aboard, sir."

"Oh yes. No. I consider that stupid, Mr Beauchamp. Why exacerbate them from the start? It'll be quite time enough to make a signal to any pursuing vessel, before they open fire. And I'll tell you something else: I'll not say which ship Prince Gorsinski's in! Halfhyde didn't think of that, did he?" Watkiss beamed and strutted to the port side of his bridge. "Damn stupid, to let the buggers know *which ship* is to be preserved!"

"Yes, sir—"

"Now what about that smoke, Mr Beauchamp?"

The escort was formed with *Venomous* ahead of the *Falls of Dochart,* and the junior ship, *Vendetta,* under the acting command of Lieutenant Prebble, taking station astern. The remaining ships were disposed abeam to port and starboard, enclosing the *Falls of Dochart* protectively as she stormed along under full press of her canvas. On the poop, Hawker was exultant at the speed his ship was making.

"Sail's not dead yet, Mr Halfhyde."

"Indeed not, and I'm glad of it. Sail made sailormen. Wooden ships, and iron men—but you know the saying, of course." Halfhyde was staring aft through his telescope. "Meanwhile, something's stirring astern."

"What?"

Halfhyde handed his glass to the mate. "The *Nikolayev*. She's weighing for sea. Someone's ticked over, after seeing the flotilla go past."

"That's not surprising."

"It is to me, and it should have been to Captain Watkiss. He should have made a signal—or perhaps it's I who am amiss."

"What signal could he have made, then?"

"Not he, Mr Hawker, nor I—but Prince Gorsinski! A signal, ostensibly from him, to say he was shifting the British warships to Balaklava, perhaps. Some time might have been gained. It's too late now."

"But you advised Captain Watkiss to let the shore know you'd captured Gorsinski. He couldn't contradict himself, could he?"

"True, if he'd adopted my civil suggestion, but he did not! How's your damage control, Mr Hawker?"

Hawker laughed. "In a sailing ship?"

"I take your point, but I fear you don't take mine. Have you a battery Aldis, for signalling?"

"No. And I don't see the connection."

"Gorsinski is our damage control, is he not—but only if the Russians know he's here! We're too distant for semaphore. How do you normally communicate with other ships at sea, Mr Hawker?"

"A blackboard in the mizzen rigging, and a stick of chalk."

"For which we're also too distant, and I'd prefer the *Nikolayev* not to bring her guns within blackboard range!" Halfhyde lifted his telescope and looked aft again; the Russian cruiser was under way now, her hoses still cascading water down her hawse-pipe as the remaining links of the cable came home, and a bow wave, small as yet, showing as a bone in her teeth. It would be some while before she could overtake, but her guns could in fact already rake the British ships from her present position. A little urgency must be dinned into Captain Watkiss to use his signal lamps towards the enemy; Halfhyde was about to ask Hawker to hoist a flag signal to attract the attention of the closer vessel on the beam, after which he would make a semaphore message, when more pressing matters intervened: there was a shout from the after poop-deck rail, followed by a revolver shot. Halfhyde swung round—just in time to see Gorsinski dropping into the ship's streaming wake.

He ran aft followed by Hawker, brushing aside the gabbled, scared excuses of the seaman on guard. Gorsinski had surfaced: his head was visible from time to time as the wake's turbulence swept over him. He was sufficiently in control of his situation to wave a fist towards the ship.

Halfhyde shouted, "Mr Hawker, the way off the ship as soon as you can! A grass line astern, and a lifebuoy." The orders were passed at once, and a boat was swung out on the davits. As the lifts were slacked away and the braces hauled the yards round, Halfhyde climbed over the lee rail of the poop. For the second time during his mission, he dived in to retrieve a man from the water, but this time with a difference: Captain Watkiss could have been presumed to want rescue, but Gorsinski would resist recapture. There was extreme danger in what the Russian was attempting, but no doubt, if he was a powerful swimmer, he had considered it a fair hope that he would be spotted from the *Nikolayev*'s decks as the cruiser came up astern.

Halfhyde's dive carried him deep. Surfacing and dashing the seawater from his eyes, he looked around with a degree of desperation. Of Gorsinski there was now no sign, but there appeared to be consternation in the flotilla, the ships seeming to hesitate as the officers of the watches saw the sail coming off the *Falls of Dochart*. The engines of one of them were moving astern, as Halfhyde could see from the surge of water boiling forward from aft along her side, and her bows were aswing towards the sailing ship. Disturbed water flowed over Halfhyde's head; he struck out towards the north, seeking Gorsinski whenever his eyes were clear enough to see, for the time being disregarding the grass line that floated aft from the poop with a lifebuoy attached to its end.

Then he saw Gorsinski. The Russian, visible only momentarily in the turbulence, was swimming strongly back towards Sevastopol and the approaching *Nikolayev*. Gasping, Halfhyde increased his own speed, making a tremendous effort to overtake his hostage before it was too late. The officers on the Russian cruiser's bridge would have guessed by now that there was a man overboard; though they would not know it was Gorsinski, they might make that assumption—if word of his earlier presence aboard the *Falls of Dochart* had reached the *Nikolayev*. That was imponderable: what was not was the overriding necessity of Halfhyde's winning a race that, after a wholly sleepless night, was taxing his strength wickedly.

• • •

"Turn her, Mr Beauchamp, turn her. Steam down the weather side of the *Falls of Dochart*." Captain Watkiss, whom all reports had reached, stared astern through his telescope. "Halfhyde saved me from the sea. I must now save him—and Prince Gorsinski. Ensure that the lookouts are vigilant. I'll have the guts of any man who fails to see a head."

"Yes, sir—"

"And call away the sea-boat's crew if you haven't seen to that already as you should have done. Swing out the falls and lower, but wait my word to slip."

Captain Watkiss, as the strong wind flapped his long shorts around his knees, was filled with all manner of bleak thoughts. Halfhyde was Halfhyde; but the loss of Admiral Gorsinski from a British ship in his flotilla could spell out the end of Watkiss's naval career, one that had not been without honour. Her Majesty the Queen was a merciless taskmistress; success in her service was all, failure brought disgrace and ignominy. Success in the result automatically justified the means, however devious, by which that result had been achieved—but failure was always visited upon the head of the senior officer responsible. To extract a British ship in accordance with orders was one thing; but to fail to extract that ship, and, whilst failing, to have kidnapped and caused the death of a member of the Czar's family, was quite another. It was possible that he, Captain Watkiss, would never make good his escape from Russian waters; and if he did . . . Watkiss was visited by an appalling vision of a disgraced post captain, fat, failed, and fifty, running the gauntlet of the vice-admiral commanding the Inshore Squadron, the commander-in-chief, Mediterranean Fleet, and all the Sea Lords of the Admiralty, before being retired to the obscurity of cheap rooms in Southsea or Plymouth, to become a nobody in plain and shabby clothes, gone forever the golden haloed glory of oak leaves, rings, and brass buttons, gone the autocracy of the navigating bridge and all the panoply of command . . .

"Damn Halfhyde!" Watkiss said through clenched teeth, bitterly.

"Sir?"

"Hold your tongue, Mr Beauchamp, and concentrate on the ship."

Gorsinski, thrashing through the rough water of the Black Sea, was no more than two fathoms ahead of Halfhyde, while the *Nikolayev*, coming up fast, was perhaps two miles to the northward. The *Falls of Dochart* lay hove-to, the so-far neglected grass line hanging over her counter, floating clear of her rudder. Her boat was pulling fast towards the two swimmers: it was just a matter of time now, Halfhyde told himself, as the blood pounded through his veins and his limbs grew desperately heavy. He plunged on; down towards him, cutting across the bows of the pulling boat, swept Captain Watkiss in the *Venomous*, his white tunic drenched with sweat despite the coldness of the wind.

"The boat, sir—"

"What damn boat, Mr Beauchamp?"

"From the *Falls of Dochart,* sir. We nearly cut it in half!"

"Stuff-and-nonsense, Mr Beauchamp. In any case, she should have altered round my stern, I have the right of way."

"Sir, I—"

"Hold your tongue." Captain Watkiss, eyes narrowed ahead, leaned out from the bridge guardrail. "Slip the sea-boat!" he cried. The order was passed down from the bridge, and in the sea-boat the coxswain knocked away the Robinson's disengaging gear so that the boat dropped the remaining two feet with a smack upon the heaving waters, its crew bearing off efficiently and then bending to their oars and giving away together to the coxswain's orders. Just as Watkiss's boat took the water, Halfhyde caught up with Gorsinski, reached out and grabbed at the collar of his uniform jacket. By this time Gorsinski was as far gone as was Halfhyde; there was no fight left in him. Long yellow teeth were revealed behind drawn-back lips as the Russian snarled furiously at his rescuer, and then a boat had come up alongside and drawn in the two men like fishes from the sea. The moment they were on the bottom boards, the boat pulled away hard, running before the menacing approach of the *Nikolayev,* which was heaving on the waters with her main and secondary armament manned and the rest of her company of seamen lining her rails, some of them with rifles aimed. As a volley of shots swept across the water, Captain Watkiss decided that the moment had come.

"Mr Beauchamp, a signal to the damn dago: *I have Prince Gorsinski in my custody and unless you cease firing he will die.* See to that at once."

"I doubt if they'll—"

"At once, Mr Beauchamp, or I shall place you in arrest." Captain Watkiss glared down into the sea: there seemed to be some confusion, but his confidence had returned. Success was going to be the outcome, the Russians simply would not risk Gorsinski's life—they might hit him by mistake, for one thing. When the firing did indeed stop, Watkiss bounced across to the standard compass in the binnacle. "D'you see, Mr Beauchamp?

I was right! Now then: signal the *Falls of Dochart* to make sail, tell the engineer maximum revolutions . . . and when Prince Gorsinski boards, he's to be brought at once to the bridge."

"Prince Gorsinski—"

"Yes, Mr Beauchamp, Prince Gorsinski. Don't answer me back, I can't bear it in my officers. It's one of Mr Halfhyde's faults . . . though in other respects he's done splendidly today." He paused: Beauchamp clearly still wished to communicate. "God give me strength. What is it now?"

"Prince Gorsinski is not boarding us, sir. He's in the *Falls of Dochart*'s boat."

"What!" Captain Watkiss went a deep, unhealthy colour. "You're a bloody liar, Mr Beauchamp!"

"No, sir, with respect, I'm not—"

"Hold your tongue." Watkiss hurried to the weather guardrail and used his telescope to sad effect: Gorsinski was indeed being hauled aboard the sailing ship, and behind him Halfhyde. Watkiss made a growling noise, his whole thick body shaking with fury barely suppressed. His fists clenched, he turned, seeking something and someone upon whom to release his feelings. Perhaps luckily, he found it. "That man!" he roared, pointing his telescope. "That damn man there, that rating! He's using the starboard ladder! *My* ladder! He's to be placed in my report, Mr Beauchamp—dumb insolence, disobedience of my orders . . ."

The *Nikolayev* steamed close to the *Falls of Dochart,* circling her and then coming up on her lee side and reducing speed to maintain station abeam. From the waist of the sailing ship Halfhyde stared up into the faces of the Russian officers on the cruiser's bridge, into the very muzzles of the heavy guns that had swung and depressed to bear on him. Gorsinski had been taken below, but his presence was now very definitely known to the officers and men of the *Nikolayev*. On the bridge, the Russian captain took up a megaphone and shouted down in English to the *Falls of Dochart*.

"Your captain, please. I wish to speak."

Hawker caught Halfhyde's eye and answered, "The captain's sick. He can't come on deck."

"Who are you?"

"The first mate."

"Yes, the first mate, I see. Where is the British naval officer, Halfhyde?"

"Here," Halfhyde answered. While his uniform dried out in the galley he was dressed in a shirt and trousers belonging to Hawker. "What do you want?"

"Your flotilla captain has threatened death to His Highness Prince Gorsinski. I wish him put aboard my ship."

Halfhyde grinned. "Not granted!"

"You are foolish, Lieutenant Halfhyde. I shall shoot my guns, and you will sink."

"So will Prince Gorsinski." Halfhyde turned away towards the poop, shrugging his shoulders disdainfully. The Russian might make the best he could of it; he would no doubt stand by all the way through the Black Sea and hope for some kind of reckoning when the ships approached the entry to the Bosporus. Walking to the after rail, Halfhyde looked back towards Sevastopol, now fast receding astern, fading into the line of grey that fringed the horizon. A large step had been taken in the pursuance of duty: the *Falls of Dochart* had been cut out with her crew intact, and the reason for her arrest and detention discovered. Orders had been obeyed, if exceeded. But there was a long way to go yet, and the Russians were nobody's fools, Gorsinski himself included. Halfhyde brooded: in a sense it had gone too well so far. He had an inner feeling that this could not last. For one thing, he was acutely aware that Prince Gorsinski could prove a two-edged sword: to carry him on into the Aegean would shatter to fragments an already much-dented diplomacy—but at what point should he be jettisoned? The moment that happened, the flotilla and the *Falls of Dochart* would be at the mercy of the Turkish guns, and as always the Turks would wish to remain on good terms with St Petersburg. The *Lord Cochrane* was one of the imponderables; Captain Bassinghorn might have deemed it prudent not to lie off the narrows for too long, and in any case Halfhyde had no knowledge of his orders from the vice-admiral in Malta. There was another thought nagging at Halfhyde's mind: as ever, a hostage was of use only whilst he lived. If the *Nikolayev* fired just one projectile at the British ships, and Prince Gorsinski died as he had threatened, what was there to prevent a holocaust?

Chapter 15

"HOW ARE YOU, SIR? You look as though you'll live!" Halfhyde looked down at the weathered face, the thick grey beard. Captain Matthews was undoubtedly out of danger.

"I am better, Mr Halfhyde, thanks be to God."

"And not to the nurse." Halfhyde glanced across the cabin at the crone, shanghaied with Prince Gorsinski and now in the dreadful throes of sobriety, munching toothless gums as the vodka dried out of her; when sober and in due course recovered, she might yet tend Captain Matthews's convalescence. "There are matters to be discussed, sir."

"Indeed there are. I gather you intend forcing the narrows, Mr Halfhyde. What about my ship?"

"At present a naval responsibility rather than yours. You'll not be held to blame if anything should go wrong. Your certificates of competency are safe, Captain Matthews."

The old man made a gesture of indifference. "Scraps of paper—"

"Years of experience, rather."

"But men are men. I am responsible for my crew. They are not to come to harm, Mr Halfhyde. Can you give me an assurance that they will not?"

Halfhyde said, "No, sir, I cannot. The risks are there and I'll not deny them."

"That's honest, at all events. I appreciate your dilemma. You have your orders. I have mine." The captain paused, staring at Halfhyde thoughtfully. "As you know, I was bound for Alexandria to pick up cotton. That is where I must go from the Dardanelles."

Halfhyde nodded. "I see no reason why you shouldn't, though the decision is my senior officer's and not mine. You may be required to enter Malta on your homeward passage, to report to my vice-admiral, and there'll be formalities when you reach the United Kingdom."

Matthews gave a hollow laugh. "Very many of them, I don't doubt! I know the ways of the Admiralty, Mr Halfhyde. And I fear much trouble."

"For yourself?"

"As master, yes. Kidnapping, shanghaiing—"

"By my act, not yours."

"By my ship, Mr Halfhyde, for which I am responsible personally. I have never ceased to be the master, even whilst in the Karnakol gaol. I have never been relieved."

"True. I understand *your* dilemma, Captain! And I may be able to resolve some part of it." Halfhyde leaned forward. "You are concerned about the presence aboard your ship of Prince Gorsinski. For different reasons, so am I. I think it is time Prince Gorsinski's benefits were spread. And for my part, I too have a ship to command, and I am not there to do so. She's in good hands—but they are not my hands, Captain Matthews. You'll understand that, I know."

"Yes . . ."

"So I propose to rejoin, and to take Gorsinski with me. It will be difficult and it will be dangerous, and it must be done without anyone seeing from the *Nikolayev.* Therefore it will be done in darkness, tonight, and without the use of boats."

"Without boats—then how?"

"I shall need to consider various alternatives, and when I have done so I shall come back to you." Halfhyde got to his feet. "I'll leave you to sleep, sir. Rest easy. I shall have a thought for your men, and my men, all the way through."

The clear eyes met his. "You are a good man, Mr Halfhyde, and a bold one too, I think. May God be with you." Captain Matthews heaved his shoulders onto his pillow and half sat up in the bunk. "A request, Mr Halfhyde. A boon, if you will be so good."

"Of course."

"My Bible. Would you bring it to me? It's in the saloon, where I'm accustomed to give readings. The top right-hand drawer of the sideboard."

Halfhyde nodded and left the cabin. He rummaged in the drawer and brought out the Bible, a heavy affair, with an embossed leather binding and with a gilt clasp. The leather was worn by much handling; the saloon would have been filled many times with the voice of Captain Matthews as he delivered his readings to his officers, whose thoughts would most probably have been many miles away and engaged in more mundane considerations than the scriptures . . . Halfhyde carried the volume back to Captain Matthews, handed it to him, and prepared to leave again.

"A moment, if you please, Mr Halfhyde." Matthews leafed through the pages, his face solemn. After a moment he extracted a sheet of thin writing paper and handed it to Halfhyde. The paper carried the house flag of the *Falls of Dochart*'s owners, with their Liverpool address, and the letter, neatly handwritten in a clerkly script, was addressed personally to Captain Matthews, care of their agents in Gibraltar. There was an instruction to enter Palermo to pick up his passenger; and a further instruction that on his homeward voyage from Alexandria he was to enter the Aegean to make a rendezvous off Mount Athos, to the north of the Gulf of Monte Santo, where six men, named in the letter, would board him from a boat. The men were Russians, and the rendezvous was to be made under cover of night, a time and a date being given.

"This," Halfhyde said, "is what Gorsinski wanted, is it not? Yet it was never found—a poor search indeed!"

"They were in God's keeping," Matthews said with simplicity. "I never doubted that He would protect them in His book. And you will see that the rendezvous is two days ahead."

"Forty-eight hours from four bells in the next middle watch, to be exact. And so, sir?"

"It can yet be made, Mr Halfhyde."

"True. But it's not my decision."

"I ask you most earnestly to inform your senior officer. Those men face certain death if they are caught, no matter what becomes of Prince Gorsinski. Well?"

Halfhyde met the gaze of the old eyes and nodded. "I shall do as you ask, once I am aboard my own ship—that is, if I can find a way of communicating without the Russians seeing."

"A way will be found—do not doubt it." Captain Matthews opened the Bible again, flattening the page with the palm of his hand. "If you would be so good?"

"In what way, sir?"

"A reading—"

"I must ask you to excuse me. I have much thinking to do."

Halfhyde backed hastily for the door, but was stopped by an upraised hand. "Sir, I—"

"It has been my custom over many years to read a passage daily to my officers at this hour. I like to think of you temporarily as one of my officers, Mr Halfhyde, and I ask you to remember we are all in God's hands, the more particularly so in the days ahead. If you will be so good?"

Halfhyde gave a sigh and sat by the bunk. As Captain Matthews read his way through a selection from Nehemiah, Halfhyde registered that the old crone was still *in situ* by the door. It was unlikely she understood more than perhaps a word or two of English, but some sense of the conversation and its inherent drama might have penetrated; she had now to be regarded as yet another possible hazard.

Vendetta was steaming in her appointed station astern of the *Falls of Dochart,* too far for any communication other than by semaphore, which could be read off by the signal personnel on the flag deck of the *Nikolayev.* Nevertheless, since the preliminary manoeuvre would be visible in any case, Halfhyde stood at the after rail of the poop and with his arms made the call sign of *Vendetta,* time and again until his antics were seen and recognized for what they were. Then he signalled: *close my weather side.* He waited; *Vendetta,* with Prebble conning her, increased speed and approached the port side of the sailing ship, holding off some two cables'-lengths on the beam. Halfhyde, equipped with a megaphone, shouted to her bridge: "Mr Prebble, can you hear me?"

There was no reaction, Halfhyde resorted once again to semaphore: *come closer.* Cautiously, Prebble brought the torpedo-boat destroyer nearer, the sea between the two ships rearing up over his decks. Halfhyde shouted again, and Prebble acknowledged.

"Full discretion, Mr Prebble." Halfhyde waved across to the lee side, indicating the Russian cruiser. "You understand?"

"I understand, sir."

"Captain Watkiss had an accident. Do you understand that, Mr Prebble?"

There was a pause, then Prebble's shout came back: "No, sir."

"Captain Watkiss had an accident whilst on passage of the Mediterranean. Ups-a-daisy, Mr Prebble, arse over tit. Got that?"

"Yes, sir."

"Two bells in the next middle watch I shall suffer something similar, plus passengers. Watch for grass. I say again, watch for grass. Understood?"

There was a wave from Prebble. "All understood, sir."

"Thank God! Resume station, Mr Prebble." Halfhyde lowered his megaphone and, turning ahead, saw the signal lamp busy from the bridge of *Venomous,* its speed seeming to reflect the anger of Captain Watkiss. Halfhyde read off the dots and dashes: *your station keeping is deplorable. Report name of your officer of the watch.* Captain Watkiss was as vigilant as ever.

Halfhyde rose from his bunk in the second mate's cabin at half past midnight. Proceeding on deck he looked around at sea and weather; the wind was still strong and there was now a lash of rain, and the waves were larger than they had been during daylight. But, after a passage slower under sail than the inward one under steam, they were now not far off the Bosporus, and the job must be done whatever the risk. Halfhyde knew that Prebble would be vigilant, and Prebble was a good seaman, a man of more experience than the average lieutenant of cadet entry. Halfhyde turned to Hawker, who had come on deck for the operation of transfer though the watch was officially in the care of the bosun in the absence of the second mate.

"Bring the grass line aft, if you please, Mr Hawker."

"You're going, then?"

"Yes. Bring up Gorsinski and the old woman in ten minutes, if you please. Hands tied behind their backs, and both to be wearing life jackets."

"If anything goes wrong—"

"Then they die, and so, as a matter of fact, do I. But nothing'll go wrong. I have God's assurance, passed by way of Captain Matthews." Hawker gave a laugh, but Halfhyde regretted the joke as soon as he had uttered it: Captain Matthews was a man of much sincerity and, somewhat to his own surprise, Halfhyde had been impressed by his quiet reading from the Bible, which had given him an inner conviction that all would indeed go well that night.

Waiting for Gorsinski and the nurse, Halfhyde paced the poop impatiently, feeling already an increase in the wind. All around there was the curious orchestra effect of a sailing ship at sea under a full press of canvas: the wind howled its eerie way through the rigging, raising different notes from braces and down-hauls, lifts and sheets and ratlines, creating a sound that accompanied a vessel without cease all the way around the world; a sound of wind and sea, of twanging harps and zithers, and the sad liquid notes of violins. Spray, lashed by the wind, was coming aboard, and the ship was heeled over to leeward at an angle of some twenty degrees, forcing Halfhyde to cling to the weather rail to prevent an undignified downhill slide.

Gorsinski, cool and disdainful as ever, was brought up in front of an armed seaman from his imprisonment in the spare cabin; behind him came the old crone, muttering and mumbling, not yet understanding what she was about to undergo— nor, for that matter, did His Highness.

"What now, Lieutenant Halfhyde? Do you wish proper professional advice in the handling of sail?"

"I think not, sir." Halfhyde waved an arm astern; the night was as dark as pitch, and the steaming lights of the *Vendetta* shone brightly through the murk, white and red and green, their position indicating that the torpedo-boat destroyer was on station, dead astern of the *Falls of Dochart*. "My ship awaits me, and you also."

"A boat, in such weather? It will need good seamanship, Lieutenant Halfhyde."

"Which is available if required, but it will not be. We go by line, sir. If you will be good enough to step clear." Halfhyde urged Gorsinski towards the after rail on the starboard side, as the hands began dragging the heavy grass line up the ladder from the waist. When the rope was coiled down on the poop, Hawker detailed men to secure Gorsinski and the old woman to it, with a two-fathom gap between them. Then the watch on deck, assisted by Hawker and the bosun, backed up the rope as Halfhyde urged the two Russians over the side. The old crone screamed into the wind, kicking out furiously in her attempts to stay aboard, but her feet were prised away from the rails with marline spikes, and down into the sea she went, behind Gorsinski, as the grass line was paid out. When the two of them were in the water, supported by the floating rope and their life jackets, Halfhyde threw a leg over the after rail, took the grass line in his hands and slid down to join his prisoners. From the poop a storm lantern shone briefly, showing its light twice, and then there was blackness, broken only by the steaming lights of the rolling vessels.

"*Up* she comes . . . with a will now, my lads!" *Vendetta's* chief bosun's mate sang out above the wind, heaving with the rest as the grass line was grappled and heaved aboard. The old crone, her teeth chattering and her body washed clean by the sea, was carried below for a welcome tot of rum. A cabin was provided for Prince Gorsinski, who seemed little the worse for the gruelling experience; Halfhyde, after a strong whisky and a hot bath, joined his first lieutenant on the bridge.

"Well, Mr Prebble, I am now resuming the command."

"I'm glad to see you back, sir."

"Thank you. We have now to consider the arrival off the Bosporus."

"What do you think will happen, sir?"

"I don't know, but we must be prepared to fight our way through if necessary."

"You don't think Prince Gorsinski will be enough?"

Halfhyde shrugged. "Time will tell, Mr Prebble. And now let us spare a thought for Captain Watkiss." He paused, staring ahead through the night towards the plunging stern lights of the vessel ahead. "I do not propose—yet, anyhow—to inform Captain Watkiss of what's been done. We shall keep our own counsel, Mr Prebble, I think!"

Prebble asked, "Why's that, sir?"

"For two reasons. Firstly, I don't want the *Nikolayev* to intercept my signals, and secondly, I have an idea that if Captain

Watkiss believes His Highness Prince Gorsinski to be still aboard the *Falls of Dochart,* we may be able in effect to double the value of our illustrious hostage!"

"I don't think I understand, sir."

Halfhyde put a hand on the first lieutenant's shoulder. "No more do I, my dear Prebble—it's just an idea, at present not properly formulated. But we shall see." He fell silent after that, and Prebble forbore to interrupt his thoughts. Those thoughts were centred upon Captain Matthews and his request to be allowed to make his appointed rendezvous; Halfhyde wished to help him rescue the Russians, but anticipated disagreement from Captain Watkiss, who would wish to make all speed out of the Aegean, if ever they got that far, rather than face a possible Russian pursuit without the benefit of a captive Prince Gorsinski . . . After some minutes Halfhyde announced that he was turning in and would be in his sea cabin if required.

"I'm to be called at dawn, Mr Prebble. By that time we shall have the entrance to the Bosporus in sight, and may be faced by the Turks."

"Yes, sir. Do you wish the ship to be at action stations at dawn, sir?"

"We'll let the dawn decide for itself, Mr Prebble. By that time, Captain Watkiss may have expressed himself."

Chapter 16

WITH THE DAWN came a lessening of the wind, and a clear blue sky, shot with pink, and dappled with scudding white clouds. Dead ahead but still distant lay the entry to the Bosporus, the buildings of Fener Keui coming up slowly as the ships approached the woodland scenery of the coast. Halfhyde looked through his telescope at the land: the narrow water between the headlands appeared empty of ships, so far at any rate.

"We'll not close up the guns' crews yet, Mr Prebble. I have an idea Captain Watkiss may intend us to look peaceful."

"For the benefit of the Turks, sir?"

"Yes." Halfhyde smiled. "I'd not like to be in the shoes of the Turkish commander—he'll have tricky decisions to make shortly! Does he offend St Petersburg, or does he offend Whitehall? Whichever way he decides, he stands to lose his head! If it were me—" He broke off suddenly. "What's Captain Watkiss doing now, Mr Prebble?"

Prebble looked ahead. The leader, increasing speed, had made a sharp turn to port, heeling his rails under as he went, and was starting to tear down the weather side of the group of ships. As Halfhyde watched in some astonishment, the coloured bunting of a disposition signal streamed up on the halliards to flutter from the leader's starboard fore yard-arm, and Halfhyde's yeoman of signals, telescope to his eye, sang out, *"Form line ahead,* sir, Falls of Dochart *to take station astern."*

Halfhyde swore. "What do we form on? Do we follow Captain Watkiss round the mulberry bush?" The leader was now swinging to port again, cutting across the stern of the *Falls of Dochart* and coming dangerously close across the bows of Halfhyde's own ship. He then swung to starboard to come down *Vendetta's* beam to leeward and Halfhyde saw Captain Watkiss standing stoutly in his bridge wing, megaphone to his lips.

"Vendetta ahoy. *Mr Halfhyde!* What are you doing aboard?"

"Commanding my ship, sir."

"Damned impertinence . . ." Speed and increasing distance took away the rest of the sentence. Watkiss swept past, heeled over to turn across *Vendetta's* stern, and came up again on the weather side. The shouted conversation was resumed. "You'll explain later, Mr Halfhyde. Frankly I fail to understand. Follow my motions into the Bosporus, and look well to your station-keeping. Maintain two cables'-lengths distance between ships. Keep in mind the shallows, which I shall pass close to but which must be avoided . . ." Once again the remainder of the message was lost to Halfhyde as Captain Watkiss sped recklessly on, making a large bow-wave, to pass his verbal orders to the remainder of the flotilla: it seemed he desired to conceal his tactical planning from the *Nikolayev.*

"What has he in mind, sir?" Prebble asked in some bewilderment.

"No doubt we shall find out, Mr Prebble, but the shallows he refers to are those we took pains to avoid when coming the other way." Halfhyde frowned in thought: an Admiralty "Notice to Mariners" received aboard before he had resumed command had warned of the recent disturbance in the hundred-fathom line that ran close to the shores of the Black Sea, a sea-bed distortion due to natural forces that had lifted the rock and formed a thick layer of soft mud to trap unwary ships. It was believed that this would be merely temporary and that the bottom would subside; but for the present it existed and it appeared likely that Captain Watkiss intended to make some use of it.

"At this moment," Halfhyde said, "I'm as mystified as you."

Watkiss proceeded ahead for the narrows once he had contacted all his ships; one by one they moved behind him, into his wake, taking up their proper distance, with Halfhyde's vessel in the rear of the line immediately ahead of the *Falls of Dochart*. The sailing ship was still flying on under all sail except for the skysails and royals, which had been furled in preparation for taking off her way as she approached the narrows; and already she had men standing by, Halfhyde saw, to let fly the sheets when the moment came to ease her speed. The *Nikolayev*, her navigating bridge crowded with officers and ratings, was maintaining her station abeam of the *Falls of Dochart*.

"The Russian's concentrating on the *Falls of Dochart*, it seems, sir," Prebble remarked.

"She is, Mr Prebble, and I think will continue to do so."

"Why's that, sir?"

Halfhyde smiled. "The answer's below, though the *Nikolayev* doesn't know that: Prince Gorsinski, Mr Prebble!"

"But Captain Watkiss, sir—*he* thinks that too—"

"Yet he's leaving the *Falls of Dochart* exposed in the rear of the line! Who knows what may lie in the mind of the good

Captain Watkiss?" Halfhyde paced the bridge with Prebble at his side. "I believe he has some nefarious plan in mind to put the *Nikolayev* into danger, some plan that he considers subtle enough to fool damn dagoes—and I can only hope he knows what he's doing." He pointed with his telescope. "There lie these recent shallows, westerly, off the Roumili Light. I shall make an estimate: the *Falls of Dochart* will maintain her station abeam to the east of the Russian, and the flotilla will prevent the Russian passing ahead of her. If the *Nikolayev* attempts to drop astern and come up on her other side to stand clear of shoaling waters, then the *Falls of Dochart* will drop back, and the Russian will be able to proceed in safety only by cutting through Prince Gorsinski."

"Or by going astern on his engines, sir."

"Yes, Mr Prebble, but then he will be faced with the prospect of Captain Watkiss getting away into the Bosporus—whereas he may be hoping to reach the channel before our ships and block the entry!"

"But the Turks—"

"The Turks are not to be relied upon, Mr Prebble, either by ourselves or the Russians." Halfhyde shrugged. "There's a large gamble ahead for all of us, and I do not propose to be caught napping. Leadsmen into the chains, if you please, Mr Prebble."

Captain Watkiss, whose own leadsmen were straining their bodies against the canvas aprons in the chains on either side of the bow as they swung their lead-lines over their heads for the cast, stood firmly at the forward guardrail of his bridge, hands behind his back and telescope under arm, as *Venomous* came within three miles of the channel for entry. Eyes narrowed, he glanced astern: his flotilla was nicely closed up, and the sailing ship was now spilling the wind out of her topgallants. Halfhyde's estimate of his intentions had been correct; and Watkiss was filled with anticipatory thoughts as he conned his command towards the buoys marking the worst area of mud. The *Nikolayev,* a much deeper-draught ship than his own, was in his view clearly bent upon beating him into the entry and then pulling herself up all standing to prevent the British proceeding. If the damn Russian was allowed to get away with that, Watkiss had told himself, the position would become one of utter stalemate, and Gorsinski would lose all his value. To keep that value intact, in Watkiss's opinion, the situation had to remain mobile. And if the *Nikolayev* could be lured or forced to stick fast in the mud, well, it wouldn't be the British that lost their mobility. Captain Watkiss was relying largely upon a degree of carelessness developing on the navigating bridge of the *Nikolayev* as the fast-moving ships neared the vital target—relying upon a degree of recklessness, the taking of chances rather than allow the British to get away with Prince Gorsinski.

Watkiss swung round to study the lie of the Russian cruiser. She was, he fancied, now making the attempt to swing easterly a little. Watkiss snapped an order: "Down twenty revolutions, Mr Beauchamp. Make the speed signal."

"Aye, aye, sir." Speed came off, the bunting flew up to the yard-arm, the rest of the flotilla eased down and added to the Russian's discomfiture as her manoeuvring space narrowed. Captain Watkiss listened to the depth reports from the leadsmen in the chains, aware that he was cutting it fine but nothing like so fine as the *Nikolayev.* He was short with Beauchamp when the first lieutenant warned, "We're approaching shoaling water, sir."

"Stuff-and-nonsense, Mr Beauchamp, we have plenty of water yet."

"I doubt if—"

"Hold your tongue. Port ten."

The last remark was addressed to the officer of the watch, who repeated, "Port ten, sir." As the wheel went over ten degrees to port, the rudder and the helm swung to starboard. The remainder of the flotilla followed the leader's movements, thus crowding the *Nikolayev* even further.

"Midships," called Captain Watkiss.

"Midships, sir."

"Steady."

"Steady, sir. Course . . . 195, sir."

"Keep her there."

"Aye, aye, sir."

As Watkiss scraped past a marker buoy, almost fouling it, a sudden hail came from the leadsman in the starboard chains: "Shoaling water ahead, sir!" Watkiss failed to hear and took no notice of his first lieutenant; his attention was now wholly directed astern, and he was bouncing on his toes with glee. The *Nikolayev* had brought up all standing and was down by the bows. Watkiss clutched the arm of his first lieutenant.

"I've damn well done it, Mr Beauchamp! Mr Beauchamp, be so good as to look astern! The damn dago's hard aground!"

Beauchamp turned: the *Nikolayev,* belching smoke and steam, was in a sorry state. All around her the water was thick and grey with mud churned up by her great ram and by the thrash and thunder of her screws; her ship's company was picking

itself up from recumbent positions, and her foremast was lean-
ing drunkenly towards the embedded bow. Even with the aid
of tugs, she wouldn't move for a week, if then.

Captain Watkiss placed his eyeglass in position and hitched
at his shorts. He was about to utter when his attention was
caught by the movement of his junior ship. Halfhyde, back in
Vendetta, was once again disobeying orders: he was hauling out
of the line to the east—and the *Falls of Dochart* had already
done the same by the look of it. It didn't really matter now,
of course, at any rate in a tactical sense, for the object of the
westerly-pressing manoeuvre had been achieved; but it was
downright disobedience of orders all the same and Watkiss
scowled blackly. About to order the making of a signal to the
Vendetta, Watkiss lurched and then went flat on his back. There
had been an appalling jerk, and a nasty grinding noise from
below; and *Venomous* now lay as deeply embedded in the mud
as did the Russian cruiser.

"One, two, three, four . . . Watkiss puts 'em all ashore."

"Sir?"

Halfhyde swept an arm around the flotilla away to starboard.
"They're *all* aground, Mr Prebble! All but us and the *Falls of
Dochart.*" He shook his head in wonder. "Obedience to orders
is of course essential, but it can be carried too far."

"Not with Captain Watkiss," Prebble said gloomily. "I'm
afraid *we'll* be the ship that gets the blame, sir—we disobeyed!"

"And remained afloat."

"Yes, sir. But to Captain Watkiss principles come first. The
principle of blind obedience is the important thing."

"To Captain Watkiss, as you said. The vice-admiral and the Board of Admiralty will never dispute the duty of a Commanding Officer to prevent his own ship standing into danger navigationally, Mr Prebble, and I am not worried." Halfhyde turned his head. "Mr Sawbridge?"

"Sir?"

"Stop engines, wheel amidships. Mr Prebble, prepare to tow aft, if you please. Yeoman, make to the *Falls of Dochart: I propose to tow you through the Bosporus to Constantinople.* Mr Prebble, pass your tow with the utmost despatch."

"Aye, aye, sir." Prebble hesitated. "What about Captain Watkiss, sir?"

"What about him, Mr Prebble?"

"Well, sir—"

"One moment, Mr Prebble, he's signalling now." Halfhyde read off the longs and shorts for himself: *you are to repair aboard immediately.*

Already in Captain Watkiss's cabin a small mountain of documents and personal gear stood stacked. Captain Watkiss, having delivered a violently-expressed rebuke for disobedience of orders, an act of virtual mutiny that Halfhyde had by no means heard the last of, waved an arm towards the stack.

"I'm coming back with you, Mr Halfhyde. I'm transferring my pennant to *Vendetta.*"

"Oh no, sir, you are not."

The eyeglass went in, firmly. "I beg your pardon, Mr Halfhyde? And who the devil are you to give *me* orders, and to seek to prevent me carrying out my duty?"

"I apologize for the words and the tone, sir." Halfhyde gave a tight bow to hide the sheer murder in his eyes. "But may I suggest that your duty lies here, with your flotilla that you have thrust into the mud? May I—"

"Hold your tongue, damn you, or I'll have you in arrest—"

"I am not having you aboard my ship, sir, other than as a passenger. I think you are a gallant officer who fears nothing, but your seamanship is an abomination. In the Mediterranean you threw yourself willy-nilly into the sea from your own fo'c'sle head—"

"A damfool cast of a heaving-line, Mr Halfhyde!"

"Which you placed yourself in the way of, sir. Earlier this morning you wove in and out of the line in utter disregard of proper ship safety, and now you have stranded four ships in possibly hostile waters, your own included. My command is not going to be blocked into the Bosporus by poor handling, sir, stuck like a duck in pondweed!"

"You are under arrest, Mr Halfhyde. Mr Beauchamp!"

"Sir?"

"Arrest this officer, Mr Beauchamp." Captain Watkiss bounced up and down on his toes. "Close arrest, if you please. A spare cabin. A sentry, armed. I've a damn good mind to have him shot. A post captain has that privilege." He stared, his eyes glassy with anger. "Damn popinjay! A mere lieutenant! Good God above us all . . . disobedience, rudeness, refusal of a direct order and I don't know what-all else! Never in all my service have I been so blatantly insulted or had my orders flatly refused." He raised his telescope in a threatening gesture. "The vice-admiral—the commander-in-chief—the Admiralty . . . God! You will die for this, Halfhyde, mark my words. Silence, sir! Hold your tongue, don't *dare* answer me back like a common seaman! I—" He broke off, his face scarlet, his chest heaving in deep breaths: a knock had come at his door and the officer of the watch stood framed in the opening. "Yes, what is it now?"

"Boats coming off, sir—"

"Boats? Where from?"

"One from the shore, sir, and one from the *Nikolayev.*"

"The devil they are!" Watkiss pulled at his lower lip, fury subsiding in the need for an immediate decision. "Now what the hell do we do, I wonder? Mr Halfhyde, what do you suggest?"

"Nothing, sir. How can I? I'm in arrest, am I not?"

"Oh, don't split hairs!"

"An officer in arrest has no standing, sir."

"Stuff-and-nonsense!"

"Am I in arrest or not, sir?"

Watkiss roared, "No, you're not! Mr Beauchamp, release this officer."

Beauchamp's mouth opened, but he said nothing; he shrugged, lifted his palms a little way, and looked helplessly at Halfhyde. Watkiss rounded on him. "Good God, Mr Beauchamp, kindly stop looking like a curate emerging from a brothel. Man the ladder, full courtesies . . . bloody dagoes! How I detest being caught like this with my trousers about my ankles! Mr Halfhyde, it's Gorsinski they'll want! Where's Gorsinski?"

"I think, sir, it's better that you don't know."

"Damn you, Mr Halfhyde, why?"

"I can't answer that yet, sir. Shall we not wait and find out a little more first?"

Watkiss fingered his jaw, eyes doubtful. "Take it as it comes, you mean?"

"Yes, sir, exactly."

"Not a bad idea, I suppose. I can't think of anything else, at all events. And in our present situation I suppose we'll have to be diplomatic towards the buggers, won't we?"

"It would be advisable, sir."

"Yes. I still can't see why you can't tell me where Gorsinski is." Anger flared again. "You're still being insubordinate, Mr Halfhyde, are you not?"

"Practical, sir. If you don't know you can't give it away inadvertantly. There are six ships Prince Gorsinski could be aboard, sir, and it takes time to search six ships. Time can still be on our side."

"Oh, damn it, I don't see how!"

"Have patience, sir." Halfhyde turned as a seaman approached the captain's door. "Here's your bosun's mate now, sir. I think the Russians are already coming alongside."

Chapter 17

THE CAPTAIN of the *Nikolayev* had come across in person; in the boat from the shore sat a resplendent Turkish officer in a multicoloured uniform, fat and smug in the stern-sheets. Both boats arrived off Captain Watkiss's ladder at the same moment; a diplomatic incident was nicely avoided by the Russian, who smiled, bowed, and waved the Turk to the foot of the ladder ahead of himself. The colourful officer, who was accompanied by a slightly-built civilian in white coat and trousers, gave a brief nod in acknowledgement of the courtesy and ordered his coxswain to go alongside.

At the head of the ladder stood Captain Watkiss, with Beauchamp and Halfhyde in attendance. There was a shrilling of bosun's calls as the fat Turk climbed to the quarterdeck: Watkiss, who had no idea whether his visitor was naval or military, or even customs, was playing for safety now.

The Turk reached the deck, stopped, glared around and then returned the British salutes. From behind the gross body came the white-clad civilian, thin, sharp-faced, bespectacled. "Captain Watkiss?" he asked in perfect English.

"Yes. And you, my dear sir?"

"My name's Frankland, First Secretary in our Embassy in Constantinople. How d'you do?"

Watkiss positioned his eyeglass and held out a hand. Taking

it, Frankland nodded towards the Turk. "General Othman Pasha has no English, so you may speak freely, Captain." At that moment the head of the *Nikolayev's* captain appeared over the side, the piping party began again, and more salutes were punctiliously exchanged. Captain Nesterov, as the Russian introduced himself, was in an ill temper and spoke plenty of English in a hectoring tone to Watkiss, blaming him roundly for forcing him onto the mud.

"Your ship, my dear sir, is your ship," Watkiss snapped. "If you put her aground it's not *my* fault. You may blame the Turks for scandalously misplacing their buoyage, if you wish."

"It is not the Turks. It is not me. It is you. You had stolen His Highness Prince Gorsinski, and I was using every endeavour to rescue him, and so I—"

"I had stolen no one," Captain Watkiss interrupted truthfully and with dignity. "And I didn't ask you to accompany me across the Black Sea, did I?" He indicated the white-suited diplomat. "Mr Frankland is Her Majesty's representative—"

"In Turkey," Frankland put in quickly, smiling blandly at Captain Nesterov.

"What?" Watkiss snapped.

"In Turkey. Not in Russia. His Excellency the Ambassador to the Ottoman Empire has no voice in St Petersburg, Captain Watkiss."

"Oh, fiddlesticks! The Queen's the Queen, isn't she, whatever set of damn . . . whichever country one's in? I expect your support, Mr Frankland, in extricating my flotilla from this attempt at illegal detention by Captain what's-his-name." Captain Watkiss shook his telescope in the Russian's face. "Tit for tat, my dear sir! I shall ask General Othman Pasha to arrest *you* now, and—"

"Come, Captain," the Russian broke in, sneering openly into Watkiss's furious face, "has not your stupid pilotage put both my ship and your flotilla into a kind of arrest already, since you have plunged us all into Turkish mud?"

Frankland, using his diplomatic training to good effect, had calmed a difficult and deteriorating situation with soothing words, and had put it into the mind of Captain Watkiss that a private conference would be an excellent idea. The several parties were now seated round the wardroom table and gin was being poured; with wonderful tact Frankland, as the only non-military person present, and therefore to some extent more impartial than the others, had persuaded Captain Watkiss to allow him the head of the table and, *ipso facto,* the chair. Captain Watkiss, at first extremely angry at the suggestion that he might take an inferior place aboard his own ship, had descended through simmer to doubt, then to a feeling of having been out-manoeuvred by devilish sharp practice, and finally to acquiesence: after all, even though she was head of both army and navy, the Queen herself was, strictly speaking, a civilian, and Frankland was her representative.

"Well, gentlemen," Captain Watkiss began.

"Er . . . Captain." Frankland coughed and smiled but his voice was firm. "The chair, I think?"

"What? Oh—very well, very well." Watkiss glared and drank some gin. "All right, Hackett," he snapped at the wardroom steward. "That'll be all. Get out and don't eavesdrop."

"Yessir." Hackett took himself off to the pantry, and the conference began. Captain Nesterov launched into a lengthy statement of the Russian case, making no mention of the reason for the arrest of the *Falls of Dochart,* but pointing the finger at Halfhyde and demanding that he be handed over to himself as representative of his Czar.

"I'll do no such thing," Watkiss stated flatly.

Frankland, lifting an eyebrow, said, "With great respect, Captain, we are here to—"

"I said I'll do no such thing. I *meant* I'll do no such thing." Captain Watkiss, his arms folded above his stomach with the tattooed snake fully visible as it climbed his forearm, glared round uncompromisingly: dagoes were dagoes, but he was a post captain aboard his own ship and had every intention of acting as such. "I demand tugs to release my ships, and I demand safe passage through the Bosporus and the Dardanelles."

"But Captain Nesterov—"

"Damn Captain Nesterov. Whose side are you on, may I ask, Mr Frankland?"

"—and General Othman Pasha," Frankland continued blandly, refusing to show his colours, "I—"

"Oh, balls to General Othman Pasha."

Frankland sucked in an angry breath. "It's lucky the general has no English, Captain. As a matter of fact, he's very well disposed towards the British." He turned to the Russian. "With all respect to you, Captain Nesterov, I feel I can say that General Othman Pasha might very well be prepared to give assistance to Captain Watkiss and even to—"

"Not to let the British through the Bosporus," the Russian interrupted. "*I* shall not allow that whatever the general has to say. One word to my guns' crews, and the British flotilla goes boom, boom." Captain Nesterov flung his hands heavenward. "Boom, boom, boom—like that!"

Watkiss got to his feet and shook a fist at the Russian.

"How dare you, sir! How dare you! By God, I'll have your guts for garters. On board my own ship—to be threatened, insulted—"

"Gentlemen, please," Frankland broke in, his eyes glassy. "Conferences are not—"

"Hold your tongue, Mr Frankland, if you please. Conferences my backside, they're all balls and bang me arse!"

"Really, Captain—"

"I said hold your tongue. Mr Beauchamp?"

"Sir?"

"All these persons are in arrest. See to it. *Close* arrest, lock and key."

"But you can't—"

"And if you persist in arguing, Mr Beauchamp, you can put yourself in arrest as well." Captain Watkiss swung round on his heel. "Now, Mr Halfhyde: you'll take your ship to sea at once with the *Falls of Dochart,* acting in execution of orders received from the vice-admiral in Malta, and you, Mr Frankland, can put that in your pipe and smoke it." A gleam lightened Watkiss's eye as an idea struck him. "That Turk. You, there. I'm taking you out of my arrest." General Uthman Pasha, realizing that he was being talked about, smiled and nodded uncomprehendingly. "He's yours, Mr Halfhyde. Put him upon your bridge as you steam into the Bosporus. Before you leave I'll send the *Falls of Dochart's* second mate across to rejoin her—the man MacAllister, you remember. Mr Beauchamp, call Hackett in and send him to the torpedo-coxswain. I want an armed party down here at the double. Take charge, if you please. Mr Halfhyde, on deck with you."

Halfhyde turned for the door and Watkiss followed, propelling General Othman Pasha before him. As Halfhyde looked back he saw incredulous fury on the face of Captain Nesterov, and Frankland looking as though he were about to burst into tears. Reaching his quarterdeck, Watkiss said, "Now then. Gorsinski. Where is he? I demand to know."

Halfhyde said, "I have him, sir."

"Aboard *your* ship, not the *Falls of Dochart?*"

"Yes, sir."

"Good! Keep him, then." Watkiss gave a chuckle. "Once you're away, I can swear blind *I* haven't got Gorsinski, can't I?"

"Indeed you can, sir. May I ask what you propose doing with the other two?"

"I don't know yet, but I think I can use them to ensure the safety of my flotilla." Captain Watkiss struck an attitude of self-sacrifice, of the officer being left behind in hostile waters. "If I fail, I shall at least have done my duty. Good luck, Mr Halfhyde, in the doing of yours. Do it well, my dear fellow." He held out a hand as the officer of the watch reported Halfhyde's boat alongside. "Take your ships in safety to Malta."

"I shall hope to, sir, but I have in mind a diversion in the Aegean."

"What?"

Halfhyde explained briefly about the men to be picked up by Captain Matthews in the *Falls of Dochart*. Captain Watkiss placed his eyeglass in position and pursed his lips.

"Revolutionaries, do you suppose?"

"It seems likely, sir."

"I don't like revolutionaries. I don't like damn socialists. There's far too much of that sort of thing."

"Human lives, sir, depending upon Captain Matthews."

"Oh, I dare say, but *socialist* lives, and that's a very different thing, is it not, Mr Halfhyde? No, I don't like scum, people who plot against their own side. It's not British."

"These are Russians, sir."

"Yes, yes, I realize that," Watkiss said disagreeably, "and that makes it worse, doesn't it? No, Mr Halfhyde, you shall not risk British lives in the interest of damn foreign socialists—"

"But Captain Matthews—"

"You shall not, and kindly don't interrupt your seniors." Captain Watkiss shook his telescope in Halfhyde's face. "Go back to your ship and carry out your orders without further blasted argument!"

"Mr Prebble," Halfhyde said as he came over the side of *Vendetta*, "you will please prepare to move out through the Bosporus." He stepped aside as the vast figure of General Othman Pasha lumbered onto the quarterdeck, smiling still. "We have another hostage, though he doesn't realize it. He's a Turkish general, by the way."

Prebble saluted. "How d'you do, sir," he said politely.

"He has no English, Mr Prebble, none at all. Have him taken to the bridge, if you please, and see to it that he's comfortable but guarded in a discreet fashion—no weapons. Try to convey that he's being given a courtesy trip to Constantinople aboard a British warship. Understood, Mr Prebble?"

"Yes, sir."

"And the ship's company to action stations. I have every reason to suppose that we may come under fire from the *Nikolayev.*"

Prebble glanced at General Othman Pasha. "If that happens, what about the Turk?"

"He may well have a nasty accident, I should think, Mr Prebble, and need to be hosed down by the fire parties." Halfhyde turned forward and climbed to his navigating bridge. Using his telescope, he scanned the waters. The *Nikolayev* would have a clear field of fire once the *Vendetta* had moved past the stranded *Venomous,* and Halfhyde had a fair idea the Russian cruisers would have been left with orders from Captain Nesterov to open upon the British ship if she moved. During his absence aboard the leader, the tow had been passed to the *Falls of Dochart* as ordered, the towing pendant now hanging slack between the ships with a safe length beneath the water. Halfhyde ordered a signal to be made by semaphore to the sailing ship, passing the orders for sea with a warning that they might be about to come under fire from the heavy guns of the *Nikolayev.*

"I shall open fire upon the Russian if he opens upon me, Mr Sawbridge," Halfhyde informed the officer of the watch. "Pass the word to the guns' crews."

"Aye, aye, sir."

"And send down for Prince Gorsinski, have him brought under guard to the bridge." Halfhyde glanced across to the starboard wing where the Turkish general sat, his enormous rump overlapping a deck chair provided by Prebble. "It may do him good to know he's no longer alone—and I fancy there may be something of interest for him to see before much longer!" Halfhyde paced his bridge, waiting for the report of action readiness to reach him; and as he paced, he pondered. Six

Russian socialists awaiting pick-up had been condemned by Captain Watkiss to a nasty death at the hands of Prince Gorsinski's aristocratic legions. In view of his assurance to Captain Matthews, Halfhyde found this a disturbing notion; and once again he thought of old Daniel Halfhyde, gunner's mate in the *Temeraire* so many years ago . . . Lord Nelson had had a convenient blind eye to which to put a telescope when the signals stood against him . . . Halfhyde's reflections were interrupted by a report from his first lieutenant.

"Ship's company closed up at action stations, sir."

"Thank you, Mr Prebble. Have an eye below for the damage control parties."

"Aye, aye, sir."

"Mr Sawbridge, the engines to dead slow ahead, if you please."

"Dead slow ahead, sir." The telegraph handles went over and the order was repeated back in acknowledgement from the engine-room. Very gently the *Vendetta* moved, taking up the tow, her course directed for the narrows. The towing pendant came up dripping water and shuddering as it took the strain; then, as the *Falls of Dochart* moved in answer to the pull, it dipped below the water once more.

"Engines half ahead." Halfhyde turned as he heard a step on the ladder, and looked round into the murderous eyes of Prince Gorsinski, who was climbing between two armed seamen under the command of a petty officer, also armed. "Good morning, sir. As you will observe, we are about to move into the Bosporus with a Turkish escort." He indicated General Othman Pasha, who rose to his feet, saluted, smiled, bowed, and dropped back into the deck chair.

Prince Gorsinski, his lip curling at the fat Turk, indicated the *Nikolayev.* "There are heavy guns against you, Lieutenant Halfhyde."

"Grounded guns, sir. Mine are mobile."

Gorsinski swore savagely. "Your nefarious manoeuvres once again, I suppose!"

"Not mine this time, sir. Captain Watkiss was responsible for this."

"And is aground himself, I see." Gorsinski spat on the deck of the bridge, the gob landing at Halfhyde's feet. "You British are poor seamen, stupid and clumsy but full of conceit—"

"Kindly be silent now, sir," Halfhyde broke in, seeing a flag hoist running up to the Russian's signal yard. "Yeoman, what's she making?"

"*Stop instantly or I shall open fire, sir.*"

"Very good, thank you." Halfhyde took another look around through his telescope. "Yeoman, warn the *Falls of Dochart* I'm about to increase speed and may alter course without further signals. Mr Sawbridge, engines to full ahead."

"Engines full ahead, sir."

The telegraph bells rang. Halfhyde watched the swing of the Russian turrets, was staring towards the guns just as they opened in a flash of orange flame, a shattering roar of reverberating din, and a heavy cloud of smoke. Glancing towards General Othman Pasha, he saw the fat Turk with his hands over his ears, trying to squeeze his gross body into a smaller target behind the frail lee of the canvas dodger. Gorsinski stood arrogantly firm, his lips parted in a sneering smile. Shells sped over the *Vendetta,* so close that their wind felt like a gale, to fall into the sea beyond and send up great spouts of water. Others fell short.

Gorsinski laughed exultantly. "What you call a straddle, Lieutenant Halfhyde! A successful ranging shot—and with the next you will be sunk!"

"You too, sir—but there'll not be another broadside from the *Nikolayev*, as it happens. Look, sir, upon what takes place when a grounded ship fires all her guns at once!"

Gorsinski followed Halfhyde's outstretched arm. The Russian cruiser, having none of the normal cushioning provided by the sea against the tremendous recoil of the main armament, had come close to sinking herself where she lay. Her upper deck was fractured, split wide open both fore and aft of her super-structure, and her already weakened foremast had gone over the side. The upheaval of her decks and the broken stalks of her turrets had thrown the gun-barrels right out of alignment, and they were pointing uselessly down into the water as the *Vendetta* steamed on for the narrows, keeping clear of the line of marker buoys, the *Falls of Dochart* still safely under tow behind her. A storm of cheering broke out from all the ships as Halfhyde, sending aloft a final farewell signal to Captain Watkiss, moved on beyond the grounded flotilla, his speed reduced now. On *Vendetta's* bridge General Othman Pasha, who had recovered his dignity when he realized there would be no more firing, executed a difficult manoeuvre: shaking his fist at Prince Gorsinski, he smiled widely at Halfhyde and managed three painful, throaty words in English: "Damfool bastard for-eigners."

Captain Watkiss would have been proud of him.

Chapter 18

THE TURKISH GENERAL fulfilled all expectations: beaming from the bridge as Halfhyde brought the *Vendetta* into the narrows past the fortifications of Fener Keui, he quelled by his colourful presence any opposition that might otherwise have come from the shore guns. The passage of the Bosporus with its tricky currents and its many forts was made without incident, and as the ships came between Pera and Scutari to approach the Sea of Marmara off Constantinople, Gorsinski was once again despatched below to the security of his guarded cabin.

"What about the Turk, sir?" Prebble asked.

"We shall put him ashore at Constantinople, Mr Prebble."

"Wouldn't he be a safeguard all the way through to the Aegean?"

Halfhyde nodded. "Yes, he would. But we have Captain Watkiss to consider. If we make off with General Othman Pasha, if we remove him from what I take to be his area of command, then the rest of the flotilla may suffer."

"Yes, sir, I follow. But what about us?"

"We still have His Highness, Mr Prebble, and the Turks appear to be friendly in any case. But time will tell. We should be off Gallipoli by nightfall if there's wind enough for Captain Matthews, and then we shall see."

"Yes, sir. Frankly, sir, I sense a trap."

"In the Dardanelles passage?"

"Yes, sir."

"You don't trust the Turks, then, Mr Prebble?"

"Well . . . do you, sir?"

Halfhyde gave a short laugh. "No further than I can throw General Othman Pasha. And we have to steam back past that torpedoed fortress."

"That's what I was thinking of, sir."

"Then think to good effect, Mr Prebble, and I shall join you. We need a stratagem—and I don't despair of finding one. In the meantime, Constantinople looms to starboard." Halfhyde turned. "Yeoman, call the signal station. Ask for a boat to be sent off for General Othman Pasha. I shall heave-to when it approaches, and lower the starboard ladder."

Smiling yet, the fat Turkish officer gabbled what appeared to be thanks at Halfhyde and then was escorted down to the quarterdeck by the first lieutenant, and seen over the side. From the bridge Halfhyde watched him disappearing across the blue water towards Constantinople's clustered white buildings, toad-like in the stern-sheets of a somewhat seedy boat. He never once appeared to have queried his being taken aboard the *Vendetta;* or at any rate he had looked content enough. Perhaps he would yet be Halfhyde's ambassador ashore; he had not liked being fired upon by "damfool bastard foreigners," and might well report unfavourably on Prince Gorsinski and his cruiser . . . Halfhyde paced the bridge in thought, as Constantinople faded away on the starboard quarter, and the torpedo-boat destroyer nosed out into the Sea of Marmara for the passage to the Dardanelles. There was a fair wind and after exchanging messages with the *Falls of Dochart* Halfhyde ordered the tow to be cast off. With a full press of canvas clothing her yards, the sailing ship made good progress, better progress than would have been prudent under tow though Halfhyde became a prey to a consuming impatience when he could not use his engines to their full power, having to reduce to the speed of the square-rigger. But all seemed well: once again the passage was made without incident, and by the time they had raised Gallipoli ahead few other vessels had been seen—and no warships. But the tension, the feeling of a trap ahead, grew throughout the ship: they were being allowed to go so far, and at the last, within a handful of miles of freedom, the trap would close.

And so far there were no stratagems.

"Won't the British Embassy take action, sir?" Prebble asked as in fading light they approached their landfall.

"I doubt it, now that Captain Watkiss has captured the First Secretary, Mr Prebble. Unless they take action against Captain Watkiss." Halfhyde put up his telescope and examined the lights from Gallipoli at the entrance to the thirty-three miles of the Dardanelles. "Still no ships in sight, but we have to steam below the fortress guns for entry. And for exit—if we get that far."

"The *Lord Cochrane* may protect our exit, sir."

"We must hope so, Mr Prebble. Send up Prince Gorsinski, if you please."

"Aye, aye, sir." Prebble turned away towards the ladder, but was called back.

"One moment, Mr Prebble. The old hag, the nurse as she calls herself with a fine conceit. How is she—sober, I trust?"

"I understand she's been suffering from seasickness for most of the time, sir."

"Seasick, on a mill-pond?" Halfhyde's eyebrows went up. "Lack of alcohol more like! Send her up as well, if you please." Prebble met his eye. "A stratagem at last, sir?"

"The makings of one, Mr Prebble, no more than that."

Halfhyde examined the old woman critically by the light of a lamp. "There are likenesses," he murmured. "She wears black, she is dumpy and fat, she has white hair arranged in a bun. She is currently very angry and shows it unmistakably. Yes, she could pass."

"For the *Queen*, sir?" Prebble asked in amazement.

Halfhyde clicked his tongue. "There is an inherent disrespect in your assumption, my dear Prebble. No, not Her Majesty Queen Victoria personally. For one of her Russian kinswomen, or one of her German kinswomen visiting Russia and, perhaps, staying with cousin Gorsinski in Sevastopol."

"And captured with him?"

"Just so, Mr Prebble." Halfhyde swung the lamp away. "I believe she may help, in case Prince Gorsinski is not enough. For all I know the Turks may be chivalrous towards women, and if they're not, they should be. Your Highness?"

"What is it?" Gorsinski, standing in his uniform in front of an armed seaman, spoke with a cold fury. "What are you doing with the old woman?"

"It is a question of what you are going to do with her, sir." Halfhyde waved towards the shore lights. "As you can see, we are about to enter the channel, and you and your kinswoman are to be our safeguard against the Turkish guns—"

"Do you," Gorsinski asked icily, "when speaking of my kinswoman, refer to the hag?"

"Who is now your fondly regarded great-aunt—or whatever. You will stand against the forward guardrail of my bridge, sir, and place an arm protectively about the shoulders of your great-aunt—"

"I shall do no such thing. I am an aristocrat. I do not clutch the peasantry."

"Tonight, sir, you will clutch at anything I order you to clutch, in the interest of our safety—yours as much as my ship's company's."

"I shall not, I say!"

"Mr Prebble, the bayonet in a little, if you please."

"Aye, aye, sir." The first lieutenant passed the order to the seaman on guard duty, and the man pushed his bayonet forward. Gorsinski gave a yelp of pain.

"To the rail, sir, at once."

"The hag smells. She is rancid."

"And very likely carries lice on her person—I agree. Nevertheless, you will clutch her lovingly or you will suffer severe bayonet damage." Halfhyde nodded at Prebble; another order was passed and once again there was a stifled cry from Gorsinski. "Now, sir—move!"

"Swine!" Gorsinski moved; the hag was pushed to his side and in obedience to orders the gold cuff-lace of Gorsinski's admiral's uniform went round the stinking body. "You will suffer for this, Lieutenant Halfhyde!"

"We shall see. Hold your great-aunt close. Mr Prebble, a yard-arm group, if you please, to shine on Their Highnesses throughout the passage."

The order was given: a leading-torpedoman came up to the

bridge, trailing electric cable from a saucer-like object with four lamp bulbs attached. This was rove to an awning stanchion and directed down upon Gorsinski and his companion: they stood out starkly as Halfhyde brought the ship into the Dardanelles below the great guns of the Gallipoli batteries. From one of them, suddenly, a searchlight shone, its beam like a knife in the night, looking for its target. The *Vendetta* moved ahead, sharply silhouetted. From the batteries came war-like sounds, shouted orders, and metallic noises as breech-blocks were slammed shut. Aboard the ship, the tension mounted: in the bright glare from the searchlight Halfhyde saw sweat pour down Prebble's face. From the old crone at the forward guardrail came a low moaning sound, a kind of keening. From the western shore a boat was seen, coming out towards the British vessels. The *Vendetta* was hailed in hesitant English from the boat's stern-sheets.

"British Captain ahoy. You must stop."

"I shall not stop," Halfhyde called back. "His Highness Prince Gorsinski would object." He spoke to the Russian. "Tell them that, sir. Be sure they understand! The bayonet is still handily placed for your rump."

Gorsinski lifted his right arm away from the old nurse and shook his fist at Halfhyde. The yard-arm group and the beam of the searchlight played upon the splendid gold lace. Halfhyde said sharply, "The arm, sir, back upon the great-aunt. And now the message, quickly."

Gritting his teeth Gorsinski called down in English to the man in the boat. "I am Admiral Prince Gorsinski, kinsman to His Imperial Majesty the Czar. I wish to proceed through the Dardanelles without hindrance."

There was a coming together of heads in the boat: a conference was in progress. Then the spokesman called back, "The
woman, who is she?"

"Careful, sir," Halfhyde warned.

Gorsinski, his face a picture, answered, "A relation visiting
me from . . ." He turned and glanced interrogatively at Halfhyde.

Halfhyde answered for him: "From Germany, a relative shared
by Their Majesties the German Emperor and the Czar, and
Prince Gorsinski. A lady from the family of Her Majesty Queen
Victoria of England. A word to the wise, whoever you may be:
there is much majesty about today, and you should have a care
for the safety of your own neck."

Stepping away from the guardrail, he looked at the dreadful old crone in Gorsinski's gold-laced grip. The searchlight,
throwing her into relief, was doing something to her silhouette:
the white hair, the bun, the black dress, the shape of the body,
even the set of the head, for currently she was a very angry old
crone—by the exercise of a little imagination Halfhyde could
almost see Her Majesty, perhaps staring disdainfully at the
unwelcome approach of poor Mr Gladstone . . . and undoubtedly there had been some effect upon the Turk in the boat. He
was now proceeding away from the British ships, back into the
shadows below the batteries.

Halfhyde laughed, and clapped his first lieutenant on the
shoulder. "The bold approach, Mr Prebble! The bigger the lie,
the more it is believed!"

"Yes, sir. Do you think it'll carry us right through to the
Aegean?"

"I hope so, but I must assume not. We remain closed up at
action stations, Mr Prebble." Halfhyde paused, and looked aft

towards the *Falls of Dochart*, coming along behind, ghost-like under a climbing moon that silvered her spread canvas as it caught the north-easterly breeze that predominated in the Dardanelles. The sailing ship spelled peace and beauty, a fit and proper base for the lofty, pious thoughts of Captain Matthews, who would no doubt be hard at prayer at this moment. But Halfhyde's thoughts were of war and screaming shells, of red fire and death along the Dardanelles, of plates that would erupt from the pressures of internal explosions as the Turkish shells drove home; and he felt that prayer might not be enough, that the Turkish God might be powerless to implement the Christian God's plea on their behalf, in face of a likely Turkish desire for revenge. Halfhyde turned back to the first lieutenant. "The fortress that I torpedoed, Mr Prebble. The Turk'll not forget that, and never mind the supposed friendliness of General Othman Pasha!"

"But the boat—"

"The boat went away, and the batteries didn't open. I know that! But this is Gallipoli, a major command where accidents—accidents to Prince Gorsinski—should not happen." Halfhyde smacked a fist into his palm. "Farther along the passage, accidents—mistakes—are much more acceptable, and the Turks don't love the Russians any more than they'll be loving us."

"No sir." Prebble frowned in concentration. "You mean, sir, that Gorsinski's presence aboard must be taken into account by the Turkish authorities here at Gallipoli, but that he won't necessarily weigh in the minds of the subordinate commanders in the forts?"

"Near enough, my dear Prebble, near enough! I say again, we must beware of mistakes made on purpose."

• • •

Farther along the narrows heavy cloud came up, obscuring the moon. Here there was no point in illuminating Gorsinski and his companion crone, and the yard-arm group had been switched off, though the two hostages remained under guard at the forward rail. Halfhyde, feeling in his bones that something was wrong, paced the bridge anxiously, looking all around at the land on either beam and at the waters ahead. One by one the lights came up and passed by: Karakova Point to starboard, flashing green every three seconds; Kodiouk to port, flashing red; Abydos Point on the starboard side of a big bend . . .

"Nothing moving about us, Mr Prebble. Nothing!"

"Yes, sir. It's as though they've closed the passage to shipping."

"Exactly, and I don't like the feel of it." Halfhyde bent to look at the chart spread out on the hinged flap at the after end of the bridge. "We're closing that fortress I shattered, it's a half-mile ahead now."

"And after that, sir—"

"After that, the last one: New Castle of Asia, one mile from the exit, and the forts guarding the narrows. They've left us alone so far. I fear our luck must run out shortly, Mr Prebble."

There was no response from the first lieutenant; the ship went onward, wind sighing through her standing rigging. They came up to the spot where the torpedoed fortress had stood; there was nothing but desolation, no sign of life whatsoever either on the banks or in the dark, placid water. From the *Vendetta*'s bridge and upper deck men stared in silence, almost in awe as they remembered. The tense voyage proceeded:

Halfhyde spoke again, his voice dropping like a knell into the silence.

"Two miles, Mr Prebble, to Koum Kaleh—and New Castle of Asia, on the eastern bank. The channel takes us close in."

"We could go westerly a little, sir."

"Only a little, not enough to make much difference. And I shall not take the risk that Captain Watkiss took outside the Bosporus, of running aground and ending up helpless under the guns." Halfhyde squared his shoulders, hands behind his back. "Warn all hands to be alert, if you please, Mr Prebble, for a sixth sense tells me we are standing into danger."

Prebble asked, "Do you know the nature of the danger, sir?"

"My dear Prebble, a sixth sense I may have on occasion, but I'm not in touch with God." The ship steamed on towards the exit into the Aegean, some three miles ahead now by the chart. The silence was broken only by the engine sounds; for the second time in that passage, Halfhyde cursed his inability to move faster. He would have liked to steam at speed past the looming fortress, racing his ship to safety beyond the range of its guns, beyond their capacity to bear upon him with their sixty-four capacious mouths—but the *Falls of Dochart* was still his responsibility, and he must husband her along the last few miles of enclosed waters at her slower speed.

The eastern bank was close now, and soon Halfhyde's telescope could pick out the battlemented walls of the fort and the massive battery below. No matter that many of those old guns threw stone: chunks of stone despatched by gunpowder could do much damage, and there were the heavy calibre guns throwing shells as well. So far as he could make out, the guns were in fact not manned; the battery stood in darkness, no lights anywhere, and there was an unready look about the place. Halfhyde took a deep breath, feeling a shake in his hands. His fears might well be groundless, but on the other hand this could be the trap they had been expecting, its closing to be signalled by a sudden searchlight beam and followed by the thunder of artillery from the shore, the moment the lulled mouse had crossed its last threshold. Halfhyde swung his telescope westerly across the Dardanelles passage, seeking, searching for he knew not what. Towards the seaward end he fancied there was a patch of deeper shadow, and he had just steadied his telescope on a point on his starboard bow when the ship gave a curious jerk and a lurch; her way checked a little and there was a violent scrape along her bottom plating.

Halfhyde swung round. "What the devil—"

"Bridge, sir!" An alarmed voice came down from the masthead lookout. "Barges, sir, swinging in on either bow!"

"A cable below . . . Good God Almighty! Mr Sawbridge, emergency full astern. Yeoman, tell the *Falls of Dochart* to back her topsails and lose way instantly. Warn her that I have sternway on and she must try to stand clear."

"What is it, sir?" Prebble asked.

"I think we've fouled a cable laid for that very purpose, and linked to ammunition lighters—and we may have tripped a timefuse too. Hold tight for your life, my dear Prebble, and may God be with us now." Halfhyde took a grip of the after rail, glanced at Gorsinski's horrified face, and began conning his ship astern to clear the *Falls of Dochart* behind. He saw that the square-rigger's canvas had been let fly, the sails spilling out their wind. The *Vendetta* dropped down dangerously towards her bow: sweat poured from Halfhyde's face, soaking into the collar of his white tunic. Now the barges were in full view; though the ship was now coming clear of the cable, the inward swing of the barges was still in being as a result of the initial pull.

A split-second later the barges blew.

There was an appalling noise like a thousand thunderstorms, an immense blast of heated air swept the bridge like a furnace-breath, and sheets of flame, red and white, green and purple and orange, sprang up and joined together as one across the *Vendetta's* retreating bows. The ship rocked violently, throwing men off their feet everywhere along the decks. Gorsinski lay in a heap with the old nurse on top of him; the blast appeared to have disrobed her partially, and her black dress was replaced by underwear of an almost equal blackness from which Prince Gorsinski was struggling to free his face. Hard along his port side now, Halfhyde found the *Falls of Dochart*, still thankfully afloat but with fire dancing along her royal and topgallant yards. As the two ships ground together Halfhyde became aware of Prebble's grasp on his arm.

"The battery, sir! They're about to open."

They were right abeam of the fortress now; Halfhyde saw the gunners at their stations, and the massive mouths of the artillery pieces swinging and depressing to bear upon him. He said, "Very well, Mr Prebble, we'll not go down without a fight. Pass the word to open, if you please."

"Aye, aye, sir!" Prebble, on the brink of giving the order, stopped with his mouth open. He seized Halfhyde's arm again, and pointed ahead. *"Look, sir!"*

Halfhyde looked: that earlier patch of deeper darkness . . .
it had moved closer and now, in the high flames of the explod-
ing ammunition lighters, stood clearly and formidably visible:
the *Lord Cochrane,* moving massively in with her great bombardment guns pointed at the fort, so close now that Halfhyde
could see on her bridge the bulky and commanding figure of
Captain Henry Bassinghorn, seeming in that moment to be as
big and sturdy as his turrets. A signal was being made rapidly
to the fort: *stand down your guns' crews instantly or I shall blow
you to Kingdom Come.*

Halfhyde skilfully manoeuvred his ship clear of the *Falls of
Dochart,* leaving little damage done to either hull. Safe, each
ship licked its wounds. Aboard the *Vendetta* the casualties were
minimal: one man killed and a number injured, by burns or
by flying metal, or from tumbles taken in the blast that had so
violently rocked the ship, wounds that the *Lord Cochrane's*
sick bay would quickly cope with; and the *Falls of Dochart*
was sailing still, if with less canvas and with two men lost in
falling from aloft, their bodies sadly broken across the gun-
wales. The fires aloft were fought by sweat and guts and superhuman effort, assisted by the *Vendetta's* hoses, and were brought
under control. The ships, led by the *Lord Cochrane,* with her
turrets still closed up for action and the drums of the Royal
Marine Light Infantry beating out in warning, steamed in total
safety past the fortresses at Cape Helles and Cape Yen Shehr,
steamed on unchallenged into the waters of the Aegean with
the fifes and drums now playing "Rule, Britannia" beneath the
flaunted folds of the White Ensign at the peak, to heave-to
beyond the narrows. Halfhyde, bidden when his ship was

brought up to report aboard the monitor, gave the facts to Bassinghorn.

"And Captain Watkiss at this moment, Halfhyde, is where?"

"No doubt still fast aground, sir."

"A muddy ending," Bassinghorn said, a glimmer of amusement in his eye.

"Yes, sir. I was wondering, sir . . ."

"What?"

"Whether we should go back for him, sir."

"Another cutting-out operation? No, Halfhyde, I think not. Enough diplomacy has been shattered as it is, and I fancy the Turks and Russians won't be anxious to shatter any more."

"They'll dig him out and let him go, sir?"

Bassinghorn said, "Captain Watkiss can be a persuasive talker, and he has the tenacity of a bulldog."

"I doubt if he'll be tactful with dagoes, sir!"

Bassinghorn wagged a reproving finger. "That smacks of disloyalty to your senior officer."

"I am never disloyal, sir."

"I know, my dear fellow, I know!" Bassinghorn smiled and pulled at his heavy beard. "Merely critical on occasions. And now I shall say something I shouldn't: I believe Captain Watkiss will talk so much and so strongly that they'll not be able to float him off fast enough! In the meantime, what about our friend Prince Gorsinski and his lady?"

"I'd prefer to retain them for a while, sir."

"Why?"

"There's a question of the men Captain Matthews was to pick up at his rendezvous off Mount Athos. Gorsinski at liberty would be a danger until that's been done, and I propose to stand by Captain Matthews until he has his passengers aboard. When that's achieved, then I'll drop my own passengers off the narrows and proceed with all despatch, to Malta."

At dawn two days later, after a successful pick-up off the 6000-foot high Mount Athos, its many convents and hermitages clustered on its sides, Halfhyde eased his engines off the Dardanelles entry and made a farewell hoist to the *Falls of Dochart,* as the sailing ship cleared away to the south for the Mediterranean and England, with her six passengers aboard. Then he made a signal to the Yen Shehr fortress and lay hove-to, awaiting transport to take off His Highness Prince Gorsinski and the hag from Sevastopol.

Gorsinski was cold but furious. "Those men in your sailing ship. Revolutionaries! You are more than ever my enemy, Lieutenant Halfhyde, an enemy of all Russia!"

"Not of all Russians, sir. There are many who stand against you."

"Peasants. Workers. Dogs! I spit." Gorsinski spat. His whole body was trembling with suppressed fury and a sense of help-lessness. His fists clenched. "They are of no account to me. You have caused immense harm, and I shall report upon you personally to my kinsman, His Imperial Majesty the Czar."

Halfhyde bowed solemnly. "A most dreadful threat." From the corner of his eye he saw a decrepit rowing-boat moving out slowly from the narrows, and he bowed again. "To the starboard ladder, Your Highness. Your bumboat is approaching. Take good care of your great-aunt."

Prince Gorsinski swung away stiffly, without further words. Twenty minutes later Halfhyde and Prebble, with a hilarious ship's company lining the rails, watched the Prince's departing back, looking like an egg in a cup as it rose above the shallow stern of his transport, caught now and again by spray from the oars. The old nurse, muttering and chattering through her toothless gums, was seated amidships and wagging a finger at His Highness, who was somewhat elaborately holding his nose clenched between thumb and forefinger, his admiral's lace glinting gold in a strong sun. Then, as the rowing-boat neared the entry to the Dardanelles and the fortified castles that dominated it, Halfhyde had the surprise of his life: into view and steaming fast for the open water came four warships, with their White Ensigns flaunted boldly from the jackstaffs.

"By God, Mr Prebble!" Halfhyde said to his first lieutenant. "Captain Watkiss is off the mud!"

"So I see, sir." Lieutenant Prebble chuckled. "And I think Prince Gorsinski is about to go aground himself."

Halfhyde looked through his telescope. Gorsinski, caught by the wash from Captain Watkiss, was wallowing and rocking violently in his bumboat, and waving a fist towards the British line, his other hand holding fast to the boat's gunwale. Then the signalling started from the leader: Vendetta *from* Venomous, *I am heaving-to. You are to repair aboard immediately.*

"Trouble, Mr Halfhyde? *I* had no trouble! I made a fuss and they responded—dagoes always do if you shout loud enough and long enough. I don't know if they understood all I said, but that damn diplomat interpreted some of it, and they sent tugs and hauled my ships off undamaged." Captain Watkiss hitched at his shorts. "That man who waved a fist at me just now. Was that not Prince Gorsinski?"

"Yes, sir."

"As I thought. That's no way to treat a prince and an admiral, Mr Halfhyde, you should have provided one of your own boats. You'll not have heard the last of Prince Gorsinski, let me tell you."

"No doubt, sir—"

"Nor of me either. Damned insubordination!"

Halfhyde raised his eyebrows. "I beg your pardon, sir?"

"Disobedience of orders! Moving out of the line like that off the Bosporus, without permission—"

"We've been into that, sir—"

"Hold your tongue, Mr Halfhyde, and don't answer me back. Disobedience of orders is a Court Martial offence—"

"I beg to disagree, sir—"

"Don't argue, if you please, Mr Halfhyde; that's fact—I said it." Watkiss flourished his telescope in Halfhyde's face. "Court Martial. The vice-admiral—"

"Will be thankful I didn't go aground as well, sir."

"What's that?"

"If I had, sir, it's at least arguable that we would all still be outside the Bosporus, awaiting Prince Gorsinski's pleasure. As it is, we appear to have won a victory."

"Ah." Captain Watkiss scratched his face, tilting it towards the sun. Gold glinted from his cap peak and from the stripes on his shoulders. "Well, I don't disagree that we're a flotilla still, and we've done our duty. I can report that I cut out the *Falls of Dochart* with her crew intact, and to that extent achieved my orders. *And* without loss to ourselves. I'm not so sure about your part in it—you'll most certainly have upset the diplomats —but I do feel I can congratulate myself, Mr Halfhyde. I run a first-rate flotilla, nobody can deny." He bounced up and down his bridge importantly. "Well, we'll not delay. Return aboard your ship, Mr Halfhyde, and then I'll make the signal to proceed in line ahead. Take care with your navigation, the Aegean's tricky and we shall find shallows."

Halfhyde looked at Captain Watkiss hard; Watkiss had seen nothing remarkable in his statement. Halfhyde said formally, "Great care will be taken, sir, I assure you."

"Good. That'll be all, then. Thank you, Mr Halfhyde."

Halfhyde saluted, turned away, and made ostentatiously for the starboard ladder from the bridge. As he set foot upon it a bellow came from Captain Watkiss, whose face had reddened and whose telescope was held aloft. "Mr Halfhyde, *not that ladder,* can't you read, that's *my* ladder!"

Storm Force to Narvik
by Alexander Fullerton

Book 1, The Nicholas Everard WWII Saga

1-59013-092-8 • 256 Pages • $13.95

McBooks Press publishes a wide range of authentic and exciting nautical fiction. See page 2 for a complete listing of all the authors and series we publish, available from your local bookstore or directly from McBooks Press. For a free catalog or to order call toll-free 1-888-266-5711 or visit www.mcbooks.com.

IN THE first seconds and minutes after the German shell struck and exploded inside his ship, Nick had been preoccupied with two questions. First, whether in her immobilised condition he might still get his torpedo tubes to bear on the enemy, and second, how long it might be before the next salvo smashed down on them.

"A" and "B" guns, meanwhile, were still firing; but the answer to that first question—and obviously, seeing it in retrospect, to the second as well—had come in a blinding, smothering snowstorm which swept down like a blanket, cocooning the destroyer in her own agony, hissing into the fires leaping from her afterpart.

The guns ceased fire. Brocklehurst reported by telephone from the director tower, "Target obscured."

It was no good thinking about getting any signals out. The foretopmast had collapsed half over the side, taking both the yards and the W/T aerials with it. MacKinnon, the PO Telegraphist, aided by PO Metcalf, the chief bosun's mate, and his henchmen, had rigged a jury aerial since then, using the stump of the foremast and the diminutive mainmast aft, but there'd been no question of trying to transmit. For one thing there were at least one enemy cruiser and two destroyers in the vicinity, and with any luck the Germans were under the impression that *Intent* had been sunk. They must have thought so, because otherwise they'd have arrived through that snowstorm to find her and finish her. So it would have been stupid to have risked alerting them to her continued existence. But in any case, with the ship's main generating plant out of action MacKinnon doubted if they had enough power on the set for it to be heard even five miles away.

The PO Tel was a tall man, black-bearded, with the soft lilt of the West Highlands in his voice. "It's voltage we're lacking more than aerial height, sir."

"Have you been listening out since you rigged the jury?"

"Aye, sir, but all we're gettin' is a load o' German."

There were no British ships anywhere near enough to have a chance of receiving them. And the signals that really mattered, the enemy reports, had been sent out before the action started.

"All right, MacKinnon. Pick up whatever you can, so we hear what's going on. We'll be in shelter in a few hours' time—we'll fix the generator and step a new fore-topmast, and you'll be in business again."

"We've no spare topmast, sir."

It was hard to concentrate on one issue for so long, when there were fifty other things to think about. Plugging slowly south-eastward: pitching like a see-saw and losing oil-fuel all the time. The stern tanks were leaking as a result of the main damage, and the port-side tanks for'ard were also leaking, presumably from near-miss damage slightly earlier. So now the only sound fuel tanks were the starboard pair for'ard and the smaller auxiliaries amidships. They were going to need oil as well as repairs.

"D'you know what that topmast was made of, PO Tel?"

"Would it be Norway fir, sir?"

"It would." Nick pointed. "And that's Norway."

But this conversation had taken place several hours later. At the start, with the ship stopped and on fire and no report yet of her machinery state or count of dead and wounded, there'd been no time for anything but coping with such emergencies as one knew about and getting ready for such new ones as might be expected. Like the weather clearing suddenly and the cruiser opening fire again. There'd be nothing to do except to shoot back—for as long as the ship floated.

Tommy Trench had gone aft to take charge of damage-control and fire-fighting. The snow still hid them, hid everything *from* them. Mr Opie, the torpedo gunner, was still standing by his out-turned tubes, and Nick had sent down for Cox, the RNR midshipman, to come up to the torpedo sights, in case visibility *did* lift suddenly and reveal their enemy. If that happened and one was quick enough . . . Well, he knew the cruiser wouldn't be lying stopped as *Intent* was; in fact the probability was that she'd be a long way off by this time. But she might be picking up survivors from poor *Gauntlet?*

Thinking of the possibility of *Gauntlet* survivors, he wondered about sending a boat to search in the direction where they'd last seen her. Both ships had been immobilised, so if there were any that was where they'd be. There'd be none alive in the water, but there might be a Carley float, something or other . . . Risk sending away the whaler in this sea? Throw sound lives after doubtful ones?

Ten or fifteen minutes after the shell had hit them Sub-Lieutenant Lyte hauled himself into the bridge with a report from Tommy Trench.

"Engine-room's a shambles, sir. Chief Stoker's trying to sort things out—*says* it's not as hopeless as it looks. There's a lot of electrical damage, but the LTOs are coping. Only the auxiliary generator's operable —or will be, Beamish says. And we're losing a lot of oil-fuel aft, so he's shut off those tanks. Other damage is comparatively minor— except for the hole in the engine-room casing—first lieutenant's getting that covered with timber and tarpaulins. But everything's in hand, sir, really." Lyte was panting: he'd paused, getting his breathing under control. "The four men who were killed are in the officers' bathroom for the moment, sir, and the two wounded—ERA Dobbs and Stoker Hewitt—are in the sickbay."

"Are they going to be all right?"

"No, sir." Lyte clung to the binnacle as the ship was lifted and flung on to her port side. "Doc says not a hope."

"On your way down, tell him I want a report as soon as possible."

"Aye aye, sir." He hadn't quite finished *his* report yet. "Most upper deck gear's smashed or burnt, sir. The only boat we have left intact is the dinghy. Whaler and motor-cutter are just charcoal. Even the Carley floats have had it. And—Mr Opie asked me to tell you he had to ditch several depth charges, when everything was burning."

That seemed to be the lot.

"All right, Sub. Thank you."

No boat for *Gauntlet* survivors, then; *that* problem had solved itself. No boat for anyone else either. Lyte told him, "Chief Buffer's clearing away the wreckage of the topmast, shrouds, and stuff, in the waist port side, sir, and he's got all the wire inboard now."

"Good." Metcalf's first thought would have been for trailing steelwire rope that might get wrapped round the screws. *If* the screws were to start turning again.

"Sub, I want to know from Beamish, *one*, how long he's going to be, *two*, what revs he thinks he'll be able to give me?"

Visibility was lifting. The snow was changing to sleet and thinning. A minute ago you couldn't see more than ten yards but he could see the ship's stem now—about a hundred feet away. And the sea beyond it, too . . .

"Lookouts!"

Gilbey on the port side and Willis on the other. He told them, "Keep your eyes peeled now. Weather's thinning. I want to know if anything's there before it sees *us* . . . Mid!"

Midshipman Cox faced round. "Yessir?"

"Ask Lieutenant Brocklehurst if he can see anything."

Cox had picked up the phone. He was short, sturdy, with a nose like a lump of putty and skin scarred by acne. He'd been a Merchant Navy cadet until 3 September 1939, and he was now just eighteen. His action station was in the plot, below the bridge, and most of the time he was employed as "tanky," assistant to the navigating officer.

He'd shoved the phone back on its bracket. "Director tower reports nothing in sight, sir."

"Keep a smart lookout yourself now, Mid."

Young Cox was a problem. Chandler wanted to get rid of him. But for the moment, the foreseeable future, there were more pressing problems . . . Visibility had stretched to about half a mile, and there was still nothing to be seen. Only the sea heaving green and angry and the clouds pressing low as if they were trying to smother it, and here and there the flurry of a passing squall. *Intent*, soaring and dropping, swinging whichever way the waves and wind pushed her, felt inert and lifeless, with no will of her own. ■